ASSASSINS OF MEXICO

LUKE RYDER
BOOK 6

JOHN G. BLUCK

ROUGH
EDGES
PRESS

Assassins of Mexico
Paperback Edition
Copyright © 2025 John G. Bluck

Rough Edges Press
An Imprint of Wolfpack Publishing
701 S. Howard Ave. 106-324 Tampa, FL 33609

roughedgespress.com

Paperback ISBN 978-1-68549-433-9
eBook ISBN 978-1-68549-532-9
LCCN 2025940152

ASSASSINS OF MEXICO

ONE

ON A SUNNY VACATION DAY, thirty-nine-year-old Kentucky Deputy Sheriff Luke Ryder stood in his gravel driveway. He stepped from the crushed stones onto his lush lawn and propped himself against an ancient white oak tree, the tallest one on his rented farm.

The odor of paint dominated the air as he gazed at his bright red barn and smiled at his paint job. Glimpsing down at his paint-splattered shoe, he saw its lace was untied.

A male Kentucky warbler sang out just as six-foot-two-inch Luke knelt to tie his shoelace. At the same instant, a shot rang out, and bits of bark rained onto his black hair. A bullet had slammed into the tree where Luke had leaned an instant before.

Luke felt a flash of fear as he dove onto sharp stones near the barn. Rocks bit into one of his hands, and pain coursed through his left side as he rolled toward the open barn door. A second bullet struck the jagged rocks. Ricocheting, the projectile whined away.

Scrambling into the safety of his large barn, Luke yanked his cell phone from his hip pocket and tapped 911.

"What's your emergency?"

"Joyce, this is Luke Ryder." Luke furrowed his brow while his brown eyes focused on the wide barn doorway. "A sniper just took two shots at me. I was by my barn. He parked a tan sedan on Elm Lane near my east fence."

"Backup's on the way. I'll call Sheriff Pike."

"Tell him I think them Mexican drug dealers are after me again."

"Okay."

That bastard better not shoot into the house and endanger Layla, Angela, and the baby.

In his mind's eye, Luke pictured little Russell, now a month and a half old, his first child. He imagined his young, African American wife, Layla, trying to raise his son and his stepdaughter, Angela, all alone. *I gotta take a shot at the shooter to scare him away, if not nail him.*

* * *

The smell of gun smoke lingered in the air. Kneeling behind a small, green sapling on Luke's property line, Mexican assassin Javier Lagos braced his Springfield 1903 bolt-action rifle on a wooden fence post. He looked through his rifle's 8X power scope.

Did I hit the gringo?

* * *

Luke shoved his phone into his hip pocket. He gulped. Glancing around the corner of the wide barn doorway toward his fence on the east side of his property, he saw the distant figure of a man with a rifle. Luke rushed from his barn by a side door behind bushes growing along the driveway. He crouched, kept low behind green leaves, and began to run toward his farmhouse.

* * *

"*Mierda*," Javier whispered in Spanish. *The cabrón's not even wounded.*

Javier's dark, wavy hair hanging down across his brow, he sighted through his scope and squeezed off a shot. The sound of it rang in his ears, and the acrid odor of gun smoke impacted his nose. The deputy kept sprinting, and Javier chambered another .30 caliber round. Before Javier could aim, Luke had opened the rear door of his house and dove inside.

* * *

Javier's fellow assassin, José Ramirez, his long, black hair dangling over his ears, stared through the getaway car's open driver-side window. A portable radio tuned to local police bands hissed beside José.

"Shots fired, 10-18. Luke Ryder's farm."

"Car Seventeen, 10-17."

"Car Eleven, 10-17, en route."

José yelled, "Let's go. *La policía* are coming."

Javier yelled. "I might get another shot at him."

* * *

Grabbing his deer rifle, Luke turned to Layla. "Get Russell, Angela, yur Beretta, and go in the basement now. Lock the door. Somebody shot at me. Police are coming."

* * *

Javier scampered to the passenger side of the stolen, tan muscle car, got inside, tossed his rifle onto the back seat, and covered the weapon with a blanket.

* * *

After running outside, Luke aimed and squeezed his weapon's trigger. The rifle's stock kicked his shoulder, and a bullet raced at the getaway car, a tan sedan.

* * *

A microsecond later, the vehicle's two rear windows shattered, and a rifle shot sounded.

Javier took a sharp breath. *That gringo damn near hit José in the head.*

As Javier slammed the front passenger-side door shut, he felt his lower back push against his seat, heard the squeal of tires, and smelled burned rubber. He gulped. "Step on it, José. Go to the Kroger parking lot."

Javier took a deep breath. *We need to switch cars fast.* He wiped sweat from his brow and sighed. He was a handsome, green-eyed man whom women found charming, energetic, and attractive until they learned he was a paid killer.

Javier glanced at his partner, José, as the man drove the sedan fast along Elm Lane. José was trembling with fear while his olive-colored face flushed.

Javier shook his head. *José lost his nerve ever since Luke swung a rake down on José's wrist and broke it months ago.* Ever since then, José had grown his hair and beard long to change his appearance.

* * *

2:06 P.M., TUESDAY, MAY 20, 2031, SHERIFF PIKE'S OFFICE

Luke's boyhood friend and now his boss, Sheriff Jim Pike, sat behind his desk in his office. He scratched his brown curly hair, accented by strands of gray, at the very moment his desk phone jangled. "Hello? Chief Pike here."

"This is Joyce at dispatch. Someone shot at Luke Ryder at his farm minutes ago. Two squad cars responded and are on the way. He thinks Mexican drug dealers are behind it."

"Is he injured?" An even-keeled man, Jim remained calm during stressful situations.

"I don't think so."

"Thanks, Joyce. Send another cruiser to Luke's house to check on Layla and the kids. I have to hang up and ask the state police to send a chopper."

"Yes, sir."

Jim reckoned Mateo Guerra, the drug czar in charge of *Nuestro Club* drug cartel, based in Tijuana, Mexico, was behind the attempt on Luke's life. Mateo hated Luke Ryder. Luke had brought down the cartel's Lexington, Kentucky, operation, and he'd killed Mateo's nephew with a crossbow.

Jim placed the phone's handset on its cradle, picked it up again, and dialed his contact at the Kentucky State Police.

Jim fingered an unlit cigar while the distant phone rang.

If I hadn't assigned Luke to go undercover at the Spicer Farm, the Mexican drug cartel wouldn't be after Luke today. Jim shifted his five-foot-eleven-inch, stocky body in his swivel chair.

A male voice answered, "Hello?"

"Hi, Rex. I need a chopper to track down a shooter. He tried to take out one of my deputies…"

* * *

Toting his deer rifle, Luke ran to his electric pickup truck, parked in his driveway on the west side of the barn which was not in the shooter's line of sight.

Luke yanked the vehicle's door open and scrambled into the driver's seat. After propping his deer rifle against the front passenger-side door, he grabbed his satellite phone. "Joyce, I'm in my truck, and I'm gonna go after the perp's tan sedan, heading north on Elm Lane. I took a shot and hit the car. He'll get on Boone Freeway at Dove Avenue."

"I'll pass it on." Luke could hear Joyce exhale. "Don't hang up."

"Okay. If Jim calls, can you patch him into my phone?"

"Yep. Our new upgrade enables it." Joyce's voice was high-pitched.

I ain't heard her so nervous before, Luke thought as he pressed his truck's accelerator pedal down too much. The pickup's wheels spun fast, throwing gravel backward into the lush grass.

Luke eased his foot up on the pedal. When the tires gripped the jagged layer of rocks on the driveway, the truck flew forward. As the metal machine gained speed, Luke's spine eased back against the driver's seat. He touched the brake pedal, and he made a sharp left turn onto County Route 54, a blacktop road, and his vehicle fishtailed. After Luke regained control of the pickup and its forward path straightened, he stomped on the accelerator pedal. The tires squealed and smoked.

After less than thirty seconds, he braked as he neared the southeast corner of his property. To avoid sliding, he turned left with care onto the gravel road, Elm Lane. It bordered his east fence. He knew going too fast on gravel was risky because a fast-moving vehicle could slide on stones as if it were traveling on ice. Peering ahead to his left, Luke saw the skinny sapling tree where the shooter had stood next to a fence post and fired his rifle. Then Luke focused his eyes northward where the road climbed a steep hill. He saw no vehicles. *The perp's gotta be on Boone Freeway by now.*

All of a sudden, Luke realized speeding and chasing a criminal were more satisfying than swallowing a shot of whiskey. Pursuing a perp made him feel more alive. His heart beat faster, and he took a refreshing breath. A recovering alcoholic, he'd learned adrenaline highs had taken the place of alcoholic lows in his life. *But I gotta be careful cuz I'm a father now.*

Still, Luke drove as fast as he dared in the middle of the gravel lane until he reached the steep hill, and then he moved into the right lane. After cresting the hill, his truck bounced as he sped another 500 feet and slowed for Dove Avenue, a blacktop motorway. He knew Dove crossed under the four-lane Boone Freeway a mile east of his location, so he turned right and pushed his truck's accelerator pedal to the floor. The pickup's electric motor thrust the vehicle forward like a jet fighter using an afterburner. In less than a minute, Luke again tapped his brakes when he neared the Boone Freeway cloverleaf.

Should I take the north or south ramp? He decided to go north because more big parking lots were on the sides of the roadway in that direction. Experience told him the shooter would ditch the getaway car in an expansive parking lot where he'd parked another car. *It's gotta be a huge lot with a crowd of cars like the one at the new Derby Shopping Center.* It was the home of three large box stores, restaurants, clothes stores, and boutiques.

In three minutes, Luke neared the Derby Shopping Center, and his satellite phone rang. It was still hooked up to dispatch. He shifted in his car seat and pulled the device from his hip pocket. "Hello, Joyce."

"Luke, Jim Pike's on the line."

* * *

Traveling north at seven miles per hour over the speed limit in a stolen tan sedan, Mexican assassins—*sicarios*—Javier Lagos and José Ramirez had passed the Derby Shopping Center on Boone Freeway a minute earlier.

From the front passenger's seat, Javier glared at José. "Go slower."

"*Sí.*"

To avoid leaving their DNA and fingerprints in the car, both men wore clear plastic gloves.

After glancing behind him at the remnants of the two back windows Luke's bullet had shattered, Javier heard the whop, whop, whop sound of helicopter props. He squinted ahead at the sky and saw a Kentucky State Police whirlybird flying south toward them on the right side of the road.

Javier's pulse rate climbed. "See the chopper? Get in the right lane under the big trees."

Tall, leafy trees lined the road.

José changed lanes and drove slower yet.

As the chopper flew over the tan vehicle, the maples hid the slow-moving automobile from the helicopter. José caught Javier's attention. "The Kroger parking lot is coming up."

The expansive Kroger parking lot was a half block ahead on the right. Within five seconds, José guided the tan sedan into a slow turn and entered the grocery store's parking area. Soon, he stopped the stolen car in the far southeast corner of the lot. Maple trees there shielded it, too, from the helicopter's view.

Earlier, Javier had cased the food store's parking area and learned security cameras did not focus on the southeast corner. This area was where he'd parked a blue compact car he'd rented with a credit card issued to a nonexistent person. Javier surveyed the rear seat of the stolen tan sedan. A blanket covered his Springfield 1903 rifle, and cube-shaped bits of broken window glass were sprinkled over the blanket. He shook his head. *Too bad I must leave the rifle here.*

José left the keys in the automobile's ignition, and then the two men exited the stolen vehicle.

José smiled at Javier. "If we're lucky, a teenager will steal it."

Javier shrugged and pushed a grocery cart away from the blue compact car he'd rented. "Let's get out of here."

José nodded as he got into the passenger side of the small blue car. "It will be a relief to nap in our room while we wait for nightfall."

Javier pictured the motel room he'd rented in a strip mall five miles away. It wasn't fancy, but he and José wouldn't draw attention to themselves while they waited there until the wee hours of the night, when they planned to make their next move.

* * *

Luke made a right turn into the Derby Shopping Center's large parking lot and stopped in a nearby space. He put his satellite phone against his right ear. "Hello, Jim."

"Where are you?" Sheriff Jim Pike sounded concerned.

"In the Derby Shopping Center parking lot."

"Did you have eyes on the tan getaway car?"

Luke sighed. "When I shot at it and hit it." He took a breath. "I bet they parked the getaway car here and switched rides." Luke heard the noise of a helicopter flying above. He spotted the state police chopper circling the blocks-long parking lot.

"I sent a cruiser to your house to check on Layla. I talked with her. She's okay." Jim cleared his throat. "A state chopper is helping to search."

"It's circlin' the parking lot above me. I'll cruise around and see if I can find the tan sedan."

"Keep me posted."

"Okay."

Luke opened his glove compartment, took out his compact binoculars, and began to scan the crowded lot.

* * *

2:20 P.M., TUESDAY, MAY 20, 2031, KROGER'S PARKING LOT

Brushing his unwashed hair away from his eyes, Kroger employee and recent high school graduate Dirk Waller glanced at the southeast corner of the grocery store's parking lot. He spotted a lone grocery cart near a tan sedan. *Why do people have to park so far away from the store and leave carts there?*

As Dirk neared the cart, he noticed a smashed rear window on the left side of the vehicle. *Somebody broke into it.* Dirk recalled the store manager had told him to call the police if he ever spotted a vehicle break-in. Dirk reached into his jeans for his phone and dialed 911.

"What's your emergency?" A woman had spoken.

"I'm in the Kroger parking lot on Boone Freeway. Somebody smashed in the back window of a car. My store manager told me to call."

"What color is the car?"

Dirk shrugged. "Kinda tan."

"What's the make and model?"

Holding his cell phone to his ear, Dirk walked around the back of the car. "It's a Ford Fox." He glanced around the right side of the car. "Hey, the other back window's broke, too."

"Is anybody near you?"

"No, I'm way off in a corner of the lot."

"Dirk, stay by the car and don't touch it. I'm sending a squad car right away."

Dirk noticed the 911 operator's voice was high-pitched now. "My boss might git mad if I'm not back in the store soon."

"We'll talk to him, and you'll be okay." The lady dispatcher hesitated. "Help us by keeping others away from the car, unless you feel in danger."

"Okay. But I'm not threatened. There ain't nobody for a hundred and fifty yards."

"Keep your phone on until the police arrive."

"Okay, ma'am."

Within thirty seconds, Dirk saw a Kentucky State Police helicopter circling above him.

* * *

2:23 P.M., TUESDAY, MAY 20, 2031, KROGER'S PARKING LOT

Two squad cars drove to the southeast corner of the Kroger parking lot and stopped by Dirk, who stood near a shopping cart and a tan, late-model Ford Fox-Tracks sedan.

Deputy Arlo Biddle exited his cruiser and walked with a slight, bowlegged gait toward young Dirk. "Son, are you the one who called 911?"

"Yes, Officer."

"Nice work." Arlo, a fair-skinned twenty-eight-year-old man with short, black hair, glanced at the tan sedan. "I'll take a quick look at this car, and then I'll ask you questions."

Dirk nodded but appeared nervous to Arlo.

Arlo glanced behind the steering wheel and saw a key in the ignition. Staring through the left rear broken window, he noticed a brown blanket covering something long and skinny. He picked up a dead branch that had fallen from the maple tree shading the parking spot.

With care, he extended the branch into the back seat and under a corner of the blanket and then lifted it. He spotted a Springfield 1903 rifle with a scope mounted above its barrel. *This is the perp's car and weapon.* He pushed the button on his two-way radio. "Joyce, we found the tan sedan and a rifle. We need a crime scene technician to examine the car."

"I'll send Alice Strom."

"Thanks." Arlo pictured Alice, a blond young lady with braided pigtails. He figured she'd search for DNA and fingerprints as well as scrutinize the scene as best she could. He knew she had a crush on Luke, just like a bunch of other women. But now Luke was taken, married a short time ago.

Arlo heard the sound of a vehicle approaching from behind him. Turning, he saw Luke driving his new truck.

* * *

2:24 P.M., TUESDAY, MAY 20, 2031, LUKE'S FARM

A squad car pulled into Luke's driveway. While Deputy Sheriff Jesse Reagan grabbed an M16 rifle and chambered a round, Deputy Lucy Bonhart pulled out her cell phone. A loose bang of her dishwater-blond hair dangling over her left temple, she tapped in Layla Ryder's mobile number.

"Hello?"

"Layla, this is Deputy Lucy Bonhart. We're in your drive-way." Lucy felt cool and collected like she always did.

Though she reckoned the perps had fled the scene, she and Jesse would follow procedure and make a thorough search of the premises. "You okay?"

"Yes, my baby, my older daughter, and I are in the basement. Luke locked the back door when he left. There's a key under the big rock by the shed."

Lucy brushed a blond bang aside. "Excellent. Deputy Reagan and I will look through the house and check the outside. When it's all clear, I'll tap on the basement door and let you know."

"Okay." Layla inhaled. "Is Luke okay?"

"Yes. We've been monitoring radio traffic. We may have located the shooter's abandoned sedan. Luke arrived at that scene to help."

"Thank God."

"We'll stay here with you until Luke comes back." Lucy glanced at the 12-gauge pump shotgun stowed inside her cruiser. "See you soon." Lucy disconnected the call and grabbed the shotgun.

TWO

A MILE NORTH of the Kroger food store, Javier and José had taken refuge in their cheap room in Mabel's Motel. José closed the room curtains, stretched out on a bedspread, and leaned against the headboard of one of the room's two beds.

Javier sat on an uncomfortable, rickety, wooden chair by a small desk and glimpsed at José. "Calling Mateo isn't going to be fun."

José shrugged. He took a bite from an apple and turned his head to peer at sunlight leaking through a crack in the curtains.

Javier felt beads of sweat begin to roll down from his armpits, tickling the sides of his chest. *Why does Mateo want to know step-by-step how the mission to assassinate Luke Ryder is going? Reporting to the jefe makes me nervous. But I should be more assertive.*

Javier pictured Mateo, who towered above most men, standing six foot three. Thin but strong, he also sported a dark beard and had prominent cheekbones. Javier imagined himself confronting Mateo, telling him the truth, not avoiding it. *Okay, Mateo, Luke Ryder did kill your sister's son, Jorge, with a crossbow. But what do you expect? You were the one who sent Jorge to kill Luke, but Jorge failed. Let me do my job, and I'll tell you when it's done. Leave me alone.*

Javier felt great during the half minute when he daydreamed how he'd face Mateo unafraid. But all of a sudden, Javier admitted he was lying to himself. Mateo was arrogant, combative, and a bully—a powerful man who would not be ordered around. Javier knew he'd never talk to Mateo as an equal, or the man might well kill him.

Staring at his encrypted satellite phone, Javier took three deep breaths and tapped out the Mexican drug czar Mateo Guerra's phone number.

Javier's pulse rate galloped as he counted the rings of Mateo's Tijuana device.

On the seventh ring, Mateo answered. "Javier, how goes it?"

Javier's heartbeat pounded at his chest wall. He gulped. "Luke Ryder dodged my bullets." Javier breathed out. "I took three shots. I had the crosshairs of my scope lined up with his upper left chest, but as fate would have it, he moved as I squeezed the trigger."

"Did you wound him?"

"No." Javier felt nauseous. "He shot back. His round missed hitting José's head by inches as we drove away. Soon cops swarmed the roads, and a police helicopter flew over us."

While Mateo did not speak for three seconds, Javier heard him suck air in and out as if he were hyperventilating.

Then Mateo spoke. "Javier, I thought I could count on you to take Jorge's place, but I'm beginning to doubt you. You and José have missed killing Luke at least two times. Once after I sent you across the wide ocean to London. There, I believe you spent my money for extravagant hotels, food, and whores."

Javier felt acid burn the inside of his stomach. "*Jefe*, boss, I apologize. Luke moved the instant I shot, or he'd be dead."

"Start attending mass once a week. Perhaps then your luck will change. How do you plan to kill Luke now?"

Javier sighed. He closed his eyes for a second and relished the brief blackness behind his eyelids. *Is this darkness what it's like to be dead?* He opened his mouth. "We'll wait two or three days and stay hidden until the police stop searching for us and watching his place." Javier wondered when the police would stop surveillance on the farm. "When we can, we'll plant a tracker on his pickup truck and study his driving habits. We'll take him out at a remote place."

"If you can place a tracker on his truck, why can't you kill him then?"

"Of course, he is familiar with his farm, and he is wary. We must make our move when and where he doesn't expect it."

"Okay. Javier. Do not fail again."

"*Sí, Jefe.*"

"I want that gringo dead more than any other man."

"It will be done." Javier heard Mateo's phone disconnect. He pictured Jorge Castro, Mateo's nephew, now a dead and buried assassin. Jorge had failed his assignment to whack Luke, and Javier figured Jorge, a cocky little *sicario,* had got what he deserved. On the other hand, Luke was a worthy adversary, a man to be respected, even if he was an enemy.

Javier's hand shook as he slipped his satellite phone into his pocket. Planting a tracker on Luke's truck would be tricky. But José was skinny, short, and as sneaky and stealthy as a cougar. Also loyal, he would follow orders even if, at times, he acted like a coward. *José can slither onto Luke's farm in the wee hours of the night and plant two trackers on the pickup in case one is discovered. If José is unsuccessful placing the trackers, well then, I'll figure out something else.*

THREE

LUKE SAT in his pickup truck fifty feet from the assassin's tan getaway car in Kroger's grocery store parking lot. Luke held his encrypted satellite phone in his palm. His mind zipped through an alternate outcome to his recent close encounter with death—an end to his life caused by a bullet with his name on it. What if he'd died? In his mind's eye, he saw his wife, Layla; his newborn son, Russell; and Layla's young daughter, Angela. They would struggle to make ends meet if he were dead and buried.

A tear seeped from Luke's right eye and raced down his cheek as his thoughts raged. He wiped away the streak of moisture from his face. Glancing across the deputies and crime scene technicians surrounding the sedan the would-be killer had stolen, Luke saw no one staring at him. He felt relieved. *Yeah, I didn't rush into a dicey situation and provoke a bad guy this time. The bastard came after me out of the blue. Even so, my odds of meeting St. Peter at the pearly gates of heaven will increase if I volunteer for more iffy assignments. Is my need for excitement and bursts of adrenaline gonna git me killed on the job?*

All of a sudden, Luke wondered if he ought to cut ties with the FBI and stop doing side jobs for the bureau. *It's been months since the Mexicans last tried to kill me in London. The FBI promised to go after the Tijuana cartel. Has the bureau made progress working with Mexican law enforcement to destroy Nuestro Club that's been gunnin' fur me? And what's the DEA doin' to help?*

Even if the bureau and the DEA were dedicated to taking down the cartel, the drug ring's headquarters was south of the border. Did the FBI and the Mexican authorities have a close relationship, or was true collaboration with Mexico a political fantasy? *I gotta git answers.*

Luke's hand hovered over his phone's contact list. As if a magnet drew his index finger downward, he tapped the name of an FBI agent, Rita Reynolds. As the distant phone rang in Rita's office in Louisville, Luke envisioned her. He'd known her since his high school days. Though now in her late thirties, she still appeared young and vibrant. Of medium build, with raven hair and brown, sad eyes, she was a rising star in the FBI. But Luke guessed she wanted something more meaningful than the FBI in her life. He scratched his dark whiskers. *She needs love. She must want it.* He sighed. *Too bad her life is speeding forward. Her job takes a lot of time, and she's gettin' older. Is she depressed?*

There was the sound of a click coming from the other end of the now active connection. "Luke. I meant to call you later today. How timely." Rita's voice sounded caring.

Luke sucked air into his lungs. "I got bad news. Somebody shot at me at the farm."

"Are you hurt?"

"No." Luke blinked and replayed in his mind's eye the instant he'd escaped a sudden, unexpected death. "I just finished paintin' the barn. I knelt to tie my shoe, and a bullet smashed into the old oak next to my driveway where I'd been leaning. He shot twice more. I called 911, ran inside the house, and snatched my deer rifle. I shot at the perp's car and blew out a couple of windows. Jim Pike sent out the cavalry, but the bastard got away. I'm sittin' next to the abandoned gitaway car in the Lexington Kroger's parkin' lot."

Luke huffed. "I think them Mexican drug pushers are after me again. I gotta know, what the hell is the FBI doin' to take down *Nuestro Club* drug ring?"

Luke realized he'd said much more at once than usual and that he was livid. He heard Rita sigh. "Luke, I've been wondering what has been happening with the cartel investigation, too. It's tough to coordinate law enforcement agencies, even in the United States. It's harder still to work with the Mexicans." Rita sounded exasperated to Luke.

Luke wondered if he'd shown Rita he was more emotional than he usually appeared on the outside. But he had to get his frustration off his chest. "Layla, Angela, or Russell could have been hit. We got to get the FBI to git off their asses and go after them SOBs."

"I hear you." Rita's voice was higher. "I promise to light a fire under the powers that be."

"Sorry I hit you with all this." Luke closed his eyes for a moment. "I value yur friendship and willingness to bend rules to help me."

Luke could hear Rita taking breaths and exhaling. "I have use-or-lose leave to burn. I can watch Layla and your kids full-time for a week when you're at work, if it's okay with you and Layla." Rita's voice sounded sugar-sweet to Luke. He was glad his outburst hadn't seemed to alienate her. He figured she knew him better than he understood himself.

Luke heard himself utter, "You don't have to do that."

"I want to. Besides, I have an ulterior motive." Luke heard her ease out a slow, even breath. "I know this is the wrong time to bring up why I was going to call you, but there's a deadline. The FBI and even the CIA need your help." Luke heard Rita inhale a lungful of air.

Luke shook his head and felt blood rush to his forehead. *You gotta be kiddin' me.* He peered through his windshield at the blue sky. "I figger it must be real urgent, if yur bringin' it up now."

"It's a matter of national security."

Luke wondered why Rita would risk upsetting him more than he was already vexed.

I gotta be nuts to consider this now. "What's the big deal?" He reckoned she could tell him about a potential bureau job because both their FBI-provided satellite phones were encrypted.

"It's complicated, but let me start by saying…" She hesitated. Luke figured she was composing her thoughts.

* * *

Rita shifted her grip on her telephone handset. She heard Luke's steady breathing on the other side of the line. *What's the best way to tell him about the FBI mission? I should start with the farm tractor he wants.*

Tapping her toes on the floor beneath her gray, government-issue desk, Rita realized her mind was speeding forward on overdrive. *I've got to get Luke to commit to this gig soon if I'm going to make it work.*

"I have a bit of unexpected good news for you. Yegor Bulot plans to ship the Belarusian tractor you wanted to your farm to arrive the day after Memorial Day."

Luke laughed. "It's hard to believe the contract I signed with the Belarus Tractor Company is valid."

Rita had to admit the situation was strange because Luke was getting to try out and maybe buy a farm tractor made in Belarus. She coughed, "The contract's legal because the UK, the US, and Belarus signed the Agricultural Pact in 2029. I hear Russia might sign the pact, too."

Rita heard Luke scratch the phone against his unshaven whiskers. Then he spoke. "The delivery's in a week."

"Tuesday, May 27." Rita ceased talking when she felt a surge of desire strike her. Though she tried to forget how much she cared for Luke, she knew she still loved him, even if he'd made Layla pregnant and then married her. Rita sighed and tried to dismiss her feelings for Luke. "I think you'll want to be there when the tractor's delivered. Yegor would like to see you then and show you how the joystick works. The Belarusian company's working to make the tractor autonomous, too, using artificial intelligence." Rita recalled watching a sales video of a farmer running the tractor remotely from his porch.

"I'll take the day off if I have to. Especially if a Belarusian KGB defector and double agent's comin' to see me."

"Yegor Americanized his name." Rita glanced at an FBI photo of Yegor on her desk. He was handsome and stocky, with black hair and eyes to match. "He goes by George Black now."

Rita recalled the detailed report she'd read about how Luke had caught Yegor at an English military proving ground in the UK back in September 2030.

Faced with years in prison, Yegor, a Belarusian KGB spy from Minsk, had defected to MI5, the UK domestic intelligence agency. Both MI5 and the UK's Secret Intelligence Service—SIS—also known as MI6, had cooperated to bring the Belarusian spy into their service. They also had worked with the FBI and the CIA to recruit Yegor as a double agent for the West.

So far, the Belarusian KGB in Minsk hadn't figured out Yegor had defected. Instead, they'd changed his name to George Black and sent him to the US to spy while he worked as a farm tractor salesman.

Rita heard Luke breathe out and ask, "Is there anything wrong with Yegor—I mean George—comin' to see me? He was itchin' to tour the US."

"There's nothing wrong with his visit. The FBI trusts him." Rita felt her stomach twist, and she gulped. "At the same time, the Belarusian KGB thinks George is still on their side. So, the FBI and the Army Counterintelligence Command will give George two or three throwaway secrets and a lot of big lies about US military capability to pass back to KGB HQ in Minsk." She paused. "Did you know the Belarus Tractor Company also makes cheap armored personnel carriers they've been selling to the UK?"

"I heard about it at the MI5 briefing when I was in London. It doesn't make sense."

Rita wondered what kind of military equipment the US was selling to Belarus, if any. "It's odd the Agricultural Pact allows the sale of military equipment as well as agricultural machines and crops among the signatory nations. But politicians often do bizarre things."

"What's all this have to do with me?"

Rita eased air from her lungs. "The FBI wants you to travel with George Black for a week and keep an eye on him when he makes sales calls out West at an Army base and then at US national parks."

"Why are y'all askin' me to do this?"

"George trusts you. He likes you." Rita stared out her window at tree branches blowing in the breeze. "In particular, we want you to watch George when he makes his first sales call at Ft. Lewis."

"Ft. Lewis?"

"It's a big Army base in the state of Washington near Tacoma. The recently reactivated 9th Infantry Division has agreed to test a low-cost armored personnel carrier the Belarus Tractor Company makes."

"So what?"

"There's a Major Jack Green at Ft. Lewis. George's Belarusian KGB handlers agreed to pay Green $60,000 in cash for secret army information. The major will give George fake information about the US Army."

"George will pay the major sixty K?"

Rita laughed. "No. George will keep the money for himself. Army Intelligence will fool the Belarusian KGB by letting Green drive a luxury automobile for free."

Rita could hear Luke snorting before he said, "Yegor—I mean George—isn't stupid."

Feeling it was the right time to try to get Luke to agree to the FBI assignment, Rita smiled. "Yep, George even convinced the Belarusian KGB to buy him and you a luxury bus tour of the national parks out West so he wouldn't have to drive from park to park."

"Sounds like fun."

Rita could visualize Luke grinning. He'd been a game warden and loved wildlife.

He must be eager to take the National Parks Tour. "So, would you babysit George for a week?" As she waited for Luke to reply, she added, "The FBI will pay you a $5,000 stipend. I talked to Jim Pike yesterday. He agreed you could take the job if you would like to do so."

"Maybe I'll do it. But why does somebody need to watch George for a week?"

"Army Intelligence doesn't yet have confidence in George. They want someone to monitor him. You're our best choice. And George genuinely wants you to go to testify how good his tractor is and to demonstrate it to national park groundskeepers."

Luke paused, bumping his phone. "As we speak, I'm watchin' out my car window. A tow truck driver's hookin' up the assassin's getaway car. I gotta worry about Layla and my kids."

Rita felt her stomach burn. *Is Luke going to say no to the mission?* "As I said, I could stay at your place for a week to guard Layla and the children. I'll bring a second agent to help, too." Rita felt her heart gallop. "And the FBI can install electronics on your fence line. The system can detect intruders and set off an alarm."

"I'll talk with Layla and let you know if we agree." Luke was silent for a moment. "If I decide to do it, when would I leave?"

"Two days after Memorial Day, May twenty-eighth. It's a Wednesday." Rita coughed. "We've made airplane reservations for you and George should you decide to do the mission."

"I'll call you back right after I discuss it with Layla."

"Excellent." Rita hung up.

FOUR

WHEN LUKE PULLED his truck into his farm's driveway, he saw a sheriff's cruiser parked near his bright red barn. Luke felt himself relax. *Lucy and Jesse are still watchin' over Layla.*

Jim Pike had told Luke that deputies Lucy Bonhart and Jesse Reagan had reported they'd searched Luke's farm and his house but had found no intruders. Luke grabbed the warm pizza box from the front passenger's seat and exited his vehicle.

Near the back door of the house, he pulled a key from his pocket. *I bet Lucy locked the door.* He slid his key into the lock and twisted it, and there was a click. "Hello, I'm home." When he pushed the door open, he saw Lucy and Jesse sitting at the kitchen table. Steaming cups of coffee sat in front of them.

Lucy smiled. "Everything's under control, Luke."

"I'm glad y'all came to secure the area." Luke set the large pizza box on the table. "Help yourselves. There's soft drinks in the fridge if you want." He glanced into the living room. "Where's Layla?"

Lucy guided a loose strand of blond hair behind her left ear. "She's in the master bedroom with the baby." Lucy blushed.

Luke bowed his head. "Thanks." He stepped toward the bedroom and opened its door.

Layla sat in a chair next to the king-size bed. Her blouse open, she was breastfeeding Russell. The baby boy snuggled near her right breast when she began to speak. "They catch anybody?"

"No." Luke sat on the bed near Layla and the baby. "I think the perps are a couple hundred miles away by now." He figured she'd be less scared if he told her that. *But those Mexican cartel guys are mad as hell at me. They could be around yet.* He sighed.

Layla glanced down at Russell, who was now asleep. She whispered, "Thank God those gangsters are gone." She stood, put Russell in his crib, and covered him with a blanket. "I'll make something to eat for us, Angela, Lucy, and Jesse."

As Layla buttoned her blouse, Luke switched off the light. "I got a real big pizza on the way home."

"I'll pop it in the oven and warm it a bit." Layla hugged Luke. "You going to ask Lucy and Jesse to stay for a while?"

"I already did. There's plenty of pizza."

Layla peered into his eyes. "Should hit the spot. I'm hungry." She blinked. "And you can tell me what you're planning to do to protect the farm."

Luke gulped. "I talked to Rita, and she has an idea how to monitor the fence line."

* * *

4:49 P.M., TUESDAY, MAY 20, 2031, MABEL'S MOTEL

José opened the mini fridge in their cheap room, removed two frozen dinners, and put one in a microwave oven. After setting the oven's timer to four minutes, he pushed the start button.

In a short time, the delicious smell of hot beef, mashed potatoes, gravy, and vegetables drifted his way. His mouth watering, José glanced at Javier. "I'm glad you bought these dinners, or we'd be starving, waiting for the cops to quit searching for us."

Javier shrugged. "Somebody needs to think ahead, consider all possibilities." Javier leaned back in an easy chair and sipped beer from a cold can.

José reopened the fridge, took out a beer, and popped the can's tab. "How will we know when the police quit searching?"

"We'll wait a day."

José wrinkled his brow. "Just a day?"

"They already think we're in another state by now." Javier puffed out a relaxed breath. "That's why they won't expect us to revisit the farm tomorrow night."

José stood up. "Are you crazy?"

"No. All we have to do is plant trackers on Luke Ryder's truck." Javier displayed a crafty, condescending grin.

"If you're going to take the chance to sneak onto the farm, why not shoot him instead?" José took a quick swig of beer.

"Shooting or trying to get in the house would cause too much noise." Javier's voice was arrogant. "We'll watch where he drives and hit him in a secluded place when he least expects it."

The microwave chimed, and José removed one dinner and placed the second one on the oven's round, glass turntable. He snapped the microwave door shut. "You've got balls to sneak onto the farm even if it turns out to be a moonless night."

Javier stood and poked José's shoulder with an index finger. "You're going to be the one to stay in the shadows and creep up on the truck."

José felt blood rush to his face. "Me? Why not you?"

Javier crushed his empty aluminum beer can. "I'm the better shot. I'll cover you. There's a reason I bought the expensive night-vision scope for the second rifle." He made a face like a man who thought he was smarter than anyone else. "Also, you are smaller, thinner, quieter, and much sneakier than I am."

José's heart was pounding. *I ought to blow Javier's brains out and tell Mateo the cops shot him.*

* * *

6:55 P.M., TUESDAY, MAY 20, 2031, LUKE'S FARM

Luke sat with Layla at their farmhouse kitchen table after the two deputies had left. His stepdaughter, Angela, was in the living room playing a video game.

Layla watched Luke smile and then bite into the last piece of pizza. Layla wasn't sure how she could bring up her concerns about the danger Luke was in.

How can I be tactful when Luke's life, my life, and our children's existence are on the line? She knew she had to use her best coping mechanism. She'd appear tough, even though underneath she felt like crying. She didn't want to lose Luke because he was one of the few men she liked, and he was her soulmate.

Layla pasted a smile on her face. "There's something important we need to speak about." She had sugar-coated her rich, feminine voice. "I'm glad you got me the Beretta and taught me how to use it." She hesitated. "But it's not enough when an assassin with a rifle shoots at you."

Luke's brow furrowed, and his smile morphed into a slight frown. "I know. I bin thinkin' on that."

"What can you do to get the Mexican drug cartel off your back?"

Luke peered down at his pizza and rubbed his whiskers. Lifting his head, he blinked and was quiet for a moment while he studied Layla's face. "I had a phone call with Rita today. She said the FBI could install an electronic system to monitor our fence line fur intruders. She'd have it done if I help the bureau for a week."

Layla felt as if Luke's eyes were probing her brain. She felt fury course throughout her body. After taking a deep breath, she said, "Isn't taking on dangerous assignments what got *Nuestro Club* after you in the first place?" She stopped talking, realizing she'd raised her voice.

"Yeah, but the FBI just wants me to babysit Yegor Bulot for a week. He's calling himself George Black now."

Layla stood and placed her hands on her waist. "If you think working with a Belarusian KGB spy is safe, even if he's switched sides, then you should reevaluate."

"It's not like you think. Rita said Yegor—I mean George —will be here in a week to drop off the loaner tractor and show me how to use it. That's the Tuesday after Memorial Day."

"What's that got to do with keeping an eye on him for the FBI?" Layla grabbed a teacup and dropped a tea bag into it.

"Yegor's going on a sales trip to peddle Belarusian farm tractors to national parks groundskeepers. The FBI wants me to go with him to demo the tractors and testify they're cost-effective."

Layla put a tea kettle of water on the stovetop and turned on the burner under it. "Why don't they send someone else?"

"George trusts me more than anybody else, and he's new to the country."

Layla sat in a kitchen chair next to Luke. "What if the sniper comes back when you're not here?"

"I think he's long gone." Luke glanced at Layla's face. "But to make sure you're safe, Rita's offered to stay here when I'm on travel, and she's a great shot. A second agent will come with her." Luke inhaled. "Plus the bureau will pay me a $5,000 stipend and all my expenses."

The tea kettle soon whistled. Layla walked to the stove.

"Why would they pay you so much for a simple babysitting job if it weren't risky?"

Luke coughed. "Since you signed the FBI nondisclosure agreement, I can tell you what I know about the job."

Layla poured boiling water into her teacup. "I'll keep it secret."

Luke drummed his fingers on the tabletop. "George is gonna meet with an Army major at a base out West. The infantry will test a Belarusian armored personnel carrier George is selling. The major's with Army Intelligence and will give George fake intelligence to pass on to the Belarusian KGB."

Layla's eyes flashed. "That's not unsafe?"

"It'll happen on a guarded Army fort."

Layla set her teacup on the oilcloth on the table, and hot tea splashed from the cup. "What about when you're not in the fort the rest of the week?"

"We'll be on a tour bus stopping at national parks. George will make sales calls during the trip. It's believed he's one of two Belarusian spies in the States, but he's on our side. I just need to talk about the tractor and drive it with a joystick."

Layla peered into her tea. *Should I say what I really think?* She had a moment of indecision and peered at Luke. "I don't believe you want to do it for the money. You like to play cops and robbers."

Luke appeared sheepish to Layla, and then he took a deep breath. "Yur right. I git shots of adrenaline from quick movin' events. That's why I like being a deputy sheriff. Do you want me to quit? I'll do it if you want."

Her chin trembling, Layla couldn't speak for a moment. Then her eyes felt like they'd burst, and her tears began to flow like they were dripping from a very leaky faucet. She wiped the wetness from her cheeks and swallowed. "I know why you like the high you get from taking chances. It's better than being a drunk. I'm glad you stopped drinking." She vacillated. "Okay, do the FBI job. Be safe. I love you."

Luke stared at the worn linoleum floor, blinked, and nodded. "Thanks. I leave Wednesday, May 28, the day after George delivers the tractor."

Layla turned in her chair, hugged him, and buried her face in his shirt. *I hope this FBI gig works out okay. Maybe he'll quit volunteering for dangerous stuff after that.*

FIVE

LAYLA WAS WATCHING a television situation comedy, *Charlie and Charley*, when Luke left his living room and went outside into his barn.

Luke pulled his satellite phone from his trousers pocket and sat on a tall wooden stool. As he scrolled through his contact list, he wondered if he was being too secretive by calling Rita from the privacy of the farm building.

He tapped Rita's name on the face of his device. The phone rang five times. "Hello, Luke. Did you speak with Layla about watching over George on his trip?" Rita's voice sounded hopeful.

"Yes." Luke sighed. "She's worried watchin' a turncoat KGB agent could be unsafe, and she burst into tears. But in the end, she agreed she was okay with me takin' the trip." Luke felt jumpy, still a bit upset by Layla's reaction to the FBI proposal. *Was that our first fight as a married couple? We both were civil and were worried about each other.*

Luke heard Rita move her phone against her ear, and then she asked, "Layla was crying?"

In his head, Luke saw a replay of Layla's show of emotion. He told himself, *She's concerned for our family's safety. I get it.* "She cried a lot." Luke was silent for a moment. "I shouldn't do any more FBI jobs after this one."

"Did you tell her how important the mission is and that George trusts you more than anyone else?"

"Yep. I gave her details about the Army info. I figure it was okay."

"That's fine. Layla signed the nondisclosure agreement." Rita waited a moment. "When I come over, I'll explain to her how this job is low-risk."

Luke wondered how well two women who were fond of him would do living together for a week. He figured Rita was unhappy he'd got Layla pregnant and married her, and he recalled Rita had made passes at him before his marriage with Layla. After those thoughts flashed across his brain, he heard himself speak. "Be careful how you talk to Layla. She's been emotional since she had the baby."

"Okay." Luke detected hesitation in Rita's voice.

Luke knew it was hard for him to deal with female emotions. *But I'm gettin' better at it. At least, I told Rita I'm not takin' any more FBI jobs after this one.*

Rita coughed. "Have any questions?"

"What's the real reason I gotta babysit George?"

Luke could hear Rita exhale two times into her cell phone's mouthpiece. "The Belarusian KGB may send a courier to pick up the bogus Army info from George. Be with George when the transfer occurs."

"Why?"

Rita paused. "Identify the second KGB guy, if you can. Take a picture of him with your phone and learn his name."

Luke stared down at his left hand. "Okay."

"Stay with George all the time."

"I can't guarantee it."

Rita sighed. "I know."

Luke stroked his scalp. "When are you gonna have the FBI set up the fence line electronic system?"

"A crew will be at your place by nine on Friday morning." She let her mind rest for a moment. "We would've had it done even if you'd declined the job."

"Thanks." Luke guessed the bureau still wanted to hire him full-time, but he knew he'd never take the job. Layla wouldn't like it, and he'd have to travel too much. He wished the FBI would stop asking him for help in the future, especially after he'd told Rita he was done doing bureau gigs. Would Rita pass the word to her superiors that he wasn't interested in being an FBI agent or doing occasional jobs for the Feds?

Rita's voice interrupted Luke's thoughts. "I told Jim Pike when the crew will install the system. He said you don't have to come in to work Friday."

"Will I hear from George before he gets here on May twenty-seventh?"

"Give him a call tomorrow. I'll text you his new number." She was quiet for a second. "Be sure to tell him about the attempt on your life, too."

"Why?"

"George is on our side now." Rita sounded like she'd choked up a bit. "He could be helpful if there's another attempt on your life."

"Maybe." Luke paused. "I gotta go."

"See you in a week. Bye."

* * *

9:00 P.M., TUESDAY, MAY 20, 2031, LUKE'S FARM

Luke slouched as he walked into the kitchen, where Layla sat while she was tapping the baby's back. Luke wondered if he'd made the right decision to go on the trip with George.

Layla moved little Russell against her chest and made strong eye contact with Luke. "What's wrong, honey?"

"Nothing." Luke leaned down and kissed his baby son's head. "I just phoned Rita and told her we'd decided I'd go with George durin' his sales trip."

Layla smiled and then embraced both Luke and Russell at the same time. She whispered in Luke's ear, "They'll pay you well for a week of work."

Luke felt warm inside. *Layla's less worried about the trip now.* "The money will help, and we'll get a free perimeter alarm system." His conscience told him that was a white lie because Rita had said the FBI would've installed the system whether or not he took the assignment.

Layla squeezed Luke's back. "Didn't you say you're leaving on May 28?"

"Yep, we'll fly to the state of Washington."

Layla scratched her head. "Be thankful we have five bedrooms. Let's invite George to stay overnight, and you can show him where to turn in his rental car."

Luke nodded. "I'll drive my truck and leave it at the airport. I can lead George to the rental returns."

Layla kissed Luke's lips. "I'm glad you asked me before deciding to go on the mission." She stopped talking for a moment. "You'll be busy getting ready to travel."

"Yeah. I gotta call George first thing after I git to work tomorrow."

SIX

CLEAR, bright sunlight beamed through the window onto Luke's desk, which sat in the large squad room near an outer wall. Because Sheriff Jim Pike had sent another cruiser to sit in Luke's driveway to watch over Layla and their children, Luke felt at ease. He figured now was the best time to call the KGB spy Yegor Bulot, who had Americanized his name. *I gotta remember to call him George Black, especially if another Belarusian agent shows up during the sales trip.*

Rita had sent a text to Luke, including George's new, secure number. Luke stared across the room and realized most of the deputies had left to go on patrol. Nobody was near him when he withdrew his encrypted satellite phone from his hip pocket and touched *George* on his contact list. *I won't talk loud.*

"Hello, Luke. It's swell to hear from you." George's Russian accent was obvious but better. "Rita said you would call." George had improved his pronunciation of English words, and his grammar had improved, too.

"Yegor—I mean George—I think you bin working on your English."

"Thanks. I took fast-track language course before I fly—I

mean, I took *an* English course before I flew here. Belarus Tractor Company paid tuition for it."

Luke noticed George had left out an *a* and a *the* from his last sentences, but his English was more fluent, and he'd spoken at a quicker pace.

I bet the KGB taught the English class. Luke liked hearing George's upbeat voice. *Despite all he's gone through, he sounds happy.* Luke moved his lips closer to his phone's mouthpiece. "Rita told me you'll be shipping the tractor to me on May twenty-seventh."

"That is okay day for you?"

"Yep."

"Your Model K tractor will get there by afternoon." Luke could hear George flip through papers. "I need deliver two more tractors to farms in Kentucky next two days."

Luke figured George had been busy making sales calls. "You sold two other tractors in Kentucky already?"

"Yeah." George laughed. "It easy to sell them. They are much less expensive than US models. Also, farmers like they can run them with remote control joystick, and later, a new AI program could run machine without human driver."

Luke realized George was a natural salesman, always on the job, praising his machines. "So, you still gonna need to send farmers here to see my Belarusian tractor?" Luke had signed a contract more than six months ago with the Belarus Tractor Company to use its Model K on his farm free of charge if he'd demonstrate it to other farmers. Luke had the option to buy the machine later.

Luke was surprised George had been quite successful selling farm machinery stateside even though he was new to the US.

Odds are George's Belarusian KGB bosses in Minsk are proud of him. With any luck, they won't figure out he's now a double agent working for the West.

If they discover his offense, they'll try to kill him. I hope the bogus info about the US Army George hands over to the KGB convinces them he's an excellent spy.

George interrupted Luke's lapse of attention. "Luke, we still have deal, and I need you demo and say Belarus Model K tractor is fine machine." George hesitated. "Besides, I can't wait see you, Layla, and new baby boy, Russell. Correct?"

"Yep. He's a healthy little critter."

"Critter?"

"Critter's a name for a living thing—like a small animal."

George laughed. "We're all little animals to start life. He will grow fast."

Luke peered out his window at a squirrel in a tree. "Time flies." He waited a moment and asked, "Do you like the US now that yur here?"

"Very much. Maybe later I quit my Belarusian job and apply to be US citizen."

Luke wondered if George would ever be able to quit the KGB. He'd have to fake his death or disappear and change his name. Luke wondered if George still drank too much vodka.

I could convince him to go to a LifeRing meeting to help him quit booze. LifeRing was sort of like AA. "George, don't eat a big breakfast the day you come here. Layla's plannin' a big country lunch for you."

"I never ate homemade Southern US lunch before. Thank you. I just drink coffee when I get up." Luke heard a beep on his phone. "I got another call. I hang up now."

Luke grinned. "See you May twenty-seventh."

"Until then." George disconnected. All of a sudden, Luke realized he hadn't told George about the sniper attack. *I'll tell him when he gets here.*

* * *

2:45 A.M., THURSDAY, MAY 22, 2031, LUKE'S FARM

The night was cold for late May. A strong breeze blew across Luke's fields of hemp. High above the farm, dense clouds blocked most of the trillions and trillions of starlight photons striking the planet over Kentucky. Even so, a few twinkling lights from distant suns poked through a break in the gloom. A sheriff's car sat in Luke's driveway, but the deputy sheriff in the cruiser had dozed off fifteen minutes ago.

Javier, the Mexican *sicario*, exited the fifteen-year-old, stolen pickup truck. He'd parked it behind dense bushes by Luke's west fence line. With care, he reached into the cargo area of the truck and removed a new sniper rifle he'd wrapped in an old rug.

José, his partner, watched as Javier attached a night-vision scope and a silencer to the weapon. José whispered, "Don't shoot the cop. If you do, and we're caught, they'll execute us on the spot."

"It doesn't happen that way in the US." Javier locked and loaded the weapon. "The sooner you plant the trackers on Luke Ryder's truck, the better. The cop could wake if you don't get moving."

José felt a chill shake his body, and the feeling wasn't due to the unusual, brisk weather. He knew he was scared, but he never wanted to show his fear to Javier.

José put on his night-vision goggles and began to follow the ditch running beside the paved highway toward Luke's driveway. As best he could, he stayed cloaked in the darkest shadows.

Then he saw Luke's new electric truck. Did it have a newfangled alarm system able to detect José's approach? José's teeth chattered, and their noise was loud. *Could a nearby person hear my clattering teeth?*

José slipped behind the bushes lining the gravel driveway. A bright light on a tall pole lit the truck, the thick hedge on the edge of the gravel drive, and the farmhouse. José crouched, lowered himself onto his belly, and low crawled under the bushes. He inched forward at a painstaking, slow rate. *Does Luke have a watchdog? I hope not.*

In ten minutes, José was next to Luke's pickup truck. Glancing through the squad car's open window, José saw a snoozing deputy.

When the lawman shifted his body, a sudden fear struck José, and he froze. José opened his mouth to better hear if the sleeping law enforcement officer was indeed waking. But the deputy began to snore, and he sounded as if he were enjoying his nap.

José eased out a slow, quiet breath. He crawled to the rear of the pickup truck, and sharp gravel bit into his stomach and hands. Taking the magnetic trackers from his breast pocket, he attached them underneath the truck's body.

I must get out of here before the cop wakes. Then a thought hit him. Had Luke installed surveillance cameras? If so, he might see José attach the trackers to the truck in a recording. Of course, he wouldn't get caught even if Luke saw him on a CCTV video tomorrow. By then, the two Mexican hitmen would be hiding in their cheap motel room again.

José realized he had to continue to be stealthy and not move too fast. *I'll be fine if I go back the same way I approached the truck — cloaked in the shadows of the thick bushes.* He exhaled a soft, slow breath. *I hope this is not a waste of time.*

Now José began to feel so scared his armpits were dripping sweat, though the cold wind blew harder. A drop of icy rain hit his forehead. *That could wake the cop in the car.* José moved faster as he crawled the last few yards to the ditch bordering the paved highway. *I must move even quicker now.*

SEVEN

LUKE STOOD in his driveway admiring a vivid green Model K tractor that had arrived on a flatbed truck at eight that morning. The farm machine's wheel hubs were bright orange.

Made by the Belarus Tractor Company, the versatile, electric-powered work vehicle included a Belarusian flag decal pasted on its hood.

Rain had dampened Luke's farm in the wee hours of the night, but now the sky was clear, and sunshine was warming his hemp fields. He felt refreshed in the rain-cleansed air.

Luke heard the driveway buzzer sound from a speaker the FBI had installed on his barn under the eaves. An electric eye the bureau's techs had attached to a post monitored his driveway entrance all the time.

Turning, Luke saw a blue, late-model electric sedan driving at a slow pace toward him over the gravel. *I wonder if Rita's here, or is it George?*

Luke squinted and peered at the driver. George Black, a.k.a. Yegor Bulot, the tractor salesman and KGB spy, was smiling. Though George's physique reminded Luke of a rottweiler, the man was as friendly as a collie. His handsome face, flashing dark black eyes, and coal-black hair appealed to women.

But he respects the fairer sex, Luke thought.

George stopped his vehicle behind Luke's pickup truck on the edge of the driveway and exited the car. "Luke, nice to see you again." He spoke with his distinct Russian accent. "Your farm is beautiful."

George extended his hand. Luke grasped it and said, "Yur as fit as a European soccer star."

George shrugged. "Funny you say that. When I took English class in Minsk, I played much football—I mean soccer."

Luke nodded. "I'm still gettin' used to calling you George Black."

"My Minsk KGB boss gave me new name. He was sure FBI would find me if I call myself Yegor Bulot." George laughed. "But would Belarusian man have the name George Black?"

Luke grinned. "Excellent question, but it'll be easier for US farmers to remember your Americanized name."

George leaned forward, and his eyes glowed. "I can't wait show you how to run tractor with joystick."

"It'll be fun."

George caught sight of a small wooden crate sitting next to the new tractor. "I help you unpack remote control."

Luke glanced at the wooden box. "I'll git a hammer and a crowbar from the barn. They packed the joystick real well."

Within five minutes, Luke had opened the pine crate. As he removed the joystick and a large computer monitor from the box, George was examining the tractor's dashboard, and he flipped a switch. "It has a full charge. I asked my technician to charge before shipping to you." He glanced at Luke. "You ready to do trial run?"

"Yep." Luke gestured at his farmhouse and its porch facing the field. "My laptop computer is there on the banquet table."

George grabbed the large monitor. "I'll attach monitor to your computer."

Luke noticed a full-size duplicate of the tractor's dashboard controls was also in the wooden box. "Do you hook this control panel to the joystick and computer, too?"

George peered backward as he carried the monitor. "Yes. Has same controls near computer, and joystick makes it easier to learn to run tractor from porch."

Working together, the men soon installed controller software on Luke's laptop and hooked up the tractor's remote dashboard and its off-the-shelf consumer joystick.

Luke gestured at the tractor. "Okay if I git in and drive it onto the grass? I can get the feel of it."

"Sure."

Luke stepped up into the tractor and sat down. It was as easy as an electric golf cart to switch on and drive.

As Luke walked back to the porch, George asked, "When is Rita going to be here?"

Luke climbed the wooden porch steps. "Lunchtime."

"I'm glad I will meet her in person." George shifted in his garden chair near the joystick. "She called me many times."

Luke sat on a lawn chair next to George. "There are a couple of reasons Rita's eatin' lunch with us." Luke gathered his thoughts. "One. She needs to brief you about meeting Major Green at Ft. Lewis. Two. She's gonna stay here and protect Layla while me and you are on the tractor sales trip."

"Why?"

"Remember how I told you two Mexican assassins from a Tijuana drug ring tried to kill me in London?"

"Yes." George drew his eyebrows closer together.

"A week ago, I was by the white oak." Luke pointed at the tree. "I bent down to tie my shoe, and a bullet hit the tree where I'd been standing."

George made strong eye contact with Luke. "Mexican drug cartel tried again?" George's accent was stronger, and he frowned.

"We think it's them again." Luke lifted his chin. "I can't

have 'em go after Layla, the baby, and my stepdaughter, Angela. If nobody were watchin' them, I wouldn't go on the sales trip."

George wrinkled his brow. "Will you carry firearm on trip?"

"Yep. I'll have two pistols."

"I expert shot. Rita will give me a gun?"

"I don't think so."

George seemed disappointed.

George is okay, even if he's a spy. "George, if you got in a shootout, that'd blow yur cover, and they're after me, not you."

"If they try shoot you, I will help you." George winked.

Luke observed him. "I bet the two hitmen fled to Mexico."

George nodded.

Luke grinned and touched the tractor joystick. "Now, can you show me how this gizmo works?"

* * *

10:02 A.M., TUESDAY, MAY 27, 2031, MABEL'S MOTEL

Javier stared at the face of his small iPad. A glowing icon representing Luke's truck on the computer's digital map showed the pickup was sitting in Luke's driveway. "He didn't go to work today." Javier began to wonder if he'd need to sneak onto Luke's farm and take another shot at the man to satisfy Mateo.

Javier imagined the ruthless cartel leader was getting more and more irritated as the days passed by and Luke was still alive. *Damn, Mateo might send someone after me if I don't take out this Kentucky deputy in another week.*

José shook his head. "For the last week, all Luke did was drive back and forth to the sheriff's department."

Javier shrugged. He didn't want José to see he was

concerned, even scared of Mateo. "Luke's going to work, and then he switches to a squad car we can't track. Today, or the next day, he's bound to drive someplace else. We'll kill him then."

EIGHT

LUKE MOVED the joystick while he peered at his computer screen and the tractor-eye TV view of his field. He watched as the heavy-duty farm machine rolled across the lawn toward his house. "Runnin' this tractor from my porch is easy." *I got used to this remote control fast. I bet Layla could learn to use it in a half hour.*

George leaned back in his chair and smiled. "Even grandmother can steer tractor with joystick and run all controls."

Luke tilted his head. "Usin' the remote control is fun, but does it make a difference?"

George stretched. "Yes. You can train tractor's AI software to follow rows of crops. After you saw robot battle tank in UK, you know we work to make AI software able to run tractor without human input. This is a secret plan."

Luke nodded and stopped the tractor next to his red barn. At the same time, a green sedan turned into his lengthy driveway. He squinted, and he saw FBI Agent Rita Reynolds waving as she drove toward the farmhouse and stopped her vehicle near George's rental car. Luke glanced at George. "Rita's here."

Of medium height, she was in her mid-thirties and attractive.

The men got up and walked across the crunchy gravel toward the agent's car. Rita got out and took two steps toward them, her hair bouncing. "Luke, nice to see you." She spoke in a soprano voice. Redirecting her attention toward the Belarusian spy, she said, "You must be George."

George dipped his chin for a moment and grinned. "I am honored to meet you in person, Miss Reynolds." Bowing a bit, he held out his hand and shook hers.

Rita's cheeks colored. "You can call me Rita." She smiled as the enticing aroma of Southern fried chicken wafted through the screen door at the rear kitchen doorway.

Luke sniffed the air. "I think Layla has lunch close to bein' ready."

Rita blinked and inhaled. "Smells delicious." She had a moment of indecision. "But before I go in, I should grab the M16 from the trunk."

"You brought an M16?"

"Yes, and two hundred rounds loaded in ten magazines."

Luke raised his eyebrows and cocked his head. "That's real firepower."

She noticed George open his mouth for a second and appear puzzled. "Didn't Luke tell you I'll be here guarding his house when you're on the trip?"

George glanced at Rita and then shrugged. "I heard there is much crime in the US. Smart to be ready."

Rita turned to Luke. "Didn't you tell me you bought a new rifle security cabinet?"

Luke nodded. "It's in the spare bedroom you'll use. I got an extra cabinet key fur you, too." He reached into his pocket and gave Rita the key. "I also bought a semiautomatic, 12-gauge shotgun that's in the cabinet."

Rita gazed at the key for a second. "Thanks." She opened her trunk and took out the automatic military rifle. "Is the cabinet big enough for two of these? I told Agent Tom Trent to bring one as well. He'll arrive after dinner and take the night watch."

"There's plenty of room." Luke took Rita's suitcase from the trunk. "I'll carry this in and show you the room." He hefted the large case and began to carry it toward the house. "The two of you agents will have enough automatic firepower to hold off a half dozen crooks."

Rita glanced at her M16. "I'll feel better having it with me."

Luke recalled he'd gone hunting with Rita when they were in high school. Even then she had been a great shot.

George stepped toward the trunk. "I help carry things."

Rita pointed at a canvas bag. "You can take the bag of extra magazines."

* * *

11:55 A.M., TUESDAY, MAY 27, 2031, MABEL'S MOTEL

Javier rested in an easy chair in his cheap hotel room in Lexington, Kentucky, drinking a beer.

Jarred by the sudden ringing of his satellite phone, Javier set his beer can on an end table near his chair. "*Hola, Jefe.*"

Javier thought he heard Mateo chewing on something crunchy, like breakfast bacon. "What progress have you made in regard to Luke Ryder?"

"José put two trackers on Luke's truck. We're monitoring his travels, but he's merely gone back and forth from the sheriff's office and his farm. There's often a squad car in his driveway." Now uneasy, Javier's voice was shaky.

Javier heard Mateo inhale through his nostrils and ease air out with a whistling sound. Then the drug czar spoke. "Do you think you can take another shot at Luke, perhaps tomorrow?"

The telephone connection was quiet for two seconds. "We could, *Jefe*, but we might miss if it's a distant shot."

Javier coughed. "I suggest we wait for a sure shot." *Was that the right answer? Am I now on Mateo's shit list?*

Javier heard liquid pouring near Mateo's phone. *Was Mateo on speakerphone? He sounded off-mike. Was he drinking whiskey, though it was 8:55 a.m. in Tijuana?* Mateo spoke. "You decide when to strike because you are the professional, but I want Luke dead soon."

"*Sí, Jefe.*" Javier's pulse now pounded as he stared at his phone, waiting for Mateo to speak.

After three seconds, Mateo said, "Next time I call, perhaps you will have a better report." Mateo disconnected.

NINE

RITA SMELLED BALES OF HAY, and she noticed their odor mixed with the clean scent of fresh air blowing through the red barn's wide doorway. She'd called a meeting because she wanted to make sure Luke and George were familiar with the details of the FBI's plan to mislead the Belarusian KGB.

Luke, George, and Rita walked to the far inside wall of the big farm building and sat at an unpainted picnic table.

Rita studied George's eyes. *Making a personal connection with George is important because he has to trust me.*

Using a gentle touch, she put her hand on George's arm. " I'm glad we've met in person. The United States is grateful to have you on our side."

George showed a warm smile. "Miss Reynolds—I mean Rita—I am lucky to be here. I love US."

Removing her hand from George's arm, Rita rested her palm on the rough, pine surface of the table. "Both the FBI and I don't want you to take chances because we want you to stay alive."

George appeared puzzled. "Spy work is chancy. If KGB finds I work for West, they will order my execution."

Rita tilted her head and made strong eye contact with George. "If you hear Minsk has learned you are working for us, promise me you will call me day or night to let me know, and we will protect you."

George nodded. "I promise."

Rita trained her gaze at Luke. "I'm worried about you, too, Luke." She felt her heart begin to throb. "You have taken lots of chances in the last two years, and you were lucky not to have been killed. Stay safe."

Luke nodded. "I'll be careful."

Rita sat up straight. "Let's get down to business." She glanced through the barn's wide opening at the blue sky above the trees lining the bright white gravel driveway. She studied George for a moment, focusing on his dark hair and handsome face. "The main objective of this trip is to convince the Belarusian KGB you have paid Major Green for useful secret intelligence about the US Army."

George winked. "Your plan will work."

Rita grinned and then peered at Luke. "If anyone has questions, stop me, and I'll answer them."

Luke raised his chin while George smoothed his shirt, both waiting for Rita to continue speaking.

Rita began. "The FBI has been working with Army Intelligence on this assignment. As instructed by the FBI, George has contacted Major Jack Green at Ft. Lewis in the state of Washington, where the 9th Infantry Division is stationed. Though he's with Army Intelligence, Major Green is posing as a member of the 9th. That division will test an inexpensive armored personnel carrier manufactured by the Belarus Tractor Company." She paused, then shook her head and smiled.

Luke cocked his head. "This whole thing strikes me as strange."

"I agree." Rita was tentative for a brief moment, seeming to gather her thoughts. "Fickle politicians from the East and West signed an agricultural trade agreement to encourage peaceful coexistence, and oddly, they also use it to justify trading military equipment. Meanwhile, we in the intelligence community continue to mistrust each other and figure out ways to deceive one another."

George rubbed his hand through his hair. "It is true. We play spy games, like when Major Green will give me fake intelligence about US Army that I will pass to KGB." He smiled. "But I say, make love, not war. Maybe I find American girlfriend." He laughed.

Rita displayed a wide grin. "You shouldn't have much trouble convincing a woman to date when you have $60,000 of the KGB's money to play around with."

Luke scratched his temple. "Does this mean a bunch of spooks on both sides will benefit from this game?"

Rita's eyes twinkled. "Yes. Secret agents in both the East and West will keep their jobs and get paid. You're getting paid, too, Luke." She glanced at George. "The FBI even helped George open a foreign bank account where he can deposit his money."

George bit his lips and sighed.

Rita folded her hands under her chin and then leaned back. "George has to maintain his cover as a tractor salesman to satisfy the KGB. The trip to US national parks will prove to Minsk he's not been detected by US intelligence."

George straightened his back. "Luke will help much cuz he will say it is easy to drive tractor with joystick." George stared through the wide barn doorway at the new Model K Belarus tractor. "Luke learned fast how to run tractor with remote control. He will answer customer questions better than me. I think I will make many sales on trip cuz of Luke." George flashed Luke a thumbs-up sign.

Rita saw Luke's smile grow wider. *Luke seems happy.*

Luke caught George's attention. "Tell me more about the bus tour."

George nodded. "It paid for by Belarus. KGB thinks I will convince you to become Belarusian agent if I treat you well. So, I bought expensive bus tour. We will stay at best hotels.

Eat at great restaurants. After we go to Ft. Lewis, we fly to Vegas. We join bus tour there. It goes 3,000 miles and visits many parks and cities."

Luke scratched his scalp. "We have to get up early tomorrow morning to get to the airport to catch our flight."

George pulled his satellite phone from his pocket. "I will set alarm. Thank you for letting me stay in spare room, Luke."

Rita observed George. He appeared excited about his upcoming sales trip.

She thought, *George did well conning the spies in Minsk. I doubt the FBI would have paid for a luxury bus trip with stops at the best hotels and restaurants. George knows how to play the spy game and have fun, too.*

Rita stood and stretched. "Let's close this meeting."

Luke got up. "I'll help George git his suitcase from his car and show him his room."

* * *

2:30 P.M., TUESDAY, MAY 27, 2031, LUKE'S FARM

Luke spotted a large suitcase in the trunk of George's rented car. *The man doesn't travel light.* As Luke reached down to grab the big piece of luggage, he glimpsed at George and said, "You packed a bunch."

Luke set the case on the gravel driveway, and George closed the trunk lid. "I live out of car." He moved toward the hefty suitcase. "I carry this."

Luke held the kitchen's screen door open as George hauled his luggage into the kitchen. "Yur room is down the hall." Luke pointed and led the Belarusian spy to a medium-sized bedroom at the end of the hallway.

I'm lucky this house has five bedrooms.

After Luke pushed the room door open, he noticed Layla had put a fancy blanket on the bed.

George rolled the suitcase across the room's rug. "Bedroom is nice. Thank you, Luke."

"Yur welcome. It's enjoyable to have visitors."

George sat in one of two chairs. "I need tell you something."

Luke's eyebrows furrowed and then relaxed, and he sat in the second chair. "What is it?"

"My boss in Minsk, Viktor, wants me recruit you to work for Belarusian KGB. That is why he agreed to give you special deal on Model K tractor."

Luke rubbed his chin and cocked his head.

George leaned forward. "I told Rita and other FBI people 'bout this. They want you to work with me on longtime basis."

Luke showed a hard smile. "Rita should have told me about this."

George peered down at the carpet. "I think she will tell you tonight, away from me." He was mute for a moment. "If you work with me against KGB, I would be honored. FBI would like it."

"I'm sure we would work well as long-term partners against the KGB, George, but I've got to talk with Rita before I decide. For now, let's just do the bus trip."

George nodded. "But there's more. KGB want to hire women to blackmail you."

* * *

2:45 P.M., TUESDAY, MAY 27, 2031, LUKE'S FARM

Luke left George to unpack in the guest bedroom and went into the kitchen. Rita held the baby in her arms and was speaking with Layla. Both women glanced up as Luke came near, and he smiled. "Russell's gettin' lots of personal attention from two women."

Rita kissed the little boy and handed him to Layla. "He's a cutie."

Luke nodded and caught Rita's attention. "I'd like to show you my little SCCY pistol. It's a great weapon of last resort."

Rita stood. "Okay."

Luke motioned for Rita to follow him outside. "I locked it up in my old pistol gun safe in the barn." He looked at Layla. "We'll be back in a few minutes."

Layla nodded.

* * *

2:48 P.M., TUESDAY, MAY 27, 2031, LUKE'S FARM

Rita sat on top of the picnic table in the barn, and Luke took a seat next to her. He glanced at a handgun safe on a rough wooden shelf on the wall. "I don't need to show you the SCCY pistol unless you really want to see it." Luke pressed the tips of his fingers together as he wondered why Rita had withheld information from him. "Why didn't you tell me George's boss in the KGB, Viktor, asked him to recruit me into the KGB?"

Rita swallowed. "I wanted to take you aside and talk about it when George wasn't around."

Luke lifted his chin. "Okay, what is it you couldn't say in front of George?"

"Army Intelligence isn't sure whether George is on our side or is feigning allegiance to the West." Rita leaned away from Luke. "What did George tell you?"

Luke sighed. "I think he told me all he knows. Said the KGB wants to set me up with a woman, take pictures of me and her, and blackmail me. He said the FBI wants me to work with the KGB as a double agent." Luke's nostrils flared. "There's no way I'm gittin' in bed with another woman. I'm not cut out to be a spy, and I won't do it."

Rita crossed her arms. "So the honey-trap-woman technique won't work on you, and George will tell Viktor that. Instead, they'll try to pay you to work for them."

"Like I said, it isn't in the cards. After this gig, I'm done working as an FBI counterespionage guy."

Rita sighed. "Okay, but the FBI is certain the KGB will try to recruit you on the trip, either through George or another way." She waited a moment and said, "Be on the alert. Just let us know what happens."

Luke nodded.

Rita squinted. "Call me every so often when George is not near. Observe him to see if he's loyal or not."

Luke felt his body relax. "I'll call you, but George is okay. He likes America."

Rita shifted her shoulders. "There's always a chance you'll change your mind about George." She coughed. "In that case, if George or someone else asks you to join the KGB, take their money." She studied Luke for a moment. "You wouldn't be prosecuted if you take their rubles. Just let me know."

TEN

A SHRILL ALARM connected to the tracker app on Javier's satellite phone sounded and woke him and José.

Javier groaned. *Damn it. What time is it?* He grabbed his mobile from the bedside table. An electronic map glowed on the phone display, depicting the vicinity of Luke Ryder's farm. Two icons representing the trackers on the lawman's truck were moving. When the trackers had first sensed the truck's movement, they had set off the app's alarm in Javier's phone. "Luke's on the move. Get dressed, José."

"*Sí.*" José pulled on his trousers while glancing at the digital clock next to his double bed.

The two Mexican assassins dressed in less than a minute, grabbed their gun cases and go bags, and tumbled into their rental car, which already held the rest of their luggage. Javier was at the wheel. "Here's my phone, José." José grasped the device. "Call out Luke's route to me."

José nodded.

Javier rolled down his driver-side window an inch. *I must hear as well as see. This could be our best chance to take out Luke Ryder.*

Javier turned to José. "I'll catch up with him and then

follow his vehicle until we find an out-of-the-way place to smoke him." Javier pushed the electric car's start button and glanced back at José. "Make sure the weapons are ready."

"*Sí, sí.*" José rubbed his eyes as Javier pressed the accelerator, and the vehicle's tires squealed. The irritating smell of burning rubber entered the auto's interior.

After fifteen minutes, José said, "Luke's turning onto Route 60, going east."

Javier's brain was running at full speed. "What's along Route 60?"

"Lexington Bluegrass Airport, shopping centers, housing developments."

Javier noted there weren't many cars on the road, but as he stared through his windshield, he saw a pickup in the left lane in the distance. He felt his muscles tighten. "There's his truck ahead." Javier pushed down on the accelerator pedal.

José bit his lip and then spoke. "Don't get too close. He might see us."

Javier glanced at the Springfield 1903 rifle propped up between José's legs. "Is it locked and loaded?"

His brow wrinkling, José took a deep breath. "*Sí,* but don't shoot him on this road. Even if traffic's light now, rush hour starts soon."

Javier stamped on the accelerator. "If we get a chance, we'll take a shot."

Glancing down at the satellite phone's display, José peered at the electronic map. "The airport's on the right."

Since he'd begun to follow Luke's truck, Javier had noticed a blue, late-model, electric sedan was close behind the truck. "You're right, José. We'll wait to shoot. That guy in the blue car's been right behind the truck for a while, and more cars are around now, too." Javier slowed and stayed far behind the blue sedan.

Luke's truck signaled and steered into the right lane, and the blue car did the same.

The traffic light at the next intersection stayed green as Luke's truck, as well as the blue sedan and Javier turned right onto Man O' War Boulevard. José rolled down his front passenger-side window. The sound of a jetliner thundered above as the plane came in for a landing.

José glanced down at the electronic map on Javier's phone. "They're going to the airport. Get ready to turn right on Terminal Drive."

Javier stared ahead as Luke's truck and the blue car turned right. "If they get on a plane, we'll try to get on the same flight. We can leave this rental here. The airport's small."

José coughed. "Drop me off where they park, and I'll follow them inside."

"Nice plan. Take your go-bag. Call me if you learn what plane they're on, and I'll catch up with you."

* * *

5:25 A.M., WEDNESDAY, MAY 28, 2031, LEXINGTON BLUEGRASS AIRPORT

Luke yawned as he drove to the rental car drop-off area at the airport. He recalled how he'd gotten up during the wee hours of the night to pace around with his fussy baby son, Russell. *I'm glad I did it. I won't see him again for a week.*

Luke glanced in his rearview mirror and watched as George pulled his blue rental sedan into a parking lot where a crowd of new automobiles sat. In less than five minutes, George walked to Luke's truck, got in, and smiled. "It fast and easy to turn in rental car in US." His luggage was already loaded in Luke's pickup truck.

* * *

5:32 A.M., WEDNESDAY, MAY 28, 2031, LEXINGTON BLUEGRASS AIRPORT

After Javier stopped his vehicle in a parking space near the rental car lot, José began to blink. He felt his nerves firing as he rushed to shove the Springfield 1903 rifle into its hard case and lock it. At the same time, Javier stowed their handguns into a separate pistol case and secured it.

Javier did the right thing when he filled out the special firearm tags ahead of time.

Though Lexington Bluegrass Airport was small compared to most metropolitan airfields, José noticed many cars had begun to arrive at the rental car drop-off point.

As Luke began to drive his vehicle toward the airport's covered, long-term parking area, José watched.

José asked, "I wonder if the guy is a friend of Luke's?"

"Maybe." Javier had put his car in gear and started to follow the truck. "He's going to park in the covered lot."

José asked, "Where are the firearm documents so we can check the gun cases?"

"In the built-in pouches on the hard cases. Put one tag on each case handle. Use the tags that match our San José, California, IDs."

José nodded. He recalled they had six sets of fake IDs, the best counterfeit documents money could buy.

At the same time Luke drove his truck through the parking area entrance, Javier stopped his rented sedan. "Get out, José. Take the pistol case and your go bag. Follow them inside the terminal and try to figure out where they're going."

"*Sí.*"

As José scrambled from the car, Javier yelled, "I'll circle around and drop off the car at the rental lot. Call if you need to."

* * *

5:38 A.M., WEDNESDAY, MAY 28, 2031, LEXINGTON BLUEGRASS AIRPORT

Luke felt a cool breeze cut through the covered parking lot as he and George pulled their wheeled luggage behind them. Luke also carried a small, locked case that held his miniature SCCY and full-size Glock pistols.

As the men headed toward the entrance doors of the terminal building, Luke was glad the airfield wasn't huge like Chicago's O'Hare or Atlanta's Hartsfield-Jackson Airports.

It won't take long to go through security.

As Luke walked inside the terminal, he scanned the signs above the airline counters that stood against the far wall of the lengthy rectangular room. In seconds, he saw the Citizens Airline logo and then glanced at George. "There's where we check our baggage."

George nodded. "I'm glad FBI travel office made airplane reservations even though I paid for tickets, but I worry KGB will find out."

Luke maintained eye contact with George. "It's fine. Rita says the FBI travel department is used to making secret arrangements." Luke pointed. "Let's go to a kiosk and print our tickets and baggage tags."

* * *

5:42 A.M., WEDNESDAY, MAY 28, 2031, LEXINGTON BLUEGRASS AIRPORT

His forehead beading with sweat despite the cool breeze, José amped up his courage. At a brisk pace, he walked through the terminal building's middle entry after an automatic door swung open. Peering ahead across the bright room, he watched as Luke and the mystery man with coal-black hair neared an array of electronic kiosks. The two men stood near the Citizens Airline ticket counter.

José reminded himself he'd altered his appearance after his disastrous encounter with Luke months before in London, England. José had attacked Luke with a knife during a murder attempt, but Luke had hit him with a garden hoe, breaking José's wrist. Since then, José had let his hair grow out from a crew cut into a long, thick mat, and he had also grown a black beard to conceal his face. He appeared older and wore a baseball cap, hiding much of his forehead.

Luke won't recognize me, José reassured himself. *I'll ease up behind him and check the kiosk screen to see what flight he's on.*

Quickening his pace, José avoided staring at Luke as the Kentucky deputy sheriff puzzled over the kiosk's on-screen buttons and instructions.

His heart pumping like a gasoline engine piston, José let go of the handle of his roller-equipped suitcase, set down his locked pistol case, and yanked his satellite phone from his hip pocket. After turning on his phone camera, he pretended to speak as he got ready to shoot bursts of three pictures per second.

The moment Luke printed a boarding pass, José touched his phone's shutter release and saw the lawman would take flight 495 to Seattle-Tacoma International Airport, leaving at 6:30 a.m. The flight's estimated time of arrival was 10:50 a.m., Pacific time.

Luke printed a second boarding pass, and José shot a second burst of pictures. Enlarging an image of the second pass, José saw the mystery man's name was George Black, and he, too, was traveling to Seattle. Both men were flying first class, so they'd sit in the front of the cabin.

Turning his back to Luke and George, José peered at his phone's contact list and found Javier's name. He touched it.

Javier answered on the second ring. "You near Luke?"

In Spanish, José replied, "*Sí*, Luke and the other man checked into Citizens Airline flight 495. It leaves at six-thirty for Seattle."

"Nice work. When you buy your ticket, get mine, too. Use our San José, California IDs. I'll be there soon."

José nodded. "Hope the flight isn't full."

"I doubt it." Javier disconnected.

* * *

5:48 A.M., WEDNESDAY, MAY 28, 2031, LEXINGTON BLUEGRASS AIRPORT

Luke glimpsed at George. *He appears relaxed but tired. We both should sleep on the flight.*

Luke handed George a boarding pass. "Let's check our baggage."

George nodded and scanned behind him, where two men, who seemed to be Latinos, spoke in low tones.

As George pulled his suitcase toward the ticket counter and baggage checking point, he turned to Luke and whispered, "There are many people here who appear to be Mexican."

Luke shrugged. "Lots of horse farm workers are from Latin America."

Luke turned and faced the ticket counter attendant, a young brunette woman. She appeared to be in her mid-twenties. He smiled and spoke. "I got a suitcase and a smaller case to check." He tapped his breadbox-size piece of luggage draped over his wheeled suitcase. "I packed two pistols in this gun case. Yur website says I should fill out paperwork and attach it." The case contained Luke's smaller SCCY pistol and his larger Glock firearm.

The young lady asked, "Could I see ID?"

Luke flipped his wallet open to display his deputy sheriff's ID card. She blushed and handed him a form. He knew his pistols had to be unloaded while in the aircraft's cargo hold. As required by the airline, he'd packed ammunition in a special container in his carry-on briefcase.

After signing the forms, he glanced behind him and saw

the two Latinos George had noticed minutes earlier. The men seemed anxious.

A second airline employee behind the counter, a black man, coughed and caught the attention of the Latinos. "May I help you?"

Fumbling with his wallet while his friend with the beard peered down at the carpet, the Latino said, "Yes. First, I must find my documents." Turning away from Luke and George, he reached into his pocket.

Luke nodded at George, and they headed toward the Transportation Security Agency passenger screening area that led to their flight's departure gate.

George had begun to hum a tune Luke figured was a Belarusian song. "You sound happy."

George's eyes danced. "This will be fine trip. You will like."

* * *

5:53 A.M., WEDNESDAY, MAY 28, 2031, LEXINGTON BLUEGRASS AIRPORT

As Javier pulled his fat wallet from his pocket, he flashed a nervous grin at the African American man behind the counter. "I would like to buy two one-way tickets to Seattle on flight 495." He sighed. *I hope there's room on the flight. If the flight's full, we won't be able to tail Luke, and Mateo will be livid.*

The counter attendant tapped on his keyboard. "You're in luck. There's still six seats left."

Javier opened his wallet. "I'll pay in cash."

The attendant nodded. "Cash is okay." He quoted the charges for the two tickets and accepted Javier's hundred-dollar bills.

Javier asked José in Spanish. "Did you attach the firearm forms?"

"Yes."

The man behind the counter handed Javier two boarding passes. "Have bags to check?"

Javier put his rifle's carrier on the baggage scale built into the row of counters. "I have this firearms case to check. The declaration tag is on it already. Also, my friend has a similar case."

The airline representative examined the tags and baggage. "You guys goin' hunting?"

Javier smirked. "Yes. We hunt a lot." He glanced at José. *Hit men are hunters. I can't wait until I get a shot at Luke. Maybe I'll take a trophy if I can. Why not? Deer hunters do.*

* * *

6:15 A.M., WEDNESDAY, MAY 28, 2031, LEXINGTON BLUEGRASS AIRPORT

Javier and José moved at a slow pace. They followed the airplane aisle toward their seats, two rows behind the craft's wings. Glancing to his right, Javier caught sight of Luke in the rear row of the first-class seating section. The lawman was facing forward and might have been able to focus on the two assassins, but Javier glanced far to his left and crouched as if to peer out of an airplane window. *Did Luke see José's face?*

After he passed Luke, Javier peeked back to his left and noticed José was staring away from Luke. *Quick thinking, José.*

As he and his fellow *sicario* found their seats, Javier breathed easier. Things were going better than he'd expected. *Luke and his friend will be among the last of the first-class passengers to leave the plane after it lands at Seattle-Tacoma Airport. We're close enough to get out not too far behind Luke, so the hunting gods are smiling down on us. Isn't Diana the Roman goddess of hunting?* Javier racked his brain, trying to remember lessons from a mythology class he'd taken in the last year of his *preparatoria* school in Tijuana.

As Javier eased back in his seat, he began to envision aiming his Springfield 1903 rifle equipped with a silencer. He peeked through its scope to put its crosshair over Luke's chest. With a gentle touch, Javier would squeeze the trigger, the weapon would fire, and the gunshot would surprise Luke. He imagined Luke falling like a puppet whose strings had been cut. *It's fortunate I bought a spare Springfield 1903 to replace the one I left in the car for the cops to find.*

Javier peered toward the front of the airplane and saw the back of Luke's head. *I'll get him.* Javier grinned, showing his coffee-stained teeth.

* * *

6:25 A.M., WEDNESDAY, MAY 28, 2031, LEXINGTON BLUEGRASS AIRPORT

Luke glanced out the jetliner's window near his seat and relaxed as the plane taxied to the runway. He turned to face forward and felt his eyelids droop, but he stayed awake. As he relaxed, he began to think. *We'll land at Seattle-Tacoma Airport before eleven Pacific time. The drive to Joint Base Lewis-McChord should take about a half hour.*

He'd studied an email Rita had sent him about the military base. Sited between Puget Sound and the Cascade Mountains, the installation was one of the biggest military bases in the US. Lewis-McChord included the Army's Ft. Lewis, McChord Air Force Base, and Madigan Army Medical Center.

As the plane climbed, Luke's eyes closed, and his body felt as if it were floating in a warm swimming pool. In his dreams, Luke saw a man in the distance with a rifle taking aim at him. A muzzle flash and the report of the weapon startled him, and he tried to dive to the ground, but he couldn't move. *Will the bullet hit me?*

ELEVEN

NEAR THE END of the long flight, George peered through the window to his left, and Luke tapped the spy's shoulder. "Let's talk about the man who may meet you during the trip to pick up the Army documents." Luke had whispered loud enough so George could hear him over the roar of the jet engines. The plane was beginning its final approach to Seattle-Tacoma Airport in the state of Washington.

George narrowed his eyes. "What do you want to know?"

Luke tilted his head to the side. "How will you recognize him?"

"Ninety percent chance Minsk send man I know." George moved three inches closer to Luke. "Also, whoever it is will use password."

"What is it?"

"I write on paper, then destroy." George wrote on the inside of a candy bar wrapper, holding his hand over it as he jotted two words. He crumpled the paper and passed it to Luke.

Straightening the note under his left palm, Luke read two words, *range* and *man*. Luke glimpsed at George. "How do you use them?"

George bit his lip and edged another half-inch closer to Luke. "Courier say first word. I say second one." George was silent for four seconds. "You only US or UK person I tell this to. I trust you."

Luke passed the wrinkled wrapper back to George. *I believe he does trust me.* Watching George shred the paper with his fingers, Luke said, "Thank you. I'll watch yur back, George."

George winked and nodded while tearing the paper into smaller and smaller bits. He dropped them into a trash bag a stewardess carried as she walked along the aisle.

Within five minutes, the plane landed ahead of schedule at 10:40 a.m., Pacific time.

Luke figured the KGB courier might meet George and him at a crowded location after Major Green had given George the secret documents. *Would the best place to do the handoff be when we go back to Seattle-Tacoma Airport to catch our flight to Las Vegas, where the bus tour starts?*

* * *

11:05 A.M., WEDNESDAY, MAY 28, 2031, SEATTLE-TACOMA INTERNATIONAL AIRPORT

Luke and George were lucky their pieces of luggage were among the first items from flight 495 to circle the baggage carousel conveyor belt. Luke and George grabbed their cases and began to walk toward a sign that read, "Rental Cars."

Meanwhile, from seventy-five feet away, Javier and José stood behind a concrete pillar next to the carousel and watched Luke and George walk toward the rental car area. Javier nudged José. "Quick, tail them to the car rental desks and rent a car. I'll be there soon, but if I'm late, follow them with your rental and call me. If I have to, I'll rent a second car and follow you."

"Okay." José turned and began to shadow Luke and George.

At once, Javier caught sight of their luggage because he'd tied yellow ribbons on their bags. With a strong voice, he said, "José." The smaller assassin turned and stopped. "I see our bags. Be there soon."

José nodded and began to power walk to catch up to Luke and George.

Javier trotted to the conveyor belt and grabbed his and José's luggage. Balancing the smaller bags atop the larger roller bags and holding the rifle case, he struggled to rush after José.

* * *

11:23 A.M., WEDNESDAY, MAY 28, 2031, SEATTLE-TACOMA INTERNATIONAL AIRPORT

After Luke slipped into his yellow rental car, he examined the rental car's GPS device. *Should be easy to use this.* He entered the address of the Joint Base Lewis-McChord main gate into the automobile navigation system.

George peered at the face of the GPS screen. "This says we should be at fort in thirty-eight minutes."

Luke nodded. *It'll take us fifteen minutes more to be cleared in by the guard and find Major Green's building.*

After leaving the airport, Luke steered the canary-colored rental car southwest on the Airport Expressway. The GPS guided the vehicle onto I-5 South and indicated a drive of thirty-six miles before taking Exit 120.

As Luke kept his eyes on the road ahead, he didn't notice the two Mexican assassins in a silver-gray, high-profile pickup truck following a hundred yards behind him.

Luke mentally reviewed the weapons he carried—his SCCY pistol, his Glock, ammunition, and a switchblade. The

FBI had cleared entry onto the fort for George, Luke, and Luke's weapons.

* * *

11:27 A.M., WEDNESDAY, MAY 28, 2031, I-5 SOUTH

Javier driving, the two *sicarios* followed Luke's bright yellow rental car. Blinking often, Javier stayed a decent distance behind Luke. "I don't want to lose him. I wish we could've put a tracker on his car." *Where the hell is he going? I must be ready to take a shot if they stop in a decent spot.*

José was taking the Springfield 1903 from its case. "I'll put on the scope and lock and load it."

Javier smiled. "You're reading my mind." *José might've lost his nerve after Luke hit him with the rake in London, but the little bastard still knows each detail of what has to be done and when to do it.*

José pulled out his compact binoculars from their case. "I'll watch them in case they get too far ahead."

Javier felt warm inside. "You're on the ball, José."

His eyes sealed against the small field glasses, José grinned. "*Gracias.*"

TWELVE

THE FEMALE GPS voice in the yellow sedan instructed, "Take Exit 120 toward Joint Base Lewis-McChord main gate."

Luke glimpsed at George. "We're here. We just gotta show the guard our IDs." *Once we git the Ft. Lewis part of this trip done, the rest of the week should be fun.*

George wrinkled his brow. "I hope guard not stop us too long."

Luke straightened his back as he steered onto the exit. "Don't worry. Rita said Army Intelligence made sure we'd go through the gate hassle-free."

After Luke got on 41st Division Drive, he began to watch for main gate road signs. A large, silver-gray pickup truck tailed Luke's yellow sedan, driving at twenty miles per hour.

* * *

As Javier followed Luke's bright yellow sedan around the

Exit 120 cloverleaf from I-5, he felt his body and mind go on high alert. "Where's Luke going?"

Through his compact binoculars, José peered left across the freeway. "I see a sign. He's heading straight for Joint Base Lewis-McChord." José paused. "It's a military base."

"We can't follow him onto a military installation. A guard will be checking IDs."

José glimpsed left at Javier. "We'll have to stake out the military gate."

Javier exhaled. "If he comes out on this street, we'll have no trouble spotting his bright yellow ride."

A fancy, red sports car began to tailgate Javier's truck, and then its driver blew his horn for two solid seconds, finally flashing Javier the finger. The assassin felt his pulse increase and his face grew red.

José stared at Javier. "Keep calm. We don't need to get into a fistfight."

Javier pulled onto a gravel strip running alongside the cloverleaf. He peered out the window at the driver, a man with messy hair and an armful of tattoos. Javier smiled and shrugged, but he whispered, "Jerk."

José continued to watch Luke's car. "No doubt he'll drive onto the fort."

Javier scratched his scalp. "If he doesn't take another exit from the fort, he'll get back on I-5. Will he go north toward the airport or head south?"

Javier figured Luke and his buddy were conducting business at the fort. *Luke won't stay there hours if they're having a meeting. But staking out the main gate exit even for an hour could be risky.* He sighed.

José took the binoculars from his eyes. "It's a fifty-fifty chance whether he'll go north or south."

Javier stared out the window at the layout of the cloverleaf. "I think Luke will go north back to the airport to fly back to Kentucky."

José glanced at Javier. "Unless you want to wait until Luke returns to Kentucky, the best time to take a shot is when he gets back on the highway. The airport is crawling with people and cops."

Javier nodded. *Little José is smart. But how can we stake out a military fort next to a freeway? We could fake a breakdown by stopping well off the edge of the cloverleaf and popping the hood open. That would work.* Javier turned his head toward José and said, "Mateo is impatient. Let's take Luke out when he gets back on the freeway going north toward the airport."

"How?"

"See across the cloverleaf where the ramp goes to north-bound I-5?" Javier pointed.

"Yes."

"We stop in the grass, open the hood, and wait."

José grasped the Springfield 1903 rifle. "How do you take a shot and not be noticed?"

Javier wet his lips with his tongue. "I'll stay down under the vehicle in the prone position with the rifle. People will think I'm working on the truck."

José's eyes gleamed. "I like your plan. The silencer will make the shot blend in with traffic noise."

Javier grinned. "It's an easy shot. If he's the one driving, he'll crash."

"He's always been the driver."

Javier cocked his head. "You sit in the driver's seat. After the shot, I'll get in, you step on it, and we'll drive north to the airport. There, we'll switch IDs and fly to LA."

José stared out the window toward the ramp leading to I-5's south lanes. "What if Luke goes south?"

"After I get back in the truck, you drive around the cloverleaf and follow him south." Javier stared at the fort across the freeway. "Good thing his car is yellow. We'll spot it and catch up."

Javier put the truck in gear and headed around the cloverleaf toward the northbound ramp.

José sighed. "We could be waiting for an hour."

Javier shrugged. "Yeah, but after we take Luke out, this nightmare is over."

* * *

12:03 P.M., WEDNESDAY, MAY 28, 2031, JOINT BASE LEWIS-MCCHORD

After getting entry badges, Luke drove his yellow sedan away from the Joint Base Lewis-McChord visitor reception building. He glanced left, ahead, and right, searching for street signs, and then began to cruise around on narrow side-roads. *There's a bunch of turns to get to Major Green's building.* The rental car GPS system didn't work on the military base. *Cuz of those terrorist threats last year, the military must've disabled GPS on the fort.*

George held a map the attendant at the visitor entry desk had given Luke. "I do not see Osborne street sign."

"I'll circle back." Luke noticed the fort was teeming with evergreen trees and verdant vegetation. Above the parklike grounds, the dark, cloudy sky was ominous. *Could be a rainstorm is on the way.* He knew the Pacific Northwest was often rainy, which helped trees and vegetation grow fast.

Driving twenty miles per hour in the right lane, Luke surveyed the side of the road. What appeared to be miniature Christmas trees grew not far from the roadway. Like hearty weeds, there were many of them the size of dandelion plants. Larger versions of the mini trees stood two feet tall or taller.

George pointed ahead. "See, the old gate of fort. Sign say, *Camp Lewis.*"

Slowing their automobile, Luke examined the old Lewis main gate as he drove past it.

George's eyes glowed. "I will study history of this fort. I like to learn about America. I want to be citizen."

Staring ahead, Luke cocked his head. "I think I see Major Green's building." Luke felt his stomach growl. "I bet he'll take us to lunch in the officers' club."

* * *

12:15 P.M., WEDNESDAY, MAY 28, 2031, GRASSY AREA ALONG I-5 NORTHBOUND RAMP

What seemed like a weak electric shock struck José when he glanced in the tall pickup truck's rearview mirror. A Washington State Patrol squad car was coming to a stop behind his rental truck in the short grass next to the I-5 ramp. The truck's hood was open.

Gulping, José hopped down from the driver's seat of the high-profile truck onto the green turf and forced himself to smile.

A tall, muscular patrolman approached and put on his hat. "You guys need me to call a tow truck?" The officer glanced at Javier's right leg which stuck out two or three inches from underneath the truck.

José tried to keep from shaking. "No, Officer. We called the rental company. They are sending tow truck." José knew his accent was thick but figured even if the lawman ran the license plate, he'd learn it was a rental.

The patrolman glimpsed at Javier's leg. "Did you hit something in the road?"

José noticed Javier scoot over his Springfield 1903 rifle to hide it under his body. Javier spoke from beneath the truck. "I'm taking a look for damage."

The officer nodded. "I'm glad you guys stopped off the freeway. Good luck. Have a good day." He tipped his hat and left.

José squatted next to Javier's leg. "What if the cop comes back?"

"No worries. Tell him we called the car rental office back, and they said the tow truck is on its way."

José stood. "Okay, I better get back in the truck in case Luke gets here soon."

* * *

12:15 P.M., WEDNESDAY, MAY 28, 2031, FT. LEWIS

After Luke and George exited their rental car, Luke felt a strong, west breeze. It had blown the black clouds east, so now they were barely visible in the distance. In contrast, the sky over the storied Army fort was now deep blue, and sunshine warmed Luke's face despite the wind. Scanning the horizon, he saw Mount Rainier. More than fourteen thousand feet tall, the volcano appeared to float like a mirage in the atmosphere. Luke knew it could erupt at any time. Scientists had detected weak quakes over the last few years near the mountain.

Luke watched as George grabbed his heavy-duty briefcase that he'd packed in his largest suitcase. Luke closed the vehicle's trunk, and the two men walked to a World War II-era building where Major Jack Green had his office on the second floor. The edifice was an elongated, two-story structure and needed a coat of paint.

Did the Army convert a barracks into an office building? Luke turned toward George. "Appears to be a barracks."

"Yeah. They do not want office to be noticed, eh?"

Luke nodded.

After climbing the steps to the second floor, Luke noticed the tiled floor was shiny and smelled of wax. He peered along the narrow central aisle and noticed offices on both sides of the passage.

Backlit and haloed by the bright sun coming through the windows, an officer in uniform stepped into the aisle and stood to face Luke. The officer took a step forward and squinted. "Are you George Black and Luke Ryder?"

Luke walked to the man and extended his hand. "Yep. Yur Major Green?"

"Yes." The major grasped Luke's hand with a strong grip. "Call me Jack. Pleased to meet you and George." He shook George's hand. "Before we start, I have to see your IDs."

Luke pulled out his wallet and flipped it open to display his Kentucky deputy sheriff's ID. While George took his

Virginia driver's license from his wallet, Luke wondered if the FBI or the CIA had smoothed the way for George to get his license.

Jack motioned toward a door near him. "Let's step into my office."

Luke guessed Jack stood five foot ten inches tall. The soldier was thin but strong and may have been in his forties. Gray hairs poked through his brown hair near his temples, and he sported a crew cut. When the major opened the sturdy steel office door, Luke noticed it had an electronic deadbolt with a keypad.

"Welcome to my humble office. Have a seat." Jack motioned to two gray, government-issue chairs by his metal desk. Let's finish official business first." He stood and turned to a heavy-duty strongbox that resembled an armored file cabinet. His body blocking Luke's view of the combination lock, Jack twirled its dial, opened the safe, and removed a large manila envelope.

Jack shoved the heavy safe door, and it closed with a clunk. "George, this is what you need. If someone asks what I did with the 60K you supposedly gave me, I bought a luxury car." Jack held the envelope out toward George.

Smiling, George took hold of it and peered inside. "Thank you, Jack."

Jack sat down behind his desk. "Your armored personnel carrier arrived yesterday. We'll test it next week and run it over rocks, through mud, and up and down steep hills."

"I am glad it came on time." George bent the metal clasps on the envelope down and slipped it into his briefcase.

Jack grinned. "I understand you guys are planning to fly to Vegas this afternoon. If you'd like to, let's drive to the officer's club for lunch." He pointed through his window at a jeep parked at the curb near the building.

Luke felt his stomach demand food. "That would be good, but we'll need to eat fast cuz we gotta leave by one to catch our flight."

Jack stood. "They have a grab-and-go serving line. You'll have plenty of time to eat."

As Luke got up, he wondered how soon a second KGB agent would meet George to pick up the secret Army documents. Would it be at the Seattle-Tacoma Airport or in Las Vegas?

* * *

1:05 P.M., WEDNESDAY, MAY 28, 2031, GRASSY AREA ALONG I-5 NORTHBOUND RAMP

Peering backward at the northbound I-5 entry ramp, José sat sideways in the driver's seat of the rented truck. His back felt strained. *Sitting this way and twisting isn't healthy.* He couldn't wait until the Kentucky lawman drove by and Javier shot him dead.

José glanced through the vehicle's passenger-side window at the sky. It was a saturated blue, and every once in a while, the strong wind shook the large pickup despite its heavy body. Training his eyes backward again, all of a sudden, he saw a bright yellow sedan getting on the ramp. Through the open window, he yelled, "He's coming."

José sucked air into his lungs, readying himself to take quick action after Javier fired his silenced Springfield 1903 rifle.

* * *

1:05 P.M., WEDNESDAY, MAY 28, 2031, I-5 NORTHBOUND RAMP

Luke turned onto the northbound ramp of I-5, heading for Seattle-Tacoma International Airport. *This trip should be easy from now on, except fur when the other KGB spy picks up the envelope from George.*

George coughed. "What time is our flight to Vegas?"

"About three. Should take two-and-a-half hours to fly to Vegas."

Left of the ramp, Luke saw what appeared to be a disabled pickup truck in a grassy area.

* * *

Javier had the jitters as he glimpsed behind him and saw the yellow sedan approaching. Lying prone on the grass beneath the pickup truck, he took a deep breath and let it out as he peered through his scope. A fraction of a second after the yellow sedan passed him, he put the sight's crosshairs over Luke's back.

With a light touch, Javier began to squeeze the trigger. A sudden jolt pushed him to his right at the same instant the silenced rifle fired, its muted sound blending into the traffic noise. The rifle's silencer caused the weapon to kick less than normal.

Damn, I missed. Must've hit the right side of the road. Javier felt as if he were drunk and the ground was in motion. *But I haven't been drinking.*

He looked behind him. *No cops.* He wrapped his rifle in a sweatshirt, rolled from under the truck, and tossed the weapon in the crew cab's back seat. "Go, José. I missed."

José pressed the accelerator pedal, and the truck leaped forward like a cheetah. "There was a temblor."

"An earthquake?"

"*Sí.* I'll turn on the radio."

"Don't lose them, José."

* * *

1:06 P.M., WEDNESDAY, MAY 28, 2031, I-5 NORTHBOUND

Luke felt the yellow rental sedan swerve sideways. He tightened his grip on the steering wheel and noticed trees on the side of the road bending sideways. It seemed like a sudden, strong wind had pushed the tree branches all at once.

Luke glanced at George. "Must be a storm comin' this way."

"I hope it not rain too much. I want to take off on time."

Luke turned on the radio. "I'll git a weather report."

Western music played on the radio, and after two minutes, Luke was about to try another station when the music stopped. "We interrupt this program to report a 6.0 magnitude earthquake struck on the Tacoma Fault. Seismologists say they believe it was felt in Tacoma and at Joint Base Lewis-McChord. We're getting calls from listeners who report store shelves collapsed, glass jars shattered, and chandeliers swayed. People say they felt sideways movements for two to three seconds. The quake was barely felt in Seattle."

George stared at the radio display. "Maybe they do not stop flights."

As if he'd been cued, the radio announcer added, "According to Seattle-Tacoma International Airport officials, the earthquake will not delay flights unless there is a major aftershock."

Luke accelerated to the speed limit and then to seven miles per hour above it. "If there's no traffic and we git to the airport soon, I think we'll be okay."

Luke didn't notice a large, silver-gray pickup truck following his yellow car as he sped along.

THIRTEEN

JOSÉ STOPPED his silver-gray pickup three cars behind Luke's yellow sedan as Luke returned his car to the Trigger Rental Agency at Seattle-Tacoma International Airport.

Javier opened the truck's passenger-side door. "I'll follow them to the ticket counter. Odds are they're on a Citizens Airline flight again."

"Okay."

Javier started to close the truck door. "Get a redcap to help you with the luggage. I'll call you."

José nodded.

Javier began to walk to a nearby set of terminal entry doors to wait for Luke and George to appear.

* * *

Tapping his foot on the concrete floor, Javier stood behind a newspaper and magazine vending machine in the covered parking lot, pretending to scan the publications. For what seemed like an eternity, he waited for Luke and George to head for the set of automatic doors leading into the terminal.

After four minutes, Javier saw the two men approach, pulling their suitcases behind them.

After his quarry passed through the wide doorway, Javier waited three seconds and, at a slow pace, followed the Kentucky lawman and his friend. Within five minutes, they neared the Citizen Airline ticket counter and kiosks.

After slipping his satellite phone from his pocket, Javier switched to its camera's telephoto lens and snapped a burst of pictures when Luke checked in for his flight.

Javier displayed one of the best pictures on his phone's screen and zoomed in on the image. *They're going to Las Vegas on Flight 987 at 3:05 p.m. I better book two tickets fast.* After accessing the Citizen Airline web page, he learned Flight 987 was full.

Glancing at the Citizen Airline ticketing area, Javier saw a Parrot Airlines sign to his left. After he stuffed his phone in his hip pocket, he walked with haste toward a Parrot Airlines agent standing behind the counter. Javier smiled. "What's your next flight to Las Vegas?"

The agent scratched his sideburn. "Flight 876. Leaves at two forty-five p.m. Arrives in Vegas at five seventeen."

"Have any tickets left?"

The agent tapped on his terminal. "A half dozen."

"I like two one-way tickets, please."

"Of course."

Javier figured if both Luke's Citizen Airline flight and the Parrot Flight 876 were on time, he and José would arrive twenty minutes before their soon-to-be victims. *If they get off their plane at a gate near ours in Vegas, we can wait and then follow them.*

Javier caught the ticket agent's attention. "Do the Parrot flights get off near the Citizens Airline gates in Vegas?"

"Yes. We have one gate in Vegas. It's next to the Citizens gate."

* * *

1:55 P.M., WEDNESDAY, MAY 28, 2031, SEATTLE-TACOMA INTERNATIONAL AIRPORT

José's phone chimed. "*Hola,* Javier."

"Hurry to Parrot Airlines ticket counter. We have a flight leaving at two forty-five p.m."

"*Sí.*"

* * *

3:10 P.M., WEDNESDAY, MAY 28, 2031, CITIZEN AIRLINE FLIGHT 987

Luke leaned closer to George as their jetliner gained altitude on its way to Las Vegas. "I'm guessin' the man who'll meet you to pick up the Army papers might show up at the airport in Las Vegas."

Luke knew the airport terminal would be crowded. It would be an ideal place for two spies to *brush pass* info from one person to the other.

Did George set up a rendezvous? He'd have to prepare the secret Army documents for a handoff and know when and where to meet a courier.

George whispered, "If man meet me at Las Vegas, I go in bar. He follow. I slip envelope to him inside newspaper."

Luke wet his lips. *It's like George to read my mind.* "Better buy a paper soon after we land."

George reached into his pocket and jangled coins. "I got change for vending machine, or I get paper from small store."

Luke nodded. "The friend you mentioned who might meet you. What's his name?"

George's hands were fidgety. With a quiet voice, he said, "Mikhail Popov."

"In case I spot him first, what's he look like?"

"Tall, thin with messy, short, black hair."

"Anything else 'bout him?"

"He teach me spy business. He is strange. Don't eat much. Skinny. Jumpy. Scans around him a lot."

Luke leaned back in his seat. "After we meet him and your transfer's done, the trip will be like a vacation."

George displayed a slow smile. "I know you will like." George sounded tired, and his English was faltering.

Luke remembered the flight's ETA was 5:37 p.m. George said it was best to take a cab to the hotel where the bus trip would depart, the Star Bright Hotel and Casino. The place was expensive and a mecca for high rollers. *Should be interestin' rubbing shoulders with the rich and famous.*

* * *

5:17 P.M., WEDNESDAY, MAY 28, 2031, HARRY REID INTERNATIONAL AIRPORT, LAS VEGAS

Javier breathed a sigh of relief as he and José exited their Parrot Airlines flight in Las Vegas after their jet had landed five minutes ahead of schedule.

Javier grinned. *We have plenty of time to get settled near the gate where Luke deplanes.* Javier hummed and glanced aside as he walked into the concourse aisle, and at once, he saw the Citizens Airline gate next to the Parrots gate.

Glancing up at an electronic flight board hanging from the ceiling, Javier saw Citizens Flight 987's ETA was 5:47 p.m., ten minutes late. He tapped José's shoulder and pointed at an overhead sign pointing the way to baggage claim. "Let's go to baggage claim. The Citizens Flight baggage carousel is next to ours."

José smiled. "We won't have to rush if our bags come off the plane fast."

Javier shrugged. "There were four people who got on after us. Chances are our luggage will be in the first bunch coming around the conveyor belt."

"That'll work in our favor."

Javier scratched his head. "The next question is, will Luke get a rental or take a taxi?"

* * *

5:57 P.M., WEDNESDAY, MAY 28, 2031, HARRY REID INTERNATIONAL AIRPORT, LAS VEGAS

As Luke walked down the jetway with George after their plane had landed in Las Vegas, Luke yawned. *Bin a busy day.* He glanced at George. "After we git to the hotel, how about we eat in the restaurant there? I'm pooped."

George walked at a slow pace. "I agree. I am hungry and tired, too."

As they entered the crowded terminal building from the jetway, Luke felt cool air inside the large building. Their airplane had been much warmer. *Out in the sun, it must be as toasty as the hottest day in Kentucky at high noon.* Staring down the wide aisle in the concourse toward baggage claim, he saw a shop with newspapers and books displayed on racks on its wall. "Don't forgit to buy a paper, George."

"I get one now."

As the two men neared the shop, Luke saw a tall, skinny man glancing around. The thin man was middle-aged with black, messy hair and appeared nervous. Luke tapped George's shoulder and gestured at the emaciated fellow. "Is that Mikhail, yur friend?"

George turned his head. "Yes. That is him." George waited a moment. "I signal."

Luke wrinkled his brow. "What about the passwords?"

"He would laugh. We know each other for many years." George lifted his arm, and Mikhail nodded and leaned against the wall near the men's room. George lifted his index finger as if to signal the KGB agent to wait a minute. Mikhail winked, indicating he understood, as crowds of people rushed back and forth along the concourse.

After George had bought a newspaper from a small shop,

he motioned with his head for Mikhail to follow. In a minute, George and Luke had found a booth in a bustling place called Barney's Bar.

George unlocked his suitcase, opened his briefcase, grabbed the manila envelope containing the secret military information, and slid it between two sections of his newspaper.

At the same time that Luke sat on the bench seat across from George, Mikhail slipped into the seat next to George, and Mikhail said something in Russian with a soft, high-pitched voice. It sounded like a friendly greeting to Luke.

George patted Mikhail's left shoulder. "We will speak English now, Mikhail. I like you meet my friend, Luke Ryder."

The very skinny KGB agent stretched his arm across the table. Luke grasped it and felt the man's sinews and bones. The spy had a strong grip, despite his anorexic appearance. Luke guessed Mikhail was in his mid-forties. Luke said, "Pleased to meet you, Mikhail."

"Likewise." Mikhail displayed a pleasant but weak smile. He'd spoken English well with a bit of a foreign accent. "George told me you are a new friend who owns a farm in Kentucky, and you are helping him sell tractors."

"Yep. I got a Belarusian tractor to show to other farmers. It's well worth the money." Luke noted Mikhail showed an easy smile.

George signaled a waitress. "You have vodka drinks?"

Her face turned rosy. "Yes. Cosmos, screwdrivers..."

George looked at Mikhail. "He and I always get Cosmos."

Luke said, "I'll have a plain ginger ale."

The waitress grinned. "I'll be back in a jiffy, gentlemen." She left for the bar.

George turned to Mikhail. "You finish read paper, if you want."

Mikhail slid the newspaper onto his lap and folded it. "Thank you. Should prove to be interesting reading." He turned his gaze across the table toward Luke. "Luke, I also work for the Belarus Tractor Company. If you can break away from farming every so often and take sales trips to help George, we'll be glad to compensate you, say $5,000 over and above the cost of each trip."

"Sounds interesting. I'll think about it." Luke waited for a second. "How can I git in touch with you?"

"George can find me. You have his phone number?"

"Yep."

After the waitress appeared with the trio's drinks, George proposed a toast. "May Belarus and US become big trading friends."

Mikhail held his glass high. "Bottoms up." He gulped his drink.

Once again, Luke wondered why the KGB spy was trying to hire him. *I know next to nothing about the US military or the government, and the KGB and Mikhail don't know I'm working for the FBI, or do they?*

* * *

6:15 P.M., WEDNESDAY, MAY 28, 2031, HARRY REID INTERNATIONAL AIRPORT, LAS VEGAS

Their suitcases next to them, Javier and José sat and waited for Luke and George to appear at baggage claim. Peering at the passing crowd, José shook his head as he thought about how Javier was giving him orders every day. *I'm tired of him pushing me around, and he's getting careless. Asks me to do risky things, like putting trackers on Luke's truck after Javier had taken a shot at him. And in London, I was the one who went after Luke with a knife while Javier sat in the car.*

His pulse pounding, José held his chin high and directed his gaze at the far end of the rows of baggage conveyors. He saw Luke stride into the luggage claim area with his stocky, tough-looking friend behind him. José turned to glare at Javier. "They're coming."

Javier smirked. "We'll take Luke out soon. Mateo will like it."

Within minutes, the two Mexican assassins watched from a distance as Luke and George snatched their belongings from the circling conveyor belt. As they began to move away from the baggage claim area, José saw the two men walk beneath a sign, "Ground Transportation."

Luke saw a line of taxicabs standing in the right lane near the terminal as he walked through the doorway onto the sidewalk. A man wearing a baseball cap and a yellow vest was talking to a woman with a suitcase. He pointed between a pair of yellow ribbons on stanchions next to the curb. "Follow the path between the yellow tapes and take the cab at the front of the line."

The woman nodded and began to pull her rolling case toward the cabs.

Luke stopped next to the taxi stand marshal. "What does it cost to take a cab?"

"It's a flat, thirty-dollar rate to the Strip."

Luke nodded, and he and George followed the woman to a second yellow taxi.

The driver put the men's luggage into the cab's trunk. "Where you going?"

As Luke opened the rear street-side passenger door, he said, "Star Bright Hotel and Casino."

* * *

Javier ran between the pair of yellow ribbons attached to movable posts bordering the curb and the line of cabs. "Let's go, José." José trailed behind Javier.

The driver of a black and white cab saw the two Mexicans running toward him. "You in a hurry?"

Javier nodded. "Yes. We'll pay extra."

The driver opened the trunk. "Okay. Where to?"

Javier watched Luke's yellow cab pull away. "The Strip." Javier tossed his luggage in the trunk and threw in one of José's bags, too. He pushed José into the back seat as the driver got behind the wheel.

In seconds, the taxi sped away from the terminal.

Javier felt his face warm up, and beads of sweat rolled down his forehead. "Follow that yellow cab."

"Which one?"

"The one in the right lane."

The driver laughed. "This is like in the movies."

Javier wiped his forehead dry. "Don't lose them."

"Yes, sir."

* * *

The sun was sinking lower in the western sky as Luke's taxi sped toward the Star Bright Hotel and Casino. Luke turned to George at the same time the cab bounced over a rough stretch of road. "Can't wait to check into the hotel, link up with the bus tour, eat, and hit the sack."

George eased back in his seat. "Belarus will pay for best meals." He glanced at the colorful neon lights populating the Vegas Strip. "Maybe I meet nice American woman."

Luke figured George was lonely so far away from his native Belarus. "You miss Belarus?"

"Not as much as UK." George's eyes glistened, and he wiped them. "I miss baroness. But she is dead."

Surprised that George, a spy, would become emotional, Luke decided to encourage him to speak about the national parks bus trip. "George, you remember all the national parks we'll see?"

"Hmm. We travel more than 3,000 miles on bus." He leaned forward. "First, we go from Las Vegas to Grand Canyon." He rushed his words. "It is big and pretty. I have trip brochure." He reached into his pocket and pulled out a well-worn pamphlet and handed it to

Luke. "Color pictures of Monument Valley are beautiful, too."

Luke opened the bent and wrinkled publication and saw images of Canyonlands and Arches National Parks. A photo of stunning, reddish natural arches in a desert landscape was impressive.

A former Kentucky game warden, Luke knew he'd like the weeklong outdoor tour of natural beauty. He sighed.

This is gonna be fun. I can't wait to breathe fresh air away from cities. I hope I'll see bears, bison, and bald eagles. "You sure know how to please, George."

George grinned, showing his bright white teeth. "Thanks." George peered from the taxi's passenger-side rear window and sighed. "Maybe on trip I find woman cuz it is time for me to settle down." The thirty-five-year-old KGB agent rubbed his hand over his face and whispered, "I made wrong choice to be spy. When I was teacher, life was boring but better."

Luke patted George's back. "I git you. I think you'll get lucky. Lots of ladies will like you."

The cab turned into the curved driveway of the Star Bright Hotel. Its colorful neon lights flashing in the shadows, the building towered above them. The sun would soon dip below the horizon, setting at 7:49 p.m.

George glanced at Luke. "Better check in hotel first, and then let bus tour guide know we are here."

Luke smiled and shot a short nod to George.

* * *

The assassins' cab driver stopped his black and white vehicle where the street met the Star Bright Hotel and Casino's driveway. Far ahead, Luke's yellow taxi driver was unloading luggage from his trunk while a bellboy stood nearby, ready to take Luke's and the other man's items into the hotel.

Javier caught his driver's attention. "Wait here until the guys in the yellow cab go inside."

"Okay."

Javier reached into his pocket and gave the driver a hundred thirty dollars in cash. "Nice driving."

* * *

7:01 P.M., WEDNESDAY, MAY 28, 2031, STAR BRIGHT HOTEL AND CASINO

After registering at the Star Bright Hotel's front desk, Luke and George scanned the large, fancy lobby area. Luke noticed two groups of people at opposite ends of the wide-open space.

George gestured with his head. "To right, I see logo over counter for Wild America Bus Tours. We check in there."

Luke nodded. *Belarus has got money to burn. Wild America excursions are the best.*

Luke estimated twenty-five to thirty people, many of them seniors, crowded around the Wild America counter. Because check-in time for the Wild America National Parks Tour was ending soon, he figured they were taking the tour, too.

As George and Luke neared the group, Luke noticed the vacationers were dressed in casual clothes. Surrounding a rail-thin woman with long, bleached-blond hair, the tourists chatted among themselves. Luke guessed the woman was in her late fifties and stood almost five foot seven inches tall. Since many in the crowd circling her were asking questions, Luke reckoned she worked for the tour company.

When Luke and George stopped near the edge of the gathering, the blond lady took notice of them. "I believe two more travelers may have joined us."

George flushed. "I and friend have reservations for national parks bus tour."

The blond lady took a step toward George. "Do you have a confirmation slip with you?"

George reached into his trousers pocket and took out a wrinkled printout. "My reservation numbers are 15605 and 15606."

Scanning a list on a clipboard she held, the lady said, "George Black and Luke Ryder, correct?"

George nodded. "I am George and my friend is Luke."

"I'm Heidi Cooke, your tour guide. Welcome." She took a breath, glanced across the throng around her, and in a loud voice, said, "The last two of our guests have arrived. So, here's our plan for tomorrow morning. I'll hand out vouchers for breakfast, which will be in the hotel restaurant. They'll begin serving at 5:30 a.m. Leave your suitcases inside your rooms with these yellow plastic tags attached to them. Your luggage will be picked up and taken to our bus for you."

Luke figured he'd carry his pistol case with him onto the bus. He raised his hand. "Kin I take a small personal item onto the bus when I git on?"

"Yes, sir. There's plenty of room in the overhead luggage rack."

As Heidi spoke, Luke began to assess her. *She's got to be well-organized and perhaps a workaholic to herd and keep track of more than twenty-five travelers. Reminds me of a high school teacher takin' us on a day trip on a school bus.*

While Heidi added more details about the trip, Luke tuned in to her description of the bus. "It's a new vehicle, painted yellow with black stripes. Reminds me of a tiger, and it's easy to spot. I suggest you be in the lobby tomorrow no later than 6:45 a.m. The bus will be in front. We'll leave at 7:00 a.m. sharp for the Grand Canyon National Park." She hesitated. "If you finish dinner soon enough, a bunch of us will meet at this desk tonight at eight-thirty. We'll walk along the Miracle Mile and ride a big Ferris wheel—the High Roller—to view Las Vegas. Wild America paid for the ride."

George's eyes lit up. "I want go." His Russian accent was

thicker than it had been earlier in the day so Luke figured George was tired.

Luke also wanted to ride the Ferris wheel. Though he felt drained and needed sleep, he wanted to survey the Vegas lights from high above the city. *I'll take pictures with my phone and text them to Layla.*

After Heidi stopped talking, the travelers began to walk away, half of them heading for the hotel's restaurant at the far end of the lobby.

Luke felt his mouth water as he envisioned a thick steak, mashed potatoes, and country vegetables on a large dinner plate. "George, I think I'm gonna get a nice rib-eye steak."

George appeared relaxed. "Me, too. Belarus pay for everything. Let's go first class."

As George and Luke neared the dining room, Luke didn't notice two Mexican men sitting on a couch on the other side of the lobby. They watched the Wild America crowd as they dispersed, going to their rooms or heading for the restaurant.

* * *

7:16 P.M., WEDNESDAY, MAY 28, 2031, STAR BRIGHT HOTEL AND CASINO

Moving behind the Wild America counter, tour director Heidi Cooke mounted a tall, comfortable director's chair. She shook her long blond hair and smoothed it with her hand. Intending to stay behind the counter until 7:30 p.m., she hoped new customers might stop by.

I could still sell a seat or two on the National Parks Tour. She pictured three empty seats in her motorcoach where more tourists could sit. Dedicated to her job, she was purposeful and wished to be useful to society. An avid travel addict, she enjoyed leading tours and educating people about the US national parks and their value.

Noticing movement to her left, Heidi turned and saw two men, whom she judged to be Latinos, approach.

Attractive with wavy black hair, the taller of the two men, who may have been in his thirties, stepped close to the counter. "Hello, ma'am." He glimpsed at the countertop and a stack of color brochures that described the company's National Parks Tour. "I noticed a crowd here earlier." He spoke with a slight Spanish accent. "They tour national parks?"

Heidi tilted her head to the side and felt her cheeks begin to turn rosy pink. "Yes, we'll leave on a luxury bus tomorrow morning at seven. I'm the tour leader."

The handsome Latino lifted his chin and picked up a flier. "This seems to be quite an exciting trip. The price is right for such a fascinating journey." He glanced at Heidi. "And it comes with many meals."

Her eyes glowing, Heidi leaned forward. "Three seats are left on tomorrow's tour, or you could book a later date." She glanced at the handsome man's companion, who was short, ugly, and skin-and-bones thin, with messy hair and plentiful black facial hair.

The taller man scratched his temple. "I'll consider taking this tour. If I decide to do it, could I sign up later tonight?"

"Of course. There's a website listed in the brochure. Simply choose tomorrow's date or another. Use your credit card to make a payment. If you decide to take tomorrow morning's tour, please be in the lobby with your luggage no later than a quarter to seven, and bring your reservation numbers."

The taller man kept the brochure. He nodded. "Thank you."

Heidi raised her index finger. "I almost forgot. If you purchase the tour tonight, you can go with us this evening on a walking tour and ride the High Roller Ferris wheel to view the city lights from above. If you can, be right here at the counter at eight-thirty."

"One or both of us may take the tour. Thanks for letting us know."

The two Latinos walked away.

Heidi studied the handsome man as he strolled toward a bank of elevators. *I wonder if I'll see him tomorrow morning.* She blinked and eased out a prolonged, soft breath.

* * *

Tapping an up button, Javier summoned an elevator. As he and José got into the lift, Javier said, "Let's be in the lobby with our luggage tomorrow morning by six-thirty at the latest."

José eyes flashed. "Why?"

"Tonight, I'll buy us tickets for the bus tour. We could shove Luke over a cliff or shoot him when it's dark."

José shook his head. "How would we get away? Steal a car?"

Studying José, Javier held his head high. *José's as ugly as a skinny dog, but he's a smart little bastard. One of us could ride the bus and do the deed, and the other could tail the bus.* "You're right, of course, José. Get us a vehicle at the Rent-A-Car office near the restaurant. Their sign says they close at nine."

José huffed. "Sure. But why don't you do it? You could pick out the kind of a ride you'd like."

Javier bit his lip. *José's getting sassy. He works for me, not the other way around, but I better not excite him. We must work together.* "I would do it, but remember, I called our friend, Liam, the pimp. He's sending a lady to meet me at my room at seven-thirty."

José took a cleansing breath. "I understand." José peered downward at the elevator's floor.

Javier smiled. "I could call Liam back and ask him to get you one, too."

"No thanks. I don't want to get VD."

The elevator door slid open, and Javier walked out toward his room. José then pressed the down button.

* * *

7:25 P.M., WEDNESDAY, MAY 28, 2031, STAR BRIGHT HOTEL AND CASINO

As Luke and George entered the hotel's restaurant and walked to the hostess, KGB spy Mikhail Popov saw them. He put a hundred-dollar bill on his guest check and slipped out the main entrance after a waitress led Luke and George to a table.

Mikhail headed to his room on the ground floor. He'd asked for it so he could make a quick departure. *Tonight, I should charge the camera in my binoculars. I'll get up early tomorrow so I can follow the Wild America bus and learn more about Luke Ryder.*

FOURTEEN

YOUNG AND ATTRACTIVE, a light-skinned Mexican woman, Regina Dorame, slipped on her vivid red dress. Wondering how many years she would need to keep turning tricks, she pictured her mother in senior care in Tijuana, sick with terminal lung cancer. Though Mama's cancer was in stage four, the fragile lady was still lucid. She'd weathered downturns and had shown an amazing ability to recover her strength, but then she would falter only to rebound again time after time. *If Mama dies, I'll grieve, but then I won't need to be a call girl. Liam won't like it, but one day, I will disappear, and he'll never find me.*

Putting on her high heels, Regina's mind was busy. *Mama's ability to fight cancer must be because her Spanish genes are strong.*

On the other hand, Regina's father had passed away two years ago. A heavy drinker, his liver had given out, though he, too, had come from a family that traced its roots to Imperial Spain. Regina's beautiful face, upturned nose, and creamy skin were in strong contrast to the features of most of her friends, whose ancestors had at least some indigenous Mexican blood.

I will stay in the US and become respectable again. When she was a teenager, she had aspired to become a nun. *What would Mother Lucia think of me now?* Regina sighed.

She left her room to meet her date, someone named Javier.

* * *

10:27 P.M., WEDNESDAY, MAY 28, 2031, LUKE'S FARM

Her mind racked with worry, Layla sat at the kitchen table and held a cup of steaming chamomile tea. Glad that baby Russell now snoozed in his crib, she sipped from her teacup.

From behind Layla, the soft sound of Rita's athletic shoes padding on the tiled kitchen floor broke the gratifying silence in the house. Rita wore a shoulder rig with her holstered FBI-issued Glock on top of her gray sweatshirt. "How are you doing, Layla?"

"I'm relaxing. Russell's an active little one." Layla glanced at Rita's big pistol. *She's got an M16 hanging next to the ancient flintlock rifle over the fireplace. Isn't a machine gun enough firepower?*

Rita pulled a chair away from the kitchen table and sat. "I thought we should talk about precautions to take until we're sure the shooter who came after Luke has left the area."

Layla sighed. "Okay."

Rita drew her eyebrows together. "I suggest you stay inside most of the time until I receive a report about the shooter's whereabouts."

Layla pressed her lips together and felt tension in her muscles. "Why?" Layla heard the ticking of the windup clock hanging on the wall. She wished time would speed up and Rita would leave.

Rita's voice broke into Layla's thoughts. "The cartel gunman could take a shot at you."

"He's after Luke, not me." Layla stared at Rita. *Rita would be happy if I died, because then she'd pursue Luke since she still loves him. I can tell by the way she watches him.*

Rita leaned closer toward Layla. "Or the cartel could try to kidnap you to get Luke to give himself up for you."

Layla stared at the kitchen window curtains that Rita had closed. *She's afraid someone could see us, shoot her, and then grab me.* Layla furrowed her brow. *I wish Luke were here.*

* * *

7:35 P.M., WEDNESDAY, MAY 28, 2031, STAR BRIGHT HOTEL AND CASINO

Sitting on his king-size bed in his hotel room, Javier uncapped a fifty-milliliter airplane bottle of scotch whiskey. He tossed its screw-on cap into the wastebasket next to a small desk.

As he began to sip the scotch, a knock sounded on his door. Tipping the small drink container against his lips, he swallowed the rest of the whiskey. *The whore Liam sent must be here.*

Peering through the peephole, Javier spied a woman in a low-cut, red, provocative dress. Her black hair was waist-long and shiny. Her pale, flawless skin was unusual for a Mexican Latina. *She seems familiar, like we've met before sometime, somewhere.*

After twisting the deadbolt knob, Javier pulled the door open.

Her red lipstick glowing, the young, attractive woman smiled. "Hello, I'm Regina, your date." She'd spoken with a Mexican accent.

"Come in, Regina." Javier felt his male parts warm as if an electric heater had blasted them.

As Regina entered the room, her mouth fell open, and a curious expression crossed her face. "Have we met before?"

"I wondered the same thing." Javier closed the door after

she had entered the room, and he locked the deadbolt. He stared into her eyes. "Are you the same Regina who lived next door to my mother's place in Tijuana in del Oro Apartments?"

Though she wore heavy makeup and fake eyelashes, Javier was impressed that her waist was still thin in contrast to her chest, the same as it had been years ago. *Yes, she's the timid Regina I knew before.*

Curvaceous, Regina stood five foot four inches tall. She blushed and spoke. "I remember you." Her skin turned redder yet. "I'm ashamed to meet you again like this."

Javier recalled how, in her teenage years, Regina had talked about becoming a nun. She'd been quite religious then—always attended mass.

What has changed her so much? Why had her life taken such a drastic turn?

Javier calculated she was now twenty-eight years old, three years younger than he. From the depths of his brain, his mind retrieved an image of her when she had been much younger. As a teen, she hadn't worn makeup and yet was stunning. He felt his body ache for her, but he said, "You don't have to do it, if you don't want to."

Regina's face was now almost as red as a ripe tomato, and Javier could feel her eyes drilling into his.

She spoke with a trembling voice. "I've always wanted you, ever since I was a teen, but you didn't pay attention to me."

Javier breathed in and out twice, peered deep into her brown eyes, and arched his back. "I did notice you. You are most beautiful." He touched her cheek with his fingertips and felt her hot cheeks.

All of a sudden, she threw her arms around him. "Take me if you want."

He kissed her lips, and she moaned. With a gentle touch, he grasped her hand and led her to the king-size bed. "May I undress you?"

Regina nodded. She appeared modest to him, though he

realized she had morphed into an experienced woman who had been disrobing for men and earning her living by whoring.

He took his time to remove her clothes, and he knew she enjoyed it. Hot and bothered, his loins demanded her.

After fifteen minutes of vigorous sex, they rested nude under the bedsheets, and Regina kissed him with her soft lips. "Javier, I do this because Mama has cancer. Treatments are expensive." Regina set her head on his chest. "I don't often enjoy my job, but with you, it's different."

Javier rubbed her back. "I'm sorry you have to do this to help your mother."

Her eyes flashed. "Liam is mean, and he treats me like a servant. I wish I could quit this." Her fawn-like eyes seemed to plead with him to do something.

Without warning, an idea came to Javier. *What if Regina took the bus tour and observed Luke and his friend? She could report details to me about what the tour would do next and what Luke is doing. José and I could follow the bus and take out Luke at the best moment.*

Javier gave Regina a tender hug. "I'm sorry Liam has ill-treated you." He stared across the room as he searched for the best words to convince Regina to take the bus tour at the drug cartel's expense. "Do you think Liam would permit you to work for me for a week?"

"What would I do?"

Javier sat up straight and grinned. "I'm a salesman in the import business. My associates in California import medications and even machinery into the US. I need someone to watch a competitor and report observations to me."

Regina glanced around the suite and rubbed her hair. "How would it work?"

Javier opened his eyes wider. "I would buy a special bus tour package of the US national parks for you. Your job would be to keep an eye on a man by the name of Luke Ryder and his colleague, who are taking the excursion. They are competitors selling items similar to ours. You would phone or text me with what you've learned. I'll be following in a vehicle to monitor the trip out of sight."

Regina swallowed twice. "It sounds like spying, but if all I have to do is send you texts and call you, it would be easy." She wavered. "I don't know."

Javier cleared his throat. "Also, my company will pay you 2,000 US dollars for a week of work. It would be a paid vacation."

Regina pulled the sheet around her. "When would I start?"

Javier sucked in a deep breath. "You'd get on the tour bus parked in the hotel's front driveway by seven tomorrow morning." Javier stopped speaking while he considered the situation. "But if you hustle, you can join a Wild America walking tour to the High Roller Ferris wheel at eight-thirty tonight. You might see Luke Ryder there."

Regina peered across the room. "Liam might get mad at me if I take time off to work for you."

"I could call him."

Regina's face turned pallid. "No. If I decide to do it, I'll call him."

Javier noticed her body began to shake a trifle. "I could talk to the CEO of my company and ask him to hire you. I've asked for an assistant, and the CEO told me he'd pay $100,000 per year to the candidate of my choice."

Regina leaned forward, and her eyes glowed. "I'll do it." All of a sudden, her voice was bubbly. "The guy who I'm supposed to watch is Luke Ryder, right?"

"Yes." Javier snatched his phone and the Wild America brochure from the desktop near the foot of the bed. "I'll sign you up now." As he logged onto the Wild America website, he pictured Mateo, the top man who ran *Nuestro Club* cartel based in Tijuana. *I'll convince him to hire her. If nothing else, she's a great lay.*

* * *

Regina wrinkled her brow and nibbled her lower lip as she watched Javier buy the bus trip for her. *What's Liam going to say? I should call him tomorrow. No, I shouldn't. He's pushy as it is, and he might be violent if I tell him I'm quitting. But I must be sure Javier will come through and give me the permanent job.*

She watched Javier write notes on a hotel tablet. An idea struck her. *I could call Liam and tell him Mama is getting worse and I must fly to Tijuana. He knows she has cancer. Then I can make two thousand dollars and wait for Javier to hire me on a long-term basis.*

She peered at her red dress on the floor beside the bed. *What about clothes and packing my bag?* Everything Regina owned was in her hotel room. Liam paid for her room and board. *I'll pack my best stuff in my biggest suitcase in the event I don't come back.*

A cautionary feeling in her stomach made her wonder. *Did I make the right decision to take this trip and maybe take a job with Javier's company?*

She recalled how, years ago, Javier had hung out with a Tijuana street gang.

They sold drugs. I'm glad he now works for a company and didn't fall in with the wrong crowd. Still, I must learn about Javier's employer before I take the job. It seems much better than it should be.

An uneasy feeling grew stronger inside her guts.

FIFTEEN

AS REGINA RUSHED to get dressed, Javier handed her a sheet of paper with her Wild America reservation number. "In twenty minutes from now, you could join the tour and get a free ride on the High Roller Ferris wheel."

"Where does the tour leave from?"

"Go to the Wild America counter in the hotel lobby and show your number to the tour guide. She's an elderly blond woman."

"Okay."

Javier peered into Regina's eyes. "If you see Luke Ryder tonight, introduce yourself to him, and you might learn something about his customers you can pass on to me. Here's a picture of Luke."

She wondered why Javier was going to follow the bus for the sole purpose of learning about Luke's customers. She scratched her hair. *Javier's sales job must pay considerable money if he's going so far as to spy on competitors.*

Riding the elevator down to the hotel lobby, Regina studied Luke's snapshot.

After rushing from the elevator, she checked a clock on

the lobby wall. She had a few minutes to catch up with the tourists who'd begun to loiter near the Wild America counter. They surrounded a bleached-blond, older woman. *She's the tour leader.*

Regina walked at a brisk pace thirty feet toward the older, thin woman. Stopping near her, Regina said, "Excuse me. Is this the Wild America tour?" Regina was aware she'd spoken with a stronger Mexican accent than she usually had.

The slender woman, who reminded Regina of a school-teacher, turned toward her. "Yes, this is the National Parks Tour. Are you the person who just signed up via our website?"

Regina held out a sheet of paper. "I did. Here's my reservation number." Regina took a deep breath and grinned. "I'm Regina Dorame."

"I'll check you in." The tour leader made a check on a printout. "If you'd like to ride the High Roller Ferris wheel, please join us on our Vegas walking tour, which starts soon from right here."

"I'd like to." Regina felt free as a bird flying from a cage and escaping into the night air. *I'm leaving the life.*

She smiled and took three steps toward Luke Ryder.

He's handsome. The other guy with him is nice-looking, too. Being a corporate spy will be exciting.

* * *

8:21 P.M., WEDNESDAY, MAY 28, 2031, STAR BRIGHT HOTEL AND CASINO

Luke stood next to George. They were waiting for the Wild America tourists to gather and walk to the High Roller Ferris wheel. Luke fingered his satellite phone in his pocket. *It's late in Kentucky, but I should call Layla.*

Luke stepped away from the gathering bunch of Wild America tourists and tapped Layla's name on his phone's display.

The phone rang twice. "Hello, Luke. How are you?"

Luke realized he was exhausted but excited. "I'm tired, but soon me and George are gonna ride a big Ferris wheel and see the Vegas lights from high up." He took a breath. "How 'bout you, hon?"

"I'm fine. I miss you, though."

Luke liked the sound of her voice, but he detected something in her tone, telling him she wasn't happy. Did having Rita in the house upset her? "Is Rita treatin' you okay?" He wished he could give Layla a hug.

Layla inhaled twice and then spoke. "Rita's fine, but says I shouldn't go outside. She's waiting for an FBI report to find out if the shooter left the area."

"I bet the bastard's long gone. Besides, I doubt if he'd take a shot at you. But better to be safe."

Luke heard Layla brush her phone against her ear. "There's no chance a shooter could get anywhere near the house without setting off the new alarm system on the fence line. Plus Rita and the other FBI agent are hanging around." Layla's words tumbled out. "And Rita's carrying her Glock in a shoulder rig and hung her M16 next to your flintlock rifle over the fireplace."

Luke knew Layla was frazzled. "I'll be back soon, babe." Luke imagined Layla and Rita glaring at each other, quarreling.

Women folk can be extra emotional and have a hard time forgettin' past spats. Layla's more tuned into emotions than I am and knows Rita still likes me. The sooner I git home, the better.

"I can't wait to be in your arms, Luke."

Luke felt his body warm up. "I wish I could hug you now." He heard baby Russell begin to cry.

Layla bumped her phone. "Russell needs me, hon."

"I hear him. Love you."

"Love you, too." Layla disconnected the phone.

Luke saw the Wild America crowd had grown bigger near the company's counter. Heidi raised both her arms and said in a loud voice, "Let's stay together and start our walk to the High Roller Ferris wheel." She paused. "We'll see it lit up against the dark sky when we're outside. It's taller than the Eiffel Tower and the Statue of Liberty."

Like a class of grammar school students, the tourists followed Heidi toward the hotel's doorway and into the seventy-degree night. Luke figured he'd wake up during the walk to the High Roller. *It's a lot cooler now than the ninety-eight-degree afternoon high was.*

* * *

Luke walked side-by-side with George past bright, multicolored neon lights with the crowd of Wild America tourists on their way to the High Roller. As Luke glanced to his left, he noticed a stunning Latina walking alongside him. Her light skin was lit by the changing rainbow of colors emitted by the gaudy signs along the sidewalk and inside shops and restaurants.

A red, tight-fitting dress accented her curves, and though her makeup was a bit much, it was well done. The way she walked, shifting her hips more than what he thought was natural, made him wonder about her intentions. *Who is she?* Despite the fact an old man in the tour group walking near her ogled her body when he thought she wasn't watching, she seemed at ease, even seeming to enjoy the codger's attention.

She turned her gaze to Luke, and he felt her eyes focus on his. Did she guess he'd been evaluating her, trying to figure out what kind of a woman she was? She'd joined the tour at the last minute, and he imagined she could be a Vegas showgirl or perhaps…

She stumbled, bumped Luke, and blinked.

* * *

George heard Luke grunt when a woman in a red dress bumped him. "Excuse me, sir." The lady spoke in a Mexican accent with a honey-sweet voice. "I was staring up at the High Roller." She nodded at the tall Ferris wheel ahead of them.

Luke shrugged. "That's okay." Even though Luke had spoken just two words, George recognized Luke's distinctive Southern drawl.

The stunning Latina now walked closer to Luke and slowed her pace to match his. "Are you from the South?"

Luke nodded. "Kentucky. You have a Mexican accent."

"I'm from Tijuana. I moved here to work as an interior decorator." She smiled at Luke. "I'm Regina. Since we're on the same tour, we'll see a lot of each other." She held her hand out to Luke, and though they were walking, he shook it.

"Pleased to meet you, Regina. I'm Luke."

"Since I told you my profession, it's your turn." Regina smiled. "What do you do for a living?"

Luke cocked his head. "I'm a part-time farmer and full-time deputy sheriff."

She avoided eye contact with him for a moment and then glanced at him, matching his pace. "What do you grow?"

"Hemp."

"What's that?"

A relaxed smile crossed his face. "You can make rope, building materials, and even plastic with it." As he talked, Luke also surveyed the towering High Roller Ferris wheel ahead.

George watched the woman's movements as she walked and talked with Luke. Despite a cool breeze, George felt his face flush and warm up. He thought in Russian. *I'm glad it is dark. No one can see my face. She is attractive, prettier than the baroness.*

George recalled the face of Baroness Anne Thorpe, who'd been murdered in London last year. She'd loved George, and he'd loved her.

I would've married her, if she'd divorced her husband.

The Latina's voice interrupted George's thoughts, and he

saw she was surveying him. Then she shifted her attention back to Luke. "Are you two guys traveling together?"

Luke nodded. "Yes. This is George Black. We're on a sales trip and a vacation at the same time."

Regina trained her eyes on George. "You're salesmen?"

George shrugged. "I am from Belarus. I sell farm tractors that Belarus Tractor Company make. Luke is farmer. He helps me show tractors to customers. Sorry for accent."

Regina cocked her head. "Don't be sorry. I also have an accent."

George thought Regina was inspecting him from head to toe. Blushing, he was glad a red neon light cast a rosy glow on his skin. Though his tongue felt like it had grown thicker, he spoke. "I ship tractors to national parks so groundskeepers can try them. Luke will use joystick to drive tractors to show how easy to do."

Regina appeared puzzled to George, so he decided to explain further. "Even a teen can use gamer joystick when sitting on chair far from tractor to drive machine. Someday, AI software can drive it without human in control."

The Latina's eyes opened wider. "I never heard of a tractor you can drive with remote control. Do you sell anything else?"

"Other farm machines."

George noted Regina seemed to be puzzled by his answer. Did she expect him to say he was also selling armored personnel carriers to the US armed forces? *Is she an agent of a third country trying to learn about the military equipment I sell? She is pretty enough to be a honey trap. Who's she working for?* Though paranoia was normal in the espionage business, George wondered if he was worrying when he didn't need to. But after a bit more thought, he concluded he wasn't being too careful. After all, he was now a double agent and had more to be anxious about than ever before.

As the group neared the base of the High Roller Ferris wheel, Heidi, the tour guide, called out. "We'll ride elevators to a boarding area where we'll get in Ferris wheel pod compartments. Docents will break us into groups before we board the pods."

George watched as Regina scooted ahead, as if she was making sure she got on the same pod as he and Luke did.

Though still wondering about Regina's intentions, George felt his desire for her grow. *She is ravishing.* He sighed as he, Luke, Regina, and other Wild America tourists entered a pod.

An attendant closed their compartment door, and as the mammoth wheel moved their pod up a bit and then stopped, Regina grabbed Luke's arm. "Sorry, Luke. I didn't expect it to stop."

George realized the next pod behind them had to be loaded, and that's why the wheel had come to a stop. *She's trying to get close to us. But why focus on Luke? I'm the spy. Perhaps she doesn't know I'm with the KGB.* George blinked. *Am I jealous of Luke? I like this woman. I must get her attention. Luke does not want her—should not because he is now a married man.*

George inched closer to Regina, who still stood near Luke, and the secret agent tapped her shoulder. "This big wheel takes half hour go round once. We will see much." He smiled at her. "A lot to do on Miracle Mile. There is big show near Planet Hollywood. Old Vegas acts. You want go with me after wheel?"

"I'd like to." Regina glanced at Luke. "Are you going to go too, Luke?"

Luke covered his mouth with his hand and yawned. "No. I'm tired, and I gotta call my wife when I get back to the hotel."

Regina turned to George and brushed her long, black hair aside with her hand. "When does the show start?"

"Next show at ten thirty. I use phone to get tickets."

Regina took a step toward George at the same time the pod began to move again, and she bumped him. "Thank you, George." She grabbed his arm. "We'll have fun."

George watched the colorful sights below them while the

wheel crept higher and higher above Las Vegas. As he viewed the flamboyant lights of Sin City from above, he fantasized how pleasurable it would be to make love with Regina. She leaned against him, and within seconds, he felt her body heat, or was it his?

Regina pointed to a huge, lighted, ball-shaped structure. "That's the Sphere. A curved LED screen covers its huge outside surface." As she spoke, the vivid, many-colored image on the skin of the Sphere changed into the picture of an Elvis impersonator. With a light touch, Regina squeezed George's hand. "They hold events and shows inside the Sphere building."

While George gazed down at the distant glow of neon casino signs, he made a pledge to himself. *I will have this woman before the end of this trip.*

As if on cue, Regina rubbed George's back in the semi-darkness. He smiled.

* * *

Heidi glanced around the dim inside of her High Roller pod. Staring through tall, curved windows, a dozen of the travelers who'd joined her bus tour chatted about the garish nighttime sights below of the Gambling Capital of the World.

After Heidi stopped scanning the tourists in the pod, she focused on a man and a woman holding hands. *Her name's Regina. Are she and the man lovers? Or had they just met?* The man was stocky but handsome. Regina wore a red dress that clung to her skin.

The dry, desert heat of the day had lessened, and the temperature was now seventy degrees at the most. *Is Regina chilly in her low-cut outfit? Is she passionate, in love?*

Heidi made a mental note. *I'll seat the two lovebirds near each other.* Like a schoolmarm, Heidi would design a seating chart for the bus that night. The passenger seating would rotate clockwise, one seat back each day. *Isn't it romantic? The lovers will be near each other throughout the trip unless I get a complaint.*

* * *

10:15 P.M., WEDNESDAY, MAY 28, 2031, LAS VEGAS

Though a brisk wind blew across the night, and the temperature had sunk to sixty-five degrees, George felt warm and confident. He smelled the odor of delicious foods as he and Regina took their time to walk to the theater through the throng of tourists and gamblers. George noticed Regina had begun to shiver, and then she sealed herself against his side. He felt her body heat rise with his, and he wondered if living in Las Vegas in the often broiling heat of the sunbaked day made people sensitive to the cool evening air. In Belarus, the climate was colder, and night temperatures often dipped into the mid-forties Fahrenheit in late May.

As they neared the ticket counter, Regina whispered, "I heard this show is thrilling. There's singing, dancing, and comics. Thank you for taking me." She kissed George's cheek.

"You're welcome." *She's wonderful. I haven't felt so fine since I dated Anne Thorpe in London.* He sighed when he recalled the night he'd found Anne dead.

Now feeling blue, George stopped at the ticket counter and told the attendant his order number. After he received his two tickets, he felt Regina link her arm with his. His recollection of Anne's classic face dissolved when he inhaled Regina's perfume, and he wished he could tell Regina how much better her touch made him feel. He felt proud and strong.

They found their seats, and Regina moved her lips close to his ear. "If I go in my room after just an evening kiss, don't think this is our last date."

George felt his spirits soar. "I understand. We both need rest."

As the theater lights dimmed, Regina rested against George's shoulder. "How did you choose Luke to demonstrate the joystick to drive your tractor?"

Again, George felt paranoid, and his mind switched to the Russian language. *The job of a spy makes one suspicious. Why is she asking this?* George heard himself say, "He is farmer. He has same joystick tractor on his Kentucky farm and will tell customers how well machine works. He is friend and is honest."

Regina rubbed his shoulder. "Being honest is important."

"He is also deputy sheriff in Kentucky."

"Oh?" Regina was silent during the show while jugglers, dancers, acrobats, and singers performed amazing acts. After the entertainment ended, Regina and George walked from the theater into the brisk outside air. George still wondered why Regina had asked questions about Luke.

She was gorgeous, but was she working for the KGB or some other espionage service? *So what if she's setting up a honey trap? I'll play her game whether or not she's a spy. She's too nice to pass up.*

* * *

11:57 P.M., WEDNESDAY, MAY 28, 2031, STAR BRIGHT HOTEL AND CASINO

Regina felt her tongue probe George's mouth as she kissed him outside of her room. Though he was a strong man, his tongue felt tender. *He's nice. Too bad he's one of Javier's competitors.*

With a soft touch, she felt George's cheek and his whiskers. Then she disengaged from his embrace. "We both need our sleep. I had a grand time, and I can't wait to see you tomorrow."

George grinned like a schoolboy. "I had excellent time, too." He lifted his arm and waved as he headed for the elevator. "See you on bus."

She grabbed her key card from her purse. Within seconds, she sat on her bed and touched Javier's name on her device.

"*Hola*, Regina." Javier sounded tipsy.

"Am I calling too late?"

"No. I'm curious what you learned about Luke."

Regina shifted on her perch on the end of the mattress and it squeaked. "Luke and his friend rode the High Roller with me and a dozen bus tourists."

"Fine work."

"His friend is George Black, a tractor salesman from Belarus, and he has a Russian accent. Luke is a deputy sheriff from Kentucky. He isn't the main salesman because he helps George demonstrate tractors."

"Where's Belarus?"

"Eastern Europe, I think. George's tractors can be remote controlled with a joystick." Regina squinted. *I'd think Javier would know his competition better than that unless Javier sells items for a large number of companies.*

"Interesting," Javier slurred.

Regina yawned. "They didn't talk about selling pharmaceuticals. If that's your main business, you don't have much to worry about."

"Our company has its hands in many businesses. Farm machinery sales are important to us, too."

Regina stared at her phone. "I can't think of anything else."

"Thanks, this is the kind of info I need. Text or call if you learn more." He disconnected.

As she stuffed her phone into her purse, Regina shook her head. "He's as drunk as a sailor on shore leave."

SIXTEEN

AS A BELLHOP ROLLED Luke's large suitcase on the sidewalk near the Wild America tour bus, Luke glanced at the vehicle's exterior. Painted yellow and black to resemble a tiger's coat, the bus was easy to spot at a distance.

Toting his carry-on luggage, Luke climbed up into the bus and saw Heidi, the tour director, standing next to the bus driver. She took a half step behind the driver to let Luke pass by. "Welcome aboard, Luke. You'll find your name on a sign above your seat."

"Thanks." Luke reckoned Heidi had to have an excellent memory to remember his name on the first day of the trip.

Three rows back on the right side of the aisle he found his and George's names written on a sticker attached to the overhead luggage rack. Glancing at the next row behind his seat, he saw Regina's name on a tag above the seat behind him. *George is lucky Regina's sittin' alone behind us. He could move back and sit with her, if he talks her into it.*

As Luke placed his locked handgun case in the overhead compartment, he peered through a side window and saw Regina nearing the bus. Earlier, when George had eaten breakfast with Luke, the Belarusian spy had spoken glowingly about his theater date with Regina, and he hadn't stopped smiling since then. *I believe George has taken a liking to her.*

Within twenty seconds, Regina walked along the aisle, neared Luke, and then stopped. She wore tight-fitting jeans and a fancy blouse, displaying her hourglass figure. "Hi." She glanced at the sign above the seat behind Luke. "I'm near you two guys." She blinked. "But I'm sitting alone."

Luke tilted his head. "I bet George could move back there to talk with you."

Regina put her purse on her seat. "Or you could sit here, if he loses interest in me."

Luke doubted a love-struck George would get tired of Regina. "He won't git bored with you." Luke stared for a microsecond at her. *It's like God built her to be a goddess. Ain't many women as pretty as she is.*

Three minutes later, George approached and caught Regina's attention and then glanced at Luke. "I have luck. Regina is sitting near us."

Regina grinned and sat straight up. "Lovely morning, George."

"It *is* pretty day, mainly cuz I see you."

Heidi approached George from behind and tapped his shoulder. "I noticed you and Luke introduced yourselves to Regina last night." Heidi then turned to Regina. "Regina, you're traveling alone, so feel free to invite others to sit with you."

Regina's brown eyes sparkled. "Thanks."

Luke watched as Heidi counted all the passengers while she walked to the front of the coach. She stopped behind the driver's seat and grabbed a microphone. "Everyone is here. We'll start on time in a few minutes. But for now, here are a few things about today's journey…"

The motorcoach began to roll from the driveway as Heidi spoke.

* * *

7:01 A.M., THURSDAY, MAY 29, 2031, STAR BRIGHT HOTEL AND CASINO

Javier had awakened José at five in the morning. José was peeved, thinking, *It's way too early.*

After breakfast, the two men had stowed their luggage and weapons in the bed of the large, gray pickup truck José had rented the night before, because the vehicle had a lockable cargo bed cover. Even so, they had put their pistols in a cardboard box on the rear crew cab seat of the pickup. Now, they sat inside the truck in the hotel's parking lot and watched. Finally, the Wild America tourists got on their bus that sat in the curved driveway near the building's main entrance, and the motorcoach began to inch forward.

Shifting his weight in the driver's seat, José put the truck in gear when the bus with the tiger-fur paint job began to move faster.

Javier glanced at the massive tour vehicle and then caught José's eyes. "Don't get too close behind them."

José nodded and appeared indifferent, but inside, he seethed. *I've been on more missions than Javier. Why's he bossing me around again?*

As the tour bus entered the on-ramp of the freeway, José was five car lengths behind the bus. It sped up, but José eased down on the accelerator with a light foot.

José peeked sideways and saw Javier's hands tremble. The larger Latino stared ahead at their quarry and then eyeballed José. "I can't wait to kill Luke. It will give me great pleasure."

José kept his eyes on the road. *Javier's too emotional and careless, and that could get me killed. I can't wait until this job's done.*

* * *

7:20 A.M., THURSDAY, MAY 29, 2031, EN ROUTE TO THE GRAND CANYON

As the bus gained speed, rail-thin tour guide Heidi Cooke stroked her bleached-blond hair, stood behind the driver, and surveyed the seated tourists. She moved her fingernail against her mike, and a scratching sound boomed from speakers embedded in the overhead luggage racks. "I hope everyone had a healthy breakfast to start your day."

She grasped a seatback near her as the motorcoach hit a bump. "Just as I will do every morning during this tour, I'll let you know what we'll do during the day."

Luke leaned forward. *I wonder what wildlife we'll see today.* A former Kentucky game warden, Luke hoped to see a wide variety of wild creatures during the three thousand-mile trip. *When am I gonna see buffalo, elk, eagles, deer?*

"Today, we'll drive more than 350 miles to our first big tour stop, the Grand Canyon's East Rim, and then we'll eat lunch at a trading post in nearby Cameron. Next, we'll drive to the canyon's South Rim and stop at three locations, where you'll have lots of time to take pictures. After our first day on the road, we'll have dinner as a group. Now, sit back and enjoy the scenery. As we go, I'll point out significant sights, and I'll also play movies. Headsets are in your seat back pouches should you decide to watch films on the TV screens strategically placed above your seats. Enjoy." Heidi shut off her microphone.

* * *

As the bus zipped along the highway toward the Grand Canyon, George, near the window, leaned sideways a bit closer to Luke. "I am glad Mikhail got envelope. Now we enjoy tour."

After studying a Wild America brochure jam-packed with colorful images of the canyon, Luke glanced at George. "The Grand Canyon's impressive."

George was staring out of the bus window near him. "I can't wait 'til I retire from Belarusian job." He focused on Luke. "We are comrades. Most people in world are peaceful and make friends with each other. How come all countries are not friends?"

Luke made strong eye contact with George. "Countries should be able to trust each other. But in each nation, there are oddballs who want to lord over everyone. They start wars, too."

George's eyes shifted to the blue sky above the wide-open landscape outside the bus window. "I was history teacher. Power-hungry men start wars far back into past." His voice was soft and quiet.

Luke stuck his chest out. "Don't feel sad. When you can, quit yur Belarusian job, stay here, and you'll be happy."

George sat up straight. "I will quit Belarusian government job soon, and after that, I can still sell tractors. These farm machines can help countries be friends."

Luke smiled. "The first step is to sell tractors to national park groundskeepers."

"I already sold tractors to national park people."

"You are busy."

"Yes. I work hard to have them shipped to some parks."

Luke glimpsed backward at Regina, who seemed to be eavesdropping.

* * *

Regina stretched forward in her seat and pinched her lips together, straining to listen to Luke and George talking. The sounds of the bus skimming over the pavement and of the whistling wind made the men's low voices hard to understand. She heard individual words, but not much that made sense.

George had said, "we…comrades…"

Regina bit her lip. *I know they're friends.*

Luke had said, "…oddballs who want to lord…"

Regina shook her head. *Snooping and listening aren't working. I must speak with them to learn something to tell Javier.* She stood, took a step forward, and focused on Luke and George. "I'm bored. Could one of you guys sit with me?"

A wide grin formed on George's face as he stood. "Excuse me, Luke."

Luke got up and made room for George to leave his seat.

Regina felt George touch her shoulder with his big hand, guiding her to her assigned seat. She noted his touch was gentle, even if his hands were big. "Want window view, Regina?"

"Yes." She sat in the seat closest to the window. "Thank you, George." She imagined what it would be like to go to bed with him.

SEVENTEEN

8:05 A.M., THURSDAY, MAY 29, 2031, EN ROUTE TO THE GRAND CANYON

AS JOSÉ DROVE THE LARGE, gray pickup truck a hundred yards behind the yellow and black striped tour bus, Javier felt stiff and rubbed the back of his neck. *Has Regina learned anything yet?*

Javier withdrew his satellite phone from his pocket. *Do either Luke or George speak Spanish? I doubt it.* Tapping with two thumbs, Javier began to type a text. "What did you learn about two men? Where, when do you stop next?"

* * *

8:06 A.M., THURSDAY, MAY 29, 2031, EN ROUTE TO THE GRAND CANYON

Regina enjoyed George's low voice and Russian accent. "Regina, you from Mexico?"

"Yes. Tijuana. It's next to San Diego, California. The two cities share fifteen miles of border." Regina's phone chirped, but she ignored a text Javier had sent.

George tilted his torso toward Regina. "What Tijuana like?"

Regina stared up at the bus ceiling as if picturing her city of birth. "Two-and-a-half million people live there." She concentrated her gaze on George. *He's handsome in a solid, rough kind of way.* She coughed. "The climate's superb, like San Diego's, and arid. There are canyons, hills, and dry creek beds." Regina reckoned Tijuana grew fast when large global companies began to make products in the city. "There was a surge of foreign investment, and businessmen built *maquiladoras.*"

George furrowed his brow. "*Maquiladoras?*" He had trouble saying the word.

"They're plants which make things for big foreign companies." She took a breath. "Even though they earn much less than US workers, the *maquiladora* workers make twice as much as average Mexican citizens."

George nodded. "In my country, Belarus, pay is low. That why tractors I sell much cheaper than US tractors."

Regina tossed her hair with her hand. "Where's Belarus?"

"Eastern Europe. Once it part of USSR, but now Belarus independent country." He stared through the bus window and studied the big sky. "Years ago, I live in big city, Minsk. I was schoolteacher and got new job."

She felt his eyes focus on hers, and euphoria tingled in her body. *He likes me, but is his desire merely physical?* At a momentary loss for words, she said, "I, too, want to switch jobs."

George hadn't stopped peering into her eyes as he spoke. "You don't like being interior decorator?"

Regina shrugged. "It's a job that allowed me to escape my neighborhood. I came from a Tijuana district called *Zona Norte*, a place where there were many prostitutes, strip clubs, and drugs. I wished to work in a respectable profession."

"So, you decide be interior decorator?"

"Yes." Regina's white lie made her feel dishonest. "I'm

bored with decorating homes for rich people, so I want to try something new."

I wonder if working for Javier's company will be satisfying. It would be better than making love with ugly men. She felt a moment of indecision, viewed George, and decided he was, without doubt, masculine.

"Boredom makes life dull." George sighed. "I hope to change jobs, too."

Regina patted George's broad shoulders. "I'm sure you'll be happier when you find the right vocation. Because we spend so much time working, it should be fun, not toil." She hoped she could enjoy a romantic life, but true love hadn't been part of her life so far. She seldom felt anything like affection or desire after she'd begun to work in the world's oldest profession. Day in and day out, she'd serviced multiple customers, often every day of the week, without feeling an emotional attachment to any of her clients. She stared at George. *He seems interested in me as a person.*

Regina remembered she'd received a text from Javier, so she opened the message, which was in Spanish. It asked, "What did you learn...?"

She tapped an answer to Javier. "Not much. Will have lunch with George and Luke in Cameron. I'll ask questions then."

* * *

8:45 A.M., THURSDAY, MAY 29, 2031, TIJUANA, MEXICO

Mateo Guerra, head of the Mexican drug cartel *Nuestro Club*, sat under an umbrella on a garden chair next to his Olympic-size swimming pool at his large estate in a Tijuana suburb. Six foot three, 210 pounds, he was thin but strong. *I must determine what my sicarios are doing.* He grabbed his encrypted satellite phone from the black, wrought iron table beside him. Tapping a phone number, he heard four rings before his hired assassin, Javier, answered.

"*Hola, Jefe.*" Javier's voice was higher than normal, as if he were nervous.

"What progress have you made with your Luke Ryder assignment?"

Mateo heard Javier cough. "We are following a tour bus he's on that is visiting national parks. We plan to make his death appear to be an accident."

Mateo furrowed his brow. *Making the murder obvious would send a message to other law enforcement agents.* He felt anger surge as his pulse rate increased. "Why not just kill him?"

"Because of our last attempt, *la policía* know we wish to kill Luke. It is best they think his demise is an unlucky mishap."

Mateo felt his fury seethe. *Calm down, Mateo.* He took four deep breaths, exhaling at a slow rate. *I must not blow up. It's crucial I keep my employees on my side.* "I trust your judgment, Javier." Mateo bit his lip.

"I have the tour's itinerary, and I also hired a woman to take the trip. She'll text Luke's movements to me. She thinks we're tracking two competing salesmen selling farm machinery and pharmaceuticals."

Mateo grasped his shot glass and sipped whiskey. "Do what you must to kill Luke. Blow him into bloody bits with plastic explosives for all I care. Tell me when it's done, and then I can party."

"*Sí, señor.*"

Mateo disconnected his phone and scratched his dark beard. *It's hard to hire outstanding help these days. If these sicarios fail, I may need to do the job myself.*

* * *

9:15 A.M., THURSDAY, MAY 29, 2031, REST STOP EN ROUTE TO GRAND CANYON

Feeling the tour bus slow, Regina peered out her window. *We're going to stop.*

Heidi, the tour director, stood up behind the bus driver as he guided his large vehicle onto an off-ramp leading to a truck stop. She switched on her microphone. "Folks, we're making a twenty-minute restroom stop. You can buy snacks or other items at the truck stop store."

After the yellow bus with black tiger stripes stopped, Luke quickly got to his feet, and George began to follow him to the bus's front exit. As they inched forward, Regina focused on George. *Could I get another date with George tonight?* She faked a stumble, bumped into him, and touched his back. "Sorry. I tripped."

George glanced backward. "No problem." He grinned like a teenage boy who beheld a prom queen.

"I'll buy you a coffee or a soft drink to make up for my clumsiness." Regina felt her heart beat faster, and a flush of desire flooded across her body. *I'll get him in bed tonight.*

"Thank you, Regina, for treating me." George's voice sounded happy.

After Luke stepped from the bus, he waved to George and Regina and began a quick walk toward the men's room.

Regina matched George's slower pace and looped her arm with his. Peering into his dark brown eyes, she said, "I don't need the restroom."

"Then I have more time to choose a drink." George grinned and pulled her closer as they neared the expansive truck stop building.

An automatic door swung open, and Regina pointed behind a counter. "There are the drinks."

An array of cold refreshments sat in a refrigerated display. Regina spotted the usual carbonated beverages as well as water, lemonade, and pomegranate juice. She watched George's eyes move back and forth as he surveyed his drink options.

George got the attention of the lady behind the counter. "I would like root beer, please. I never drink it before." She opened the glass door of the cold storage case and placed a plastic bottle of root beer on the countertop by George.

Regina's fingers touched her parted lips. "You don't have root beer in Belarus?"

"Maybe, but I like Uzvar."

Regina raised her eyebrows. "Uzvar?"

"It family drink for holidays. Made from dried fruits—apples, pears, cherries, plums. Also, honey." George sighed with a faraway look in his eyes.

Regina moved closer to him. "Must be delicious." She looked at the woman behind the counter. "Since you don't have Uzvar, I'd like lemonade." Regina pulled a crisp fifty-dollar bill from her purse and paid for the drinks.

As Regina and George walked toward the store's exit, Regina didn't notice Javier was standing in the crowded building's back corner, staring at her and George from behind a tall shelf.

* * *

9:40 A.M., THURSDAY, MAY 29, 2031, EN ROUTE TO GRAND CANYON

As the bus with the tiger-fur paint job sped toward the East Rim of the Grand Canyon, Regina's eyes closed. She relaxed and napped, enjoying the soft darkness behind her eyelids. Her head had slipped sideways and rested against George's right arm, and she felt his soothing warmness.

A buzzing vibration jarred her awake. Reaching into her tight-fitting jeans, she straightened her leg and wrested out her phone. Staring at the device, she saw a text had arrived from Javier. *What's Javier want? I suppose I'll send him more info about Luke's background.* She'd talked a great deal with Luke and George before she'd dozed off.

Certain Javier's text was in Spanish, she opened the message. It read, "Where will the bus stop next?"

With her two nimble thumbs, she tapped a response in Spanish. "First, East Rim. Lunch at Cameron Trading Post. Last, South Rim stops."

George touched her shoulder. "Who you text?"

Regina jerked her head up and focused on George. "My sister. She wants to know about the trip."

George nodded.

As Regina peeked at her phone, Javier sent another text. "What hotel will you stay at tonight?"

Regina wrote, "Not sure."

"Find out. We'll meet in your room."

Regina blinked and felt the skin around her eyes tighten. She tapped a reply, "We better not. Luke's room is close to mine. Tourists are in block of suites."

In mere seconds, Regina's phone signaled Javier had sent another text. "Too bad." A moment later, Javier added, "Have new report?"

Regina stared out the window of the speeding tour bus. She recalled what Luke had said a few minutes ago. Tapping with quick movements of her thumbs, she wrote, "Luke is Kentucky deputy sheriff and hemp farmer. George is from Belarus—sells farm tractors. Luke demos tractors. Drives them with joystick. These guys dangerous? Seem harmless."

Within fifteen seconds, Javier sent another text. "Men no threat. Find out where you stop at South Rim."

Regina typed, "Okay."

Regina glanced at Heidi, who sat in the front of the bus behind the driver. *I need details about the trip so I can text Javier more info.* Regina tapped George's shoulder. "I'm going to stretch my legs." She studied George's eyes. "And I might as well ask Heidi about our East and South Rim stops."

George stood to let Regina move into the aisle. Brushing

her silky, dark hair with her fingertips, she stepped into the bus's walkway.

As the motorcoach bounced over a bumpy stretch of the road, Regina shuffled forward and grabbed the luggage rack over Heidi's seat behind the driver. "Heidi, could you tell me about the stops at the Grand Canyon?"

Heidi's eyes glowed. "At the East Rim, we'll visit the Desert View Watchtower Overlook for twenty minutes. You'll love scanning the canyon far below us and seeing its many colors." She rested her voice for a moment. "A lady architect, Mary Colter, designed the tower, which was built in the 1930s. It resembles a castle tower and has a view of the Colorado River as it snakes its way a mile below, like a ribbon winding through the reddish canyon."

Regina grinned. "Sounds pretty."

"After we eat lunch at a trading post, we'll drive to the South Rim, and the bus will stop at three places to observe the canyon." Heidi spoke fast, showing her excitement.

Heidi then handed Regina a thick pamphlet with a dozen stunning photographs of the Grand Canyon. Regina wondered if Javier had a copy of the booklet, which included the trip itinerary. If so, why had he been asking about the next stops on the tour?

Maybe he's worried the bus might not always stick to its planned route. Strange he didn't take the tour himself, even if he and Luke had known each other in the past. Oh well, why worry about it? I'm getting paid to take a free vacation.

Heidi spoke, interrupting Regina's thoughts as she thumbed through the fancy Wild America publication. "We'll stay the night at a national park hotel at the South Rim."

Regina showed Heidi a happy face. "Thanks." *Corporate espionage is a fine way to make money and have a vacation at the same time.* Regina felt more relaxed than she had for years.

As Regina returned to her seat, she decided to send the Wild America URL to Javier. *Then he won't keep asking me about tour stops.*

She neared George, who stood to give her access to her window seat. *I can't wait to slip into bed with George.* Brushing George's body as she scooted past him and sat, she felt his eyes focus on her. As if a magnet pulled her toward him, she leaned against his side, her knees weakened, and her body ached for him.

EIGHTEEN

THE WILD AMERICA bus was nearing the East Rim of the Grand Canyon in Arizona, twenty miles east of the Grand Canyon Village at the South Rim.

Luke studied the faces of the other tourists aboard the bus. Most were older, retired people, but two couples were younger, well-off foreigners. Luke believed one couple spoke French while another pair conversed in German.

As Luke observed his fellow tourists, he thought, *They're excited, talkin' a lot, even over their chair backs.* He realized the group had begun to bond and show camaraderie. They'd revealed it by how they interacted, displaying beaming faces. Luke felt his excitement grow, as well. As a smile formed on his lips, he reckoned his carefree attitude had put him at ease.

After guiding the bus into a parking lot near the canyon edge, the driver stopped the massive vehicle.

Heidi stood. "Folks, enjoy your first glimpse of the Grand Canyon. Be sure to visit the Desert Watchtower by the rim."

* * *

Within five minutes, Luke stood with George and Regina next to the tower. It could've been part of a medieval castle, Luke reckoned. He estimated the orange stone structure was seventy feet tall. With four levels of tiny windows overlooking the chasm below, the rough, cylindrical edifice seemed to teeter on the edge of the chasm. Luke turned to George. "If there was an earthquake like they had yesterday in Washington, would this tower fall down?"

George shrugged. "It be okay. Was here many years, since 1930s."

The three entered the tower, and Regina browsed in a gift shop there. After taking a glance at the items on display, Luke went outside to peer over the stony cliff where occasional small trees and shrubs grew on its edge. He surveyed the wide, sweeping view to his right and spied the Colorado River, weaving its way from the east following the bottom of the chasm.

Luke tilted his head back. The big sky was deep blue, and white clouds took their time to drift eastward above the landscape.

Peering down again, studying the cliff edges, Luke saw piles of rock and geologic layers of sediment. He heard footsteps on the rocky surface behind him. Turning, he noticed Heidi with a dozen Wild America tourists.

All of a sudden, Heidi eyeballed an Asian man inching toward the cliff edge, straining to snap digital images. She raised her arm and spoke with a firm voice to her flock of tourists. "Folks, don't do what that guy's doing because people die every year doing stupid stuff like that."

At the same moment Heidi pointed at the Asian man, he slid without warning and, by chance, stopped his movement. Exhaling, he released a nervous sigh and, with caution, moved backward to a safer place.

Luke wondered how many inattentive people had slipped over the cliff and died a violent death at the Grand Canyon, their bodies smashing against the rough, stone-and-dirt natural wall.

Heidi's loud voice cut into Luke's thoughts. "The Grand Canyon National Park has 1,900 square miles. The East Rim's open twenty-four hours a day, every day of the year."

Luke wondered how weak the lighting was after dark because he didn't see any streetlights. *Do people go too close to the mile-deep abyss even on moonless nights?*

After surveying the stunning canyon for another fifteen minutes, the Wild America tour group met at the tiger-striped tour bus. Heidi stood outside the motorcoach, counting the passengers as they climbed inside the large vehicle. Once everyone was aboard the bus, sitting in their seats, she moved to a position behind the bus driver. "Next, we're going to have lunch at Cameron Trading Post."

The bus began to move.

Luke didn't notice two men sitting in a large gray pickup truck at the far end of the parking lot. One man, Javier, peered through a pair of compact binoculars. He lowered them as José pressed down on the truck's accelerator and began to follow the tour bus.

NINETEEN

THE MOTORCOACH SPED toward the Cameron Trading Post near the Little Colorado River Gorge while Luke's stomach growled.

Lunch is late coming. As his belly began to demand food even more, he noticed a sign over a long, flat building in the distance.

Faced with flat stones and encircled by a protective overhang, the edifice displayed a horizontal sign atop its roof that read *Motel, Indian Arts & Crafts, Dining Room.* A smaller sign said *Cameron, established 1916.*

As the bus slowed, Heidi raised her microphone to her lips. "We've arrived at the Cameron Trading Post. I suggest you eat lunch first in the post dining room and then browse the eight-thousand-square-foot gift shop. There are Native American rugs and trinkets, Hopi pottery and jewelry, Apache baskets, and Plains beadwork. You may want to watch as a woman weaves Navajo rugs."

Luke heard the coach's air brakes sound, and the massive vehicle stopped.

Heidi spoke again. "We'll assemble at the bus no later than two fifteen."

Luke got up and turned to George and Regina. "I'm taking Heidi's advice and heading for the dining room. Y'all wanna join me?"

George pumped his head up and down. "Yes. I hungry."

Regina latched onto George's arm. "I'll stick with you guys."

A short walk later, Luke, George, and Regina entered the Grand Canyon Restaurant. The dining area was expansive, its floor covered with Native American rugs, while fancy, old cabinets adorned many of its walls. Tribal art, baskets, and pottery added a Southwestern aura to the space. As Luke peered at the ceiling, a waitress saw him stare upward, and she grinned. "The ceiling's overlaid with pressed tin."

Luke nodded. "Thanks. Nice to know." The odor of delicious Navajo food made his mouth water.

After Regina sat, Luke watched her grab a menu and study it. "They have Navajo tacos. I'll try one."

George appeared puzzled. "What is taco?"

Regina cocked her head. "Order one. You'll like it."

Luke chose Navajo fry bread covered with ground beef, beans, green chiles, lettuce, tomatoes, and cheddar cheese.

After the three ordered, Luke focused on the view of the Little Colorado River Gorge through a window. Meanwhile, Javier and José sat in the corner of the large room with their backs to Luke and his two companions.

* * *

12:53 P.M., THURSDAY, MAY 29, 2031, CAMERON TRADING POST

Though Javier had asked the hostess to seat José and himself in the far corner of the large, crowded dining area, José felt nervous being in the same room with Luke. As José followed the hostess and Javier to a table, José heard the noise of chatting people grow louder.

When they stopped in a less crowded part of the restaurant, José detected less noise, making him feel better, but still jittery. After he sat facing away from Luke, George, and Regina, José leaned forward and peered down at the table-top. He bit his lip.

Goddamn Javier. Luke has never seen him, but Luke saw me in London when I went after him with a knife. Just because I've grown a beard and let my hair grow long doesn't mean he won't recognize me.

José whispered in Spanish. "Javier, why take a chance and eat lunch in the same room with Luke?"

"We must not lose him. After eating, we could get lucky and shoot him when he's alone."

José shook his head and glanced around the jam-packed room. "Where?"

Javier cocked his head. "Perhaps in the bathroom."

"It'll be as crowded as the dining room." José sighed. *I'm being led by un estupido.*

Javier grinned. "In any case, we must eat to maintain our strength. He won't see us."

José felt his jaw muscles tighten. *Javier's carelessness will get us killed one day if we don't kill Luke first.* José's temples throbbed.

Javier turned his eyes toward José. "Our next best chance may well be at the South Rim." Behind him, he saw Regina across the room for a fleeting moment.

* * *

Regina sipped a cup of coffee after finishing her lunch. Staring across the room, she caught sight of Javier as he glanced at her, and her eyes widened.

Javier's watching. I should send him a text to prove I'm working. She got a brief view of a short, skinny Latino man sitting next to Javier for a fraction of a second before he turned away to stare out a window.

Regina got George's attention. "Excuse me. I'm going to the ladies' room." She snatched her purse and stood.

George turned up the corners of his lips and nodded.

As she walked toward the restrooms, Regina passed Javier's table, turned her head, and winked. He made a quick head movement to indicate he'd seen her.

Once in the restroom, Regina went into a stall, closed its door, and sat on the closed toilet seat lid. Reaching into her hip pocket, she pulled out her mobile phone and began to text Javier. "My report. Our tour will watch sunset at rim. George and Luke will demo joystick tractor for Grand Canyon groundskeepers after dinner at night. Tractor has headlights. I'll try to see sales pitch."

Twenty seconds later, Regina's phone signaled Javier had sent a text. "Nice work. If you go, record video of demo, even though it's after dark."

Regina's two thumbs tapped a quick, "Okay, if I can get George to invite me to demo."

"Great," Javier texted.

She stood, peered in the bathroom mirror, and brushed her hair. She visualized George in his underwear in her hotel room. *I better get back to the table.* She rushed from the restroom. *We should walk through the gift shop. It's huge.*

* * *

Javier sat as still as a stone on his chair.

José cocked his head. "Anything wrong?"

A wicked smile crossed Javier's lips. "No. Regina said the Wild America tour group will watch the sunset at the South Rim today. We'll go after Luke then."

Javier sat up straight. "We need to test-fly the new drone after the tour bus stops at the South Rim this afternoon to do a dry run." He took a sip of coffee and licked his lips. "We'll see if there are any drawbacks to my plan."

José scratched his scruffy, black beard. "When's sunset?"

Javier tapped the display on his satellite phone and then peered at a website. "Seven forty-four."

TWENTY

THE WILD AMERICA motorcoach left the Cameron Trading Post after most of the travelers had bought souvenirs.

While the bus gathered speed, Luke saw Regina hold a T-shirt up to her chest. An artistic, silkscreen graphic of the Desert Watchtower was on the garment's front.

Regina focused on George. "How do you like it?"

"Nice. Can't wait see you in it."

Luke decided Regina could make any kind of clothing appear attractive if she wore it.

As the Wild America motorcoach came closer to its second Grand Canyon stop, Luke saw three elk and four mule deer.

After the bus driver parked in a lot close to the edge of the mile-deep canyon near Mather Point, Heidi explained the Grand Canyon is widest and deepest there.

When Luke stepped down off the bus, he felt a fresh, clean breeze blow across his face. *Sure beats polluted city air.* He craned his neck to stare up at the saturated, deep-blue sky and sucked in a lungful of energizing air.

After walking five minutes toward the canyon's rim with George, Regina, and the rest of the Wild America tourists, Luke stared across the colorful scene. Heidi had stopped the group next to a brownish metal fence at the edge of the yawning gorge. "We're at Mather Point."

Luke felt elation flood his body and uplift his spirits. He listened as Heidi spoke. "Because it's a clear day, you can see thirty miles east and sixty miles west along the canyon. Glimpse down, and you'll see Phantom Ranch and lots of crisscrossing trails."

As Luke studied the depths, formations, and colors of the canyon, Heidi said, "From sunrise to sunset, the landscape's hues change in a dramatic way."

Hearing a camera click, Luke glanced to his left and saw a group of tourists. Because his mother was from Naples, Luke was sure the people were speaking Italian. An Italian man began to lean over the railing, taking pictures while he peered straight down over the cliffside.

He's nuts. If he loses his balance, he'll fall over the edge and die. Luke shook his head.

When he heard a whop whop whop sound, Luke turned toward the racket and saw a yellow helicopter hover over the middle of the deep gorge. Abruptly, the whirlybird swooped down toward the Colorado River, more than 5,000 feet below. Squinting, Luke scanned north across the wide canyon and spied a second aircraft, a red light plane flying east.

Heidi stepped close to Luke and caught his attention. "Helicopters and fixed-wing aircraft fly tourists to sightsee, but I think you can view as much from the rim."

Luke nodded. "Sure is pretty." He peered down and saw sightseers riding mules down a steep trail into the canyon. "Hope they don't slip."

Heidi grinned. "Mules are sure-footed, and riders don't have to steer them. That's Bright Angel Trail, leading to Phantom Ranch on the canyon floor. The visitors spend the night there and return on the South Kaibab Trail."

Luke glanced at Heidi and smiled. "If I knew how to paint, this would be a fine place to set up an easel."

Heidi pointed toward layers of rock that made up the canyon walls. "Those strata are geologic records. They go back millions and millions of years."

Luke eyed the horizontal layers of rocks. "How old's the canyon?"

"The most accepted theory is it took the Colorado River six million years to carve the gorge. But a recent study leads some scientists to think the west end of the canyon could be seventy million years old because an older river, running west to east, eroded it."

Luke scratched his beard. "Were dinosaurs around here then?"

Heidi cocked her head. "Dinosaurs died out about sixty-five million years ago. The ferocious, meat-eating Tyrannosaurus Rex lived around here."

Luke stood still as he gawked at the canyon wall, and then he spoke. "It's always been a dangerous place, even if it's real pretty." He studied the many angles of natural walls and bands of rocks. There were chocolate hues, light vermilions, purples, greens, and oranges. Shifting his eyes, he drank in the vibrant beauty.

Heidi winked at Luke and stepped to one edge of her crowd of Wild America tourists. "Let's head for the next vista point."

Luke inhaled clean air into his lungs and began to follow Heidi. His brain busy, he recalled both the Asian tourist and the Italian sightseer who had taken unnecessary chances on the edge of the canyon.

* * *

4:04 P.M., THURSDAY, MAY 29, 2031, SOUTH RIM, GRAND CANYON

The Wild America tour group traveled to a second parking lot on the Grand Canyon's South Rim.

After José followed the bus into the lot, he parked his gray pickup truck 150 yards from the yellow and black striped tour vehicle.

Javier leaned forward and peered at the Wild America tourists as they exited the bus. "It's time to test the drone camera."

He reached behind him and snatched his hobbyist-model drone from the truck's back seat. He'd bought the mini whirlybird at a big box store in Las Vegas and had charged the mini aircraft's batteries in his Las Vegas hotel room. "I must practice flying it and learn how its camera works."

José glanced at the small flying machine. It was a foot in diameter and had four helicopter-like props. "I'll watch the drone video on my phone while you fly it."

"Let's hope its camera is sharp." Javier opened the pickup's front passenger-side door, reached up, and placed the drone on the truck's roof. "See a picture on your mobile, José?"

"Sí." José gazed at his phone's display and saw a close-up view of a small patch of the truck's gray roof.

Javier fingered the drone controls, flew the drone up into the air, and peered at the sharp picture on his controller's video screen, which revealed a drone's-eye view of the parking lot. "I've flown another kind of drone before. This one's easier to use."

Squinting and leaning closer to his mobile phone, José stared at the aerial picture on the device's display. "It's sharp. I can see everything."

Javier glimpsed at José. "I want to test how hard it will be to find Luke in the crowd." Javier watched his controller's video screen as he flew the tiny aircraft above the rim, following its edge. "I see Luke walking behind the thin, blond tour leader."

* * *

4:07 P.M., THURSDAY, MAY 29, 2031, SOUTH RIM, GRAND CANYON

Luke followed Heidi as she led her group of Wild America sightseers to a viewpoint on the canyon's edge where there was no fence. She gestured toward a tall, wedding-cake-like formation of rocks on a finger of land poking into the mammoth ravine 400 yards distant. "You can get a great view if you don't go too close to the rim."

Luke figured if someone ventured too near to the canyon edge and slipped, the person would slide downward on a layer of loose dirt and gravel and fly over the lip of the gorge. He noticed a thin tree eight feet from the edge of the rim.

That's a safe place to stand and get a fine view.

With caution, he worked his way to the skinny tree and grabbed its scrawny trunk with his left hand. Moments later, a man with jet-black hair and sunburned pink skin, dressed in Bermuda shorts, neared the canyon edge to Luke's right. Luke realized the man was not on the Wild America tour.

The man raised a large digital camera as if to prepare to peer through its viewfinder. His back foot slid on loose pebbles. Losing his balance, he dropped his expensive camera and lunged after it as it skidded away, sliding toward the precipice. Luke, while still holding onto the small tree, stretched and grabbed the back of the photographer's belt and stopped his forward motion. An instant later, his camera rolled over the edge.

As Luke held onto the man's belt, the man yelled, "What the hell did you do? My camera's worth two grand." He spoke with a strong New York accent.

The skinny tree trunk cracked, and Luke slid his left hand down to its roots, driving a splinter into his palm. With his right hand, he pulled on the protesting man's belt as the tourist slipped farther and fell on his rear end. Small rocks and dirt plummeted downward to the distant floor of the gorge. Luke pulled the man next to him. "You damn near died, mister." Luke spoke with a strong Southern drawl while his heart pounded at double its normal rate.

The man stood and brushed dirt from his shorts, as onlookers seemed to be relieved the man wasn't hurt. "You goddamn hillbilly. I ought to slap your face. Because of you, I lost my camera and all the pictures I took."

Luke rose and shook his head in disgust as he stared at the obnoxious New Yorker.

I shouldn't say anything more.

Luke figured that after just saving the arrogant man from sure death, it wouldn't be wise to get into a fistfight on the edge of the steep cliff.

With an unexpected, fast move, the man pushed Luke, but Luke grabbed the thin tree again.

Feeling blood rush to his face, Luke glimpsed down around him and saw foot-size patches of solid rock. He stepped on the sections of flat stone to move away from the canyon's edge. At the same time, the New Yorker in Bermuda shorts followed Luke and yelled, "I'm going to teach you a lesson."

Seconds later, with a stone wall now between the two men and the cliff, the aggressive man swung his fist at Luke. Luke dodged the blow.

His nostrils flaring, Luke felt sweat bead on his forehead.

I had enough of this. After slapping the man's left cheek, Luke also smacked the man's right cheek. Blood oozed from the New Yorker's nose and lips.

Stepping back, the defeated man rubbed blood from his nose. "Stop. I had enough."

A half dozen tourists and Heidi halted near the two men. Then Heidi spoke. "I saw it all, and I shot a video." She stared at the once belligerent New Yorker. "You can walk away, no questions asked, or I can call the rangers and have you arrested."

The man raised his hands. "I'm leaving."

As the New Yorker strode away, Luke thought he heard a drone-like buzz.

With fire in his eyes, George neared Luke and stared at the retreating aggressor. "If he did not leave, I beat him to pulp."

Luke patted George's shoulder. "Thanks, George." A fanlike hum made Luke eyeball the sky. "Hear that, George?"

"Yeah. What is it?"

Luke pointed. "A drone. Not a great place to fly it."

George furrowed his brow, and the rest of the busload of Wild America tourists gathered around Luke and Heidi.

* * *

All of the Wild America tourists formed a circle around Luke, Heidi, and George. Luke surveyed them and saw the motley group of people from across the country and the world display concern.

One of Luke's fellow Wild America tourists, a heavy, older Texan who could've been a professional football player because of his tall, bull-like body, stepped up to Luke. "You did the right thing slappin' the rude guy. You saved his life, and see what thanks he gave you. You should call the cops."

As he felt his breathing slow, Luke focused on the Texan. "Thanks. But there's no need to call the police. The man learned a lesson."

Grasping her cell phone as if ready to call 911, a thin French woman spoke up. "Still, the authorities should be called."

"Folks, I'm a deputy sheriff on vacation. If I wanted to, I woulda made a citizen's arrest. It's over now. But y'all, I thank you fur your concern."

Heidi held up her right arm. "Okay, folks. Let's move to the next viewpoint."

Regina interlocked her arm with George's. As the group of tourists followed Heidi around the canyon rim, Luke once again heard a drone buzzing above them.

* * *

Lagging behind Heidi and many of the Wild America tourists, George, Regina, and Luke surveyed the deep, multi-colored Grand Canyon gorge below them. As a gentle wind wafted across Luke's face, Regina walked aside to take a wide shot of the canyon.

Again, a high-pitched, humming buzz grabbed Luke's attention. He glanced up and saw a hobbyist-class drone a foot in diameter flying five feet above them, following Heidi's group. Glancing at George, Luke said, "It's illegal to fly drones in national parks. The pilot could git six months in jail and a $5,000 fine."

George shook his head. "Odds are one careless person is in each group of thirty."

All of a sudden, the drone zoomed upward and away from the cliff edge. In seconds, the tiny aircraft disappeared at the same time as two park rangers came into view 200 yards away.

Luke sighed. "The air's clear and clean. Makes me wanna sleep outside tonight."

George spread his arms wide and high, closed his eyes, and stretched. "I love this country. I feel free sometime, but not all time."

"What do you mean?"

George crossed his arms. "I am like a canary in cage after you and MI5 caught me." He peered at the dusty ground. "Then I switch sides like pro football player. Now I am falcon and work for Western nations. I fly free, but only to hunt, maybe kill prey." George winced and coughed. "I need to leave the life of the spy."

Luke was mute for a moment and then spoke. "I git it."

George had a faraway look in his eyes. "I can't wait to quit spy game."

"I think you need to wait."

George leaned on the railing close to him and gazed into the distance. "What if I tell Mikhail I work for West? Then I not useful to FBI or MI5. KGB would not want me anymore."

Luke avoided eye contact with George. "Wouldn't the UK and US say you broke your deal with them? Would they arrest you? Would the KGB kill you?" Luke rubbed his hand on his trouser leg.

"I know spy craft. I would disappear in crowd. Change name. Get low-paying job. Then I be free."

Luke scratched the back of his neck. "Maybe you can avoid running and hiding."

"How?"

"Work for the FBI a while more. Keep giving the KGB false intelligence about the US military. Save the KGB bribery money the US won't take, just like you kept the $60,000 the KGB gave you to bribe Major Green."

George tilted his head backward and stared at the sky for a moment. "You are right. I must be patient."

* * *

4:23 P.M., THURSDAY, MAY 29, 2031, SOUTH RIM, GRAND CANYON

Javier sat with José in their rented truck. Staring into the video screen of his drone's controller, Javier guided the tiny aircraft to a landing next to the pickup's front passenger-side door. After glancing around, he saw no one was watching, and with a quick motion, he opened his door and snatched the drone. *That was easy enough.* He felt relief once the miniature whirlybird was in his hands.

After plugging the drone into one of the truck's USB ports to charge the small craft's batteries, Javier placed it in its cardboard box, closing its flaps. He took notice of José, who appeared nervous. "Nobody will see it in the box."

José exhaled. "I'm glad." He glanced out the driver-side window across the parking lot. "We damn near got lucky when the tourist pushed Luke."

Javier rubbed his chin. "Luke's luck is about to end."

José peered down at the truck's floor mat. "Mateo's impatient."

Javier blinked. "Mateo should know hunting requires patience."

Staring at the cardboard box containing the drone, José spoke. "Since you've test-flown the drone, do you think it'll be able to see Luke when dusk comes?"

"Sí, even if it's at night. The machine has infrared vision."

José squinted. "So we'll try at sunset for sure?"

"Yes." Javier leaned sideways in his seat and observed José for five seconds. *Will José be up to the task? He'll have to do the deed because he doesn't know how to fly the drone.*

José's face appeared red even under his tan. "Why not just shoot him?"

"It would be evident he'd been shot, and it would be hard for us to get away. The roads in the park are narrow and twist around like spaghetti."

José shook his head and raised his chin as his nostrils flared. A vein in his throat throbbed.

Javier took note of José's body language. *After this job, I'll tell Mateo José's lost his courage. He no longer has a spine. I must ask for another partner.*

TWENTY-ONE

EN ROUTE to another spot on the Grand Canyon's South Rim, Luke scanned the scenery for more wild animals, like the elk and mule deer he'd seen earlier that day. He smiled. Viewing deer and other wildlife was one of his favorite pastimes and the reason why he had so enjoyed his previous job as a Kentucky game warden.

The bus came to a stop in a parking lot within walking distance of the canyon's edge. As Luke stepped off the bus, he detected the slight odor of smoke in the soft breeze. A smoky haze was drifting eastward. He turned to Heidi. "Smells like a fire." He recalled an airline magazine article about the drought impacting the West, dehydrating the land until much of it had dried to dust.

Heidi stroked her long, bleached-blond hair. "I got a report a wildfire is west of us. It's cutting visibility but should make for a vivid, orange-red sunset. We'll watch tonight's sunset at seven forty-four from the rim near the Bright Angel Trailhead."

Regina stepped closer to Heidi. "There's a fire?"

Heidi nodded. "We didn't have enough rain this spring across the West, and weeds and trees are dry as tinder."

Luke noticed George had walked to the path by the parking lot. The spy's mobile phone rang, and he peered at its face. As he answered, he waved Luke to approach him.

When Luke stopped near George, the man was speaking into his phone. "Thank you for inviting us. I tell colleague Luke Ryder. He will demo joystick control." George nodded. "Thanks." He appeared to relax as he ended his call.

Luke blinked. "What's happening?"

George's smile grew wider. "South Rim chief groundkeeper invited us to dinner at eight-thirty. After we eat, we will demo joystick and nighttime control of tractor. It arrived two days ago. Groundkeeper drove it in normal mode. He likes machine even without joystick control." Luke noticed George shift his weight back and forth from one foot to the other.

Luke couldn't contain his grin. *George's excitement is contagious.* Luke took a step closer to George. "You think the park will buy the tractor?"

George laughed, and his face flushed. "They buy it and two more."

Luke grabbed George's hand and shook it. "Congrats."

Regina, from behind Luke, moved forward and latched onto George's shoulder. "George, I heard the great news about your tractor sales." Her face was upturned, and she focused on George's eyes.

George placed his arm around Regina's waist. "I got good news for you."

"What?"

"Groundkeeper invite me, Luke to dinner at eight-thirty. I ask if you can come. Groundkeeper said yes."

"It'll be cool."

George focused on Regina's eyes. "You can watch night demo of tractor, too, if you like."

"I'd love to." Regina gave a quick hug to George, and Luke saw him make strong eye contact with her.

Luke rubbed his chin. *George has taken a liking to that*

woman. He needs to fill the hole in his heart left after Anne, the baroness, died.

Heidi waved to Luke, George, and Regina. "I'll walk to the rim with you folks and show you where the geologist is giving a talk about the canyon's history. George was on a phone call, so I waited for you."

* * *

Luke sat down on a sun-warmed, flat stone overlooking the canyon below. Standing with his back to the cliff edge, a US Park Service geologist was lecturing the Wild America tour group about the geologic history of the canyon. "Two billion years ago, igneous and metamorphic rocks formed, and then layers of sediment fell on top of the old, base rocks. Some layers are made from drifting sands, others from limestone formed from the shells of sea life."

The toasty, dry air felt relaxing, and Luke's eyelids slipped downward and closed. The droning lecture faded from his awareness and sounded like a distant hum. *I'm sleeping, but I don't care.*

All at once, he saw a dreamy vision of his wife Layla, and he leaned closer to her and kissed her tender lips.

Layla spoke. "I miss you. Can't wait 'til you're back from the FBI gig. Is the money you earn worth it?"

Luke felt someone shake his shoulder. Luke's chin collapsed forward against his chest, and he awoke.

George peered at him. "You sleep like baby. I'm glad you rested before demo tonight."

Luke caught sight of the rest of the Wild America group. Four or five of them had begun to follow Heidi toward another canyon viewpoint.

Glimpsing far to his left, Luke saw a finger of land sticking out from the lookout into the gorge. In the distance, people on the tip of the point appeared to be the size of black ants. They stood behind a metal fence and surveyed the canyon from their high perch.

After catching up with the rest of the tour group, Luke, George, and Regina stopped by a rock wall. As Luke gawked at the vast canyon to his left, he saw a zigzagging dirt trail descending the canyon wall.

George reached into his breast pocket and pulled out a map of the park. "That is South Kaibab Trailhead. It heads down into canyon. Yaki Point is north." He pointed to his right. "If we had time, we could walk thirteen miles on the paved path following South Rim."

Luke noticed Heidi had worked her way through her brood of tourists toward him.

She's payin' lots of attention to us. Could be she likes George.

Heidi pointed at the dirt track. "The South Kaibab Trail is the main way to hike down into the canyon, but it's hot, and there's no shade or water. It's steep, difficult, and tiring when you walk back up."

George's body seemed to sag. "I think I will not hike down. We might be late for special dinner with Grand Canyon groundkeeper."

Heidi scratched her cheek. "So you won't be at the catered dinner tonight at eight with the rest of the tour group?"

George glanced at Luke and Regina and then focused on Heidi. "I forget to tell you. I am tractor salesman. At many national parks, I talk to park officials to sell them tractors. Tonight, Luke, me, and Regina will dine with chief groundkeeper. Then we demo tractor after dark."

Heidi touched her lips with her index finger. "Because you'll miss my announcements during tonight's group meal, I'll email you details about tomorrow. We'll pull away from our hotel at 8:00 a.m. to head for Monument Valley."

George smiled. "Thanks."

Heidi glanced leftward toward the Visitor Center at Mather Point. Beyond that, a bit farther west, was the Verkamps's Visitor Center and the hotel Wild America had booked for Heidi's group. She pointed west. "Tonight, we'll stay in the El Tovar Hotel. If you arrive late there, call me, and I'll give you your keys." She handed George, Luke, and Regina her business cards. "There's free time until dinner." She paused. "Your map shows you where the park shuttle bus stops are in case you decide to follow the rim a little farther." Heidi checked her watch. "I'm taking a two-hour mule ride. Want to go?"

Luke shook his head. "I gotta call my wife."

George said, "Regina and me will walk and take shuttle bus along rim."

Heidi smiled, waved, and left them.

Regina said, "I see a bathroom. Be right back."

* * *

Regina opened a bathroom stall, sat on the toilet lid, and smelled ammonia. *The restroom must've just been cleaned.* Phone in hand, she tapped Javier's name on her contact list. Javier's phone rang five times.

"*Hola*, Regina. Any news?"

"George invited me to the tractor demo after dark tonight, but I'm not sure where it is yet. I'll shoot a video for you."

"I'll be anxious to see it. Anything else?"

"We'll watch the sunset as a group from the rim near the Bright Angel Trailhead." She took a quick breath. "Thank you for the gig. I'm having fun."

Regina heard Javier bump his phone. "I'll text you the number of my boss, Mateo Guerra. After the tour is done, please call him. When I told him how well you're doing on the job, he said he'd love to speak with you."

Regina's heart pounded faster. "Does he want to talk to me about working for your company?"

"I think so. I bet he'll invite you to his estate outside of Tijuana in order to interview you."

Regina felt blood rush to her face. "Thank you for helping me, Javier." She felt her heart pounding.

"It's my pleasure, Regina. Talk to you later."

"Bye."

* * *

5:00 P.M., THURSDAY, MAY 29, 2031, SOUTH RIM, GRAND CANYON

Javier shifted in the front passenger seat of his rented pickup truck. As he stuffed his satellite phone into his hip pocket, he glanced at José, who sat in the driver's seat. "Regina told me Luke's tour group will view the sunset from near the Bright Angel Trailhead." Javier rubbed the stubble on his chin.

José blinked. "You said sunset's about quarter to eight, right?"

"Sí."

Staring at Javier, José cocked his head. "I wager there will be a crowd watching the sunset. How do we know Luke will be near the edge?"

"We don't know." Javier was staring at his phone's display. "Right now, I'm checking out the street view of the rim near Bright Angel Trailhead. The best thing we can do is prepare."

José nodded.

Javier noticed there was a parking area near the Bright Angel Lodge. *I wonder if I can book a room in the lodge. I could fly the drone from there while José jogs on the rim trail. I might be able to watch through a window, too.*

Javier searched the internet for the Bright Angel Lodge. He soon viewed pictures of the main lodge building and separate one-story cabins where ninety rooms were scattered between the large lodge and the canyon rim.

A relaxed smile crossed Javier's lips. "Perfect."

José sat up straight. "What?"

"If I can book a room at the Bright Angel Lodge, it's next to the rim. I can fly the drone from there. After you kill Luke, you can run back from the rim and be inside within less than a minute."

José rolled his eyes and shook his head. "Why do I have to take the biggest chances?"

Javier studied José's eyes with a laser-like stare. "I know how to fly the drone. You don't. It's our single option."

José sighed. "Okay, okay." He held his hands up.

After three minutes, Javier booked a room at the lodge. He figured someone had canceled their reservation at the last moment because the cabin he booked had a view overlooking the canyon. *I can't wait until sunset when Luke's eyes will close for the last time.* Javier felt himself form a devilish grin.

* * *

5:12 P.M., THURSDAY, MAY 29, 2031, SOUTH RIM, GRAND CANYON

As Javier and José stepped from their pickup truck, Javier considered it lucky José had found a parking place in a lot close to the Bright Angel Lodge. They walked around the back of the vehicle, and José opened the truck bed cover over the rear cargo area. He unzipped his suitcase and removed jogging clothes, white socks, and a pair of running shoes. He put these items in a white plastic garbage bag. At the same time, Javier was grabbing underwear and a magnetic vehicle tracker from his case and putting them into another trash bag.

Javier looked at José and winked. "Now we're ready for a quick getaway if Luke dies."

As the men neared the front entry of the large Bright Angel Lodge to check in, Javier was impressed with the old-fashioned, rough-hewn beauty of the place. Its gable roof overhung a wide front porch. Large adze-carved logs supported the porch part of the roof, while a stone siding covered the building's front, exterior wall.

Once inside the lodge, Javier spotted a large fireplace made of what he reckoned were local stones. Gazing around the building's interior, he saw more log construction. Logs made up a major part of the building as well as limestone rock.

As he and José neared the check-in desk, Javier stopped and removed a credit card from his wallet. Hector Castro, one of Javier's aliases, was printed on the back of the plastic card.

A young woman with dark brown hair in braids greeted the two men. "How may I help you, gentlemen?"

Javier displayed a cheerful face. *I should appear innocent and harmless.* "We're checking in. I reserved a room with my credit card. My name's Hector Castro." He handed the young lady his card.

Within two minutes, the woman had received Javier's advance payment and returned his card. She smiled. "You're fortunate you scored a cabin near the rim. From the back window, there's a great view."

Javier put the credit card back in his wallet. "Lady Luck is on our side today." He winked at the attractive young woman.

* * *

After the two assassins entered their rented cabin, José sat in an easy chair and put his feet up on a hassock.

Standing nearby, Javier reached into his white plastic trash bag and grasped a magnetic vehicle tracking device the size of a silver dollar.

Lucky I spotted where the Wild America bus is parked. If nobody's there, this is the best time to plant the tracker. He turned to José. "I'll be back soon." He held up the tracker. "I'll put this on the bus."

José nodded.

Five minutes later, trying to appear casual, Javier walked at a slow pace toward the yellow and black striped bus. He glanced around and saw no one nearby. After reaching into his trousers pocket to take out the vehicle tracker, he knelt and pretended to tie his shoe.

Again scanning the area, Javier didn't see anyone close to him, so he slapped the magnetic tracker under the motor-coach's huge body. *Now, in case we don't nail Luke tonight, we can still follow the bus from a mile back or more. He won't see us tailing the motorcoach and get suspicious.*

Javier stood and walked toward his rented cabin at the Bright Angel Lodge. *I hope José regains his courage. We need to finish off Luke tonight.* Javier gritted his teeth.

* * *

7:34 P.M., THURSDAY, MAY 29, 2031, SOUTH RIM, GRAND CANYON

Javier peered through his compact binoculars at José. The short, thin man, dressed in jogging clothes, loitered behind bushes not far from the canyon's South Rim, trying to hide from view. Javier wasn't sure if José had attached his earbud speaker to his satellite phone yet.

Speaking into a lavaliere microphone clamped to his shirt, Javier asked José, "Hear me okay?"

"*Sí.*" José's voice emanated from the speaker on Javier's mobile phone, which rested on the mattress of one of the cabin's two queen-size beds.

Javier was proud he'd plotted how to oversee Luke's murder using satellite phones and a drone. Earlier, he'd concealed his consumer-model drone outside by the east wall of his rented cabin and behind a small, stunted tree.

Placing his field glasses aside, Javier sat at the room's small desk near the drone controller on the desktop. The mechanism's display showed a live feed from the drone's infrared-enabled video camera. He stared at the close-up TV view of grass blades underneath the tiny, idle aircraft.

Glancing away from the controller, he saw the orange-red sun was low on the horizon while the smoky, western sky was crimson, the color of blood.

Touching the controller's buttons and joystick, Javier launched the drone. Watching a live video feed of the flying machine's downward view as the aircraft soared skyward, Javier's eyes glowed. *All that's left is to spot Luke and tell José when and where to strike.* Javier couldn't contain the grin spreading across his lips.

* * *

7:44 P.M., THURSDAY, MAY 29, 2031, SOUTH RIM, GRAND CANYON

A sudden drop in temperature cooled Luke and the rest of the Wild America tour group as they watched the reddish ball that was the sun dip below the horizon. The distant sky was a deep, flaming red with streaks of orange, and the sky's zenith displayed saturated purples and dark blues.

The smell of smoke triggered Luke's brain to flashback to visions of the many times he'd camped in Kentucky's woods, watching his glowing campfire flicker in the growing darkness of dusk.

Luke felt a tap on his shoulder as the cool nighttime breeze picked up speed. Turning, he saw Heidi's face in the quick-fading light. Her voice helped return him to the here and now. "The wildfire smoke's drifting toward us on a west wind. The haze helps the sun's rays color the sky."

Nodding in the darkness, Luke said, "Yep." He saw a reddish glow reflect from Heidi's bright blond hair. Staring past her, the big, crimson sky appeared surrealistic, like a desert view of an unexplored planet in a distant galaxy.

Feeling as free as a soaring hawk, Luke considered, *If only I had wings.* He reckoned he could swoop downward and enjoy multiple shades of orange, burgundy, and purple decorating the rugged canyon walls. Feeling fearless, relishing the moment, he stood on the edge of the rim, away from everyone else except for Heidi.

Heidi whispered, "This view makes me want to be here forever."

"Me, too." Luke widened his eyes, trying to see deeper into the dim light to take in the fading colors. From his position on the cliff edge, he didn't notice a lone jogger approaching at a slow pace through the darkening gloom.

* * *

7:46 P.M., THURSDAY, MAY 29, 2031, SOUTH RIM, GRAND CANYON

Javier stared at the video display on the drone's controller. A night-vision infrared image of Luke and the rest of the Wild America tour group showed them standing at the very edge of the chasm. Better yet, Luke was alone on the rim of the cliff, peering at the sunset. Javier grinned and laughed, though he was alone in the cabin. *This is working out better than I thought it would. Luke's fascinated with the sunset. His eyes are not adjusted to the darkness, and he won't see José coming.*

Javier spoke into the microphone attached to his shirt. "Do it, José. Luke's near the edge. He won't see you in the dark."

The satellite phone resting on the queen-size mattress sounded. "*Sí.* Wish me luck."

"You will succeed, *amigo.*"

Javier heard José's breathing grow rough as the skinny man began to jog and then gather speed. Javier grinned. *This job gives new meaning to the term* bump off.

* * *

7:47 P.M., THURSDAY, MAY 29, 2031, SOUTH RIM, GRAND CANYON

Reducing his speed to a slower pace, José felt jittery as he squinted through the dim, dusky light. *There aren't streetlights here. How can I see Luke?*

Now near the Wild America tour group, José felt his heart firing like a Gatling gun. Twenty feet from the tourists, José caught sight of Luke.

Now running at top speed, José veered toward Luke, who stood close to the rim. Taking care not to propel himself

over the edge with Luke, José feigned a trip, slipped sideways on the hard, dry ground, and threw his right leg at
both of Luke's feet. In a split second, the big Kentucky
deputy sheriff flew toward the cliff edge while José skidded
in the opposite direction on his left leg like a baseball player
sliding into home plate.

Pain coursed through José's rump as the rough surface
slammed across his upper leg and butt. *Did I skin my ass?*
José scrambled to his feet and ran away as fast as he could.

* * *

A jolt of pain stabbed at Luke's right ankle as he tumbled
down over the rim of the deep chasm. Aware someone had
run into him, he had felt unstoppable momentum drive him
over the edge. A primal, involuntary scream leaped from his
lips. Now airborne, he wondered what his last memory of
life would be. Grasping the rough cliff side with both his
hands, he felt the rocky surface sandpaper them.

As his right arm banged against and around a thin tree
growing from the canyon wall, he fell into a crevice. His
body stuck in it inches from a drop to the canyon floor far
below him. Panting, he gulped air and tried to calm down.
As he peered up at the dark, star-studded sky, he gasped and
then yelled, "Throw me a rope."

His ankle throbbing, he felt small rocks and dirt bounce
off his body and plummet downward. He reckoned he was
twenty-five feet down from the rim of the side of the cliff.

The beam of a penlight shining down lit the crevice
around him. "I called 911." George's Russian-accented voice
sounded calm.

"Thanks, George." Luke realized his voice was higher
than normal. "I ain't sure how stable the rocks are."

Luke caught sight of Heidi's blond tresses, partly lit by
George's miniature flashlight. "Luke, the rangers are
coming." Her voice was shrill, and she sounded beyond
stressed.

Luke sucked in a deep breath. "Thanks," he yelled. *Them Mexicans must've followed me. I gotta call Rita when I git outta this fix.*

A large clump of dirt and rock broke loose from under Luke's left foot, crumbled, and fell into the black void beneath him. *I hope someone throws me a rope pretty soon.*

Luke didn't want to admit he was scared.

* * *

7:50 P.M., THURSDAY, MAY 29, 2031, SOUTH RIM, GRAND CANYON

As he stared into the video screen on the drone controller, Javier watched Luke tumble over the canyon's rim. Javier yelped.

Finally, we got the son of a bitch.

The Mexican assassin let out two slow breaths, fumbled for a moment with the drone controller, and guided the miniature aircraft over José, who was sprinting west on the rim trail. Javier yelled into his lavaliere microphone. "José, you did it. Great job."

Leaning over the small desk where the controller sat, Javier heard the sound of José's wheezing coming from the satellite phone's speaker. The device sat on the bed behind him. José gasped and then said, "A ranger is running toward me."

Javier stared at the infrared image on the controller display. At once, he saw a park ranger nearing José. Within two seconds, Javier flicked the drone controls and sent the small whirlybird into a dive toward the advancing ranger.

* * *

7:53 P.M., THURSDAY, MAY 29, 2031, SOUTH RIM, GRAND CANYON

José heard the whine of Javier's drone as it flew at the ranger, whose silhouette was outlined by the darkening, fading red sky on the horizon. As the ranger dove to the surface of the rim trail, José turned left. He heard the high-pitched buzz of the miniature whirlybird decrease in volume as the small flying machine zoomed Kamikazi-style down toward the Colorado River thousands of feet below.

I must run faster to get back to the room. He felt irritating pain as his skinned left leg and butt chafed against his jogging outfit. He turned left through bushes, and branches scratched his face. Squinting ahead through the murky night, he could just see the shape of the cabin he and Javier shared. *We better get out of here before the cops start investigating.*

Slowing his pace as he neared the cabin door, José breathed in and out, in and out. *I'm glad this job's over.* He opened the cabin door.

* * *

8:01 P.M., THURSDAY, MAY 29, 2031, SOUTH RIM, GRAND CANYON

Fast-approaching spotlights blinded George's vision as they seemed to rush toward him and the rim trail where Luke had fallen over the edge. As George's eyes adjusted to the focused beams, George saw the light came from two bright yellow park service pickup trucks. They had slowed and now were inching their way toward a crowd of people peering over the cliffside.

Three or four spectators held flashlights illuminating Luke and the crevice where his fall had ended.

Dressed in yellow sweatshirts and orange helmets, four men scrambled from the two trucks. One raised his arms. "Let us through, people."

Aiming a powerful LED flashlight, the first man in yellow to arrive at the rim's edge peered down at Luke. "Stay strong, sir. We're going to lift you with special equipment."

Regina and Heidi next to him, George watched as the men set up an apparatus made of three telescoping poles, ropes, and a pulley. The rescuers placed the contraption on the rim of the cliff. Resembling an upside-down letter V, two of the poles dug into the dry dirt and rocks. A third pole extended horizontally across the point where the two supporting poles met.

After attaching a harness to a rope dangling from the horizontal pole, the men lowered the harness to Luke and then pulled him up to safety. Letting out three deep breaths, Luke brushed the dust from his jeans, smiled, and concentrated his gaze on the four men who'd rescued him. "Thanks, fellas."

A spontaneous cheer erupted from the gathering crowd.

George stepped up to Luke. "I will cancel robo-tractor demo."

Luke shook his head. "I'm okay. After I eat, I'll be raring to go." He flexed his left hand and licked a skinned patch of his left palm. "Lucky I work on the farm and my hands have callouses."

George grabbed his phone and glanced at Luke. "I will call groundkeeper and delay dinner and demo."

George rubbed the back of his neck. He thought in Russian. *Luke's hiding the fact he was scared, but who wouldn't be terrified?*

* * *

8:01 P.M., THURSDAY, MAY 29, 2031, BRIGHT ANGEL LODGE CABIN

As José tapped on the cabin door, Javier turned the interior lights off.

When José entered, Javier threw his arms around the short, wiry man. "You're fearless again. Nice work."

As José's smile faded, he wrinkled his brow. "We better get moving. Even if it was dark, people saw me slide into Luke."

Javier put the cabin key on a dresser. "You're right. Let's go."

After stuffing their few belongings into their white plastic trash bags, the two men stepped into the night. Javier closed the cabin door, and they walked to their pickup truck.

Within three minutes, José had guided their vehicle at the speed limit toward the park exit. He asked, "What about the whore you hired to watch Luke?"

Javier shrugged. "She'll call or text and say Luke's dead. I'll tell her she did an outstanding job and to call Mateo."

José wrinkled his brow. "You think the cops will ask her questions?"

"I doubt it."

TWENTY-TWO

FLOODLIGHTS MOUNTED on two yellow pickup trucks lit the wider area where Luke had slipped over the canyon rim. As Luke sat resting on a large boulder, he selected FBI Agent Rita Reynold's name on his satellite phone contact list. He heard her phone ring six times.

"Hello, Luke. It's almost a quarter after eleven here. Everything okay?"

"No. I damn near died."

"What?"

Luke waited to speak as he relived the incident during which he had come close to death. "At dusk, a man ran into me, tripped on my ankle, and I flew over the canyon edge. Lucky I fell into a crevice twenty-five feet down. Rescuers pulled me up with a harness and ropes."

"Are you hurt?"

"Just scuffed up." Luke figured he wouldn't tell Rita he still felt jumpy after he'd been scared shitless.

"The rangers catch anybody?"

"Not yet." Luke waited a beat. "I didn't see the guy who tripped me. But I think it was the Mexicans sent by Mateo Guerra."

Rita hesitated. Luke figured she was thinking of what to do next. She began to speak. "The FBI has jurisdiction on federal land, so I'll send FBI agents to investigate."

"What'll I tell the park rangers?"

"Don't tell them you suspect Mexican cartel assassins tried to kill you. If the rangers approach you before I phone them, call me. I'll tell them the FBI's taking over the investigation."

"Okay."

Rita was silent for three seconds. "How do you know the Belarusian KGB didn't try to kill you?"

"I met the KGB courier, Mikhail Popov. He's a friend of George's who picked up the Army info. He tried to recruit me and offered to pay me $5,000 for each tractor sales trip."

"Wow. Play along with him. We'll discuss how to handle him later." Rita yawned. "But still, we'll investigate to rule out the KGB. Describe Mikhail."

"Skinny, tall, about forty years old. Has a slight Russian accent. I snapped a pic of him with my phone when George and Mikhail weren't watchin'."

"Excellent. Text it to me." For a moment, Rita was silent.

"Anything else?"

"Tell anyone else who asks that you think a jogger ran into you by accident in the dark, and he panicked and ran away. We need to keep our inquiry under wraps. I don't want the KGB to get spooked, pun not intended."

"Okay. I gotta go with George to eat dinner with the Grand Canyon chief groundskeeper. After that, George and I will demo the Belarusian tractor for the national park folk."

"Are you sure you're up to it?"

"Yep."

"You'll demo when it's dark?"

"The tractor's got headlights."

Luke heard Rita take a quick breath. "When I'm calling the rangers, will you phone Layla?"

"Is she awake?"

"She's sound asleep."

Luke sighed. "Let's not worry her tonight. I'll call her tomorrow." Luke coughed. "But I gotta tell George about the Mexican assassins ASAP."

"Okay, George is on our team." Rita hung up.

Luke was worried Rita and Layla might be on each other's nerves in the close quarters of his farmhouse. He reckoned Rita still had a crush on him, even though he'd married Layla.

Luke shook his head. *And when Layla hears the Mexicans tried to kill me again, she's gonna be angry with Rita fur sure because she recruited me to take the job escortin' George.*

Luke caught sight of a young ranger who started to walk toward him. The light from the flood lamps on the yellow rescue trucks backlit the man's figure. "I heard you had a close call, sir. Could you tell me what happened?"

Luke gazed at the ranger. "An FBI agent asked me to refer all questions about this incident to her."

The youthful ranger appeared puzzled. "Who?"

"Agent Rita Reynolds. I'll call her for you." Luke tapped Rita's name on his phone.

"Hello, Luke."

"Hi, Rita. There's a ranger with me who needs to talk with you."

"Okay."

Luke handed his phone to the baffled ranger.

* * *

8:16 P.M., THURSDAY, MAY 29, 2031, EN ROUTE FROM THE SOUTH RIM

José guided his rented pickup truck through the inky darkness and away from the Grand Canyon South Rim.

As Javier and José neared Arizona State Route 64 South, Javier's eyes were dancing while he sang at the top of his lungs to a popular Mexican song blasting from the radio.

Without warning, Javier abruptly stopped singing and turned down the radio's volume.

His eyes wide, José gazed to his right at his partner.

Javier frowned and peered down at the floor of their speeding vehicle. "I should call Mateo."

"You should."

His hands shaking, Javier grabbed his encrypted satellite phone and tapped in Mateo's phone number. After seven rings, he heard Mateo's voice. "Javier, I suppose you have news to report about Luke Ryder."

"*Sí, mi Jefe.* At last, Luke is dead."

"Fabulous. How did he die?"

"At dusk, Luke was watching the sunset from the canyon rim. José jogged by and tripped Luke, who slid over the edge. It was murky dark by then, and José ran away to our cabin room. We left a few minutes ago."

"You're sure he's dead?"

"He had to fall hundreds of meters. No one could survive such a fall."

After pausing, the cartel boss spoke. "I am pleased. Be sure to get another vehicle in case the authorities conclude Luke's death was not an accident."

"*Sí.* We'll return to Tijuana soon."

"Come to my villa, and we'll have a drink."

"Thank you, *Jefe.*"

* * *

9:00 P.M., THURSDAY, MAY 29, 2031, THE SOUTH RIM, GRAND CANYON

Regina, George, and Luke stood on the wide front porch of the Bright Angel Lodge. Peering into the ebony night, Regina caught sight of a tall, thin man with stringy, gray hair tied in a ponytail, and tanned, rough skin. He approached George, who stood near the top of the porch steps. She reckoned the weathered man was in his late fifties.

The older man stepped closer to George. "I'm Tom Topaz. Are you George Black?"

"Yes, sir." George grasped the man's hand and shook it with Old World vigor, and then he gestured toward Regina. "Tom, this is my friend, Regina." George glanced at Luke. "And this is Luke Ryder. He will demo joystick tractor."

Tom extended his leathery hand to Luke, and the two men shook hands. "Luke, I heard you had a close call." He glanced at Luke's scratched hand.

"I was lucky."

"I'll say. I'll buy you a drink. Bet you need one."

Luke grinned. "Thanks, but I'm in a program. I drink ginger ale, though."

The wrinkles in the man's weathered face furrowed as he smiled. "Then I'll get you a ginger ale to wet your whistle."

"Thanks, Tom."

The four of them walked into the lodge and headed for its bar and grille, and Tom glanced at George. "I hope this place is okay with you. I figure we'll get served fast. I like the burgers here."

Regina figured it was fortunate George could still demonstrate the tractor after Luke had come close to falling to his death. After the group ordered their food, Regina stood and blinked. "I'll be back soon."

The men chatted as she headed for the ladies' room. She fingered her cell phone that was in a side pocket of her purse. *I should call Javier to tell him I'll be filming the tractor demo a little late because of Luke's accident.*

She entered a stall and latched the door. Touching Javier's phone number, she heard ring tones and sat on the toilet lid. "Hello, Regina. Any news?" She heard a Mexican tune playing in the background.

"Yes. One of your competitors, Luke, came close to dying." She thought she heard Javier gasp.

Javier said nothing for a full three seconds, and then he sounded as if he'd panted. "What happened?"

"It was dark, and somebody ran into Luke near the rim

of the canyon by mistake. Luke slipped over the side, but he fell into a crevice. Guys from the park threw a rope and a harness down about twenty or thirty feet to him and pulled him up."

Regina heard Javier breathing hard. "Was he hurt?"

"Just scratches. Tonight, he's still going to demo how to remotely control George's tractor with a joystick."

Javier sounded like he'd gulped. "I'm glad he is okay. I don't wish harm even to my competitors." He stopped talking and was quiet for a moment. "What happened to the person who bumped him?"

"The rangers seem to think the man panicked and ran away." She added, "It was a hit and run, but not with a car."

She wondered what Mexican song was playing in the background as she waited for Javier to say something more. "Did you get a clear view of him?"

"No, it was dark. But I saw he had unkempt hair and was short and skinny. He could've been Mexican." Regina hesitated, wondering if she'd seen the man somewhere before. He'd seemed somewhat familiar. She spoke again as if on autopilot. "He could've been a drunk runner."

"Did you say drug runner?"

Regina laughed. "No, I said maybe he was drunk, *borracho*."

She heard Javier cough, and then he asked, "Anything else?"

"No. I'll send you the movie of the demo."

"*Gracias*. I must hang up."

Regina heard his phone disconnect.

He sounded quite upset about Luke. Javier is handsome, but he hasn't seemed caring before even when I knew him at school.

She stood, left the bathroom stall, and walked into the dining area. *I can't wait 'til the demonstration is done. How can I convince George to be with me tonight?*

When she arrived at the table where George, Luke, and Tom sat, she saw they'd begun to eat, and her roast beef sandwich and cola were there, too.

Tom nodded at her. "Sorry we started before you came back, but this place closes at nine-thirty."

Regina felt her stomach crave food. "I don't mind eating fast." She smiled.

She almost felt George's eyes as he surveyed her, and her body tingled when he spoke. "Tom set up demo area near railroad track. It close by. It won't take long time to show tractor. I know you are sleepy." George smiled.

Regina felt blood rush to her cheeks. *George is so sexy.*

She noticed Luke turn to Tom. "Good thing you put off the demo 'til ten. Any chance you could make a quick stop at El Tovar Hotel so we can pick up our room keys from the tour director?"

"No problem."

* * *

12:15 A.M., FRIDAY, MAY 30, 2031, LEXINGTON BLUEGRASS AIRPORT, KENTUCKY

Two FBI agents soon found Luke's pickup truck in the long-term parking area.

Agent Walter Moore tapped his partner's shoulder. "There it is by the concrete post."

"I see it," said Karen Andrews.

As they neared Luke's truck, Walter surveyed the area. "Nobody's here." He realized Lexington Bluegrass was a small airport, and few flights landed after midnight. He watched as Karen held a mirror under the truck's body.

She stood and peered at him. "I found a tracker."

Walter pulled an evidence envelope from his lapel pocket. "Here. Remove it and bag it while I take pictures."

Karen nodded and put on a pair of nitrile gloves.

Walter dug his mobile phone out of his pocket and activated its camera. "I'm ready."

As Karen knelt and removed the magnetic vehicle tracker, Walter shot pictures.

Karen smiled as she wrote on the evidence bag and then said, "If we're lucky, we'll find DNA."

Walter scratched the whiskers on his chin. "Take another peek at the rest of the underbody with your mirror. Do a preliminary scan for explosives. I'll request a team to do a further check on the truck with an explosive detection dog. After that, we'll tow it. Who knows what those cartel guys did to Luke's pickup."

TWENTY-THREE

TOM, the chief groundskeeper, stopped his large, white sedan at the curb near El Tovar Hotel.

As Luke opened the front passenger-side door, he felt a burning pain on his left palm where he'd scraped it on the cliffside when he'd fallen over the canyon's rim. "Thanks, Tom. Our tour director, Heidi, will be thankful we showed up before bedtime to git our keys."

Tom saluted Luke and smiled. "I'm sure she needs her beauty sleep. Being a tour director's a tough job."

After Luke, Regina, and George stepped into the lobby, George pulled out his cell phone. "I call Heidi to get keys." He tapped his cell phone. "Hello, Heidi. This George. Could you give keys to me, Luke, and Regina? Sorry we are late." George listened to Heidi. "Okay, be at your room soon." He disconnected and glanced at Regina.

Before George could say anything more, Regina raised her hand. "I volunteer to get the keys. Heidi might be in her nightgown."

A relaxed smile crossed George's face. "She in Room 203."

Luke showed a slow smile. *I gotta tell George about*

the Mexicans before something else happens. As Regina headed for a flight of stairs, Luke pointed to a couch in the lobby. "Let's sit. I got somethin' important to tell you."

George wrinkled his brow. "Is it about your fall?"

As they sat, Luke glimpsed at George. "Yep. It wasn't an accident."

George opened his mouth to speak and then waited for a moment. "Who you think did it?"

"Mexican drug cartel assassins."

"You do not suspect KGB?"

"No. Mikhail offered me a job to help you sell tractors."

George nodded with vigor. "Belarusian KGB likes you." He was silent a moment. "You going take KGB job?"

"I don't know. Rita would like that. But I don't want to be a game piece in a global checkers game."

George peered down at his feet. "Yeah. I know what you mean. We are just checkers."

Luke sighed. "Why do regular people get caught doing the biddin' of governments when all they want is to live a satisfying, peaceful life?"

George glimpsed at Luke. "You not going take KGB job and work for FBI at same time like me?"

"I gotta think on it. Layla don't like the idea." He was undecided about what to say next. "To answer yur original question…" Luke's facial features tightened. "Ever since I helped bust up that Tijuana drug cartel's operation in Lexington, they bin after me."

George's eyes bugged out. "They from Tijuana?"

"Yep. The cartel's called *Nuestro Club*. It's run by Mateo Guerra."

George blinked. "Regina is from Tijuana."

Luke shrugged. "There are millions of people livin' in Tijuana. Bein' from there don't make her a cartel member."

George drew his eyebrows together. "I have been too long in spy business. My gut says be careful."

Luke sighed. "Regina seems like a nice woman."

"Yeah. I like. She could be honey trap. But I will find out. I like her a lot."

Luke saw motion out of the corner of his eye. As he turned, he caught sight of Regina approaching.

Regina stopped by the men. "Here you go." She handed key cards to Luke and George.

George stood. "Better we not let Tom wait. We can do demo fast. Then go to bed." The KGB spy eyeballed Regina, and Luke noticed she blushed.

* * *

10:00 P.M., THURSDAY, MAY 29, 2031, SOUTH RIM, GRAND CANYON

Luke stared out into the night as Tom stopped his large sedan near the Mule Barn, a short distance south of the Bright Angel Lodge near Village Loop Drive. Tom clicked the car's unlock button and glanced at his passengers. "I had your tractor and joystick set up here."

Luke, George, and Regina stepped from the car and followed Tom, who switched on his flashlight. After they walked thirty feet, Luke saw the old groundskeeper train the flashlight beam on the new Belarusian Model K tractor.

Luke turned to George. "It appears you sent attachments to Tom that's not included with my Model K."

George nodded. "Yeah. Besides stronger headlights, we added side and back floodlights and a robot arm water sprayer."

Luke wondered why anyone would want to have a robotic water arm on a farm tractor.

Tom walked to the tractor. "We couldn't read the Russian instructions for the water hose hookups. But the pictures in the manual are great, and the guys figured it out."

George patted the tractor's seat. "I get company translate to English." He hesitated, "If wildfire happens, spray arm is great to fight flames."

Luke rubbed his beard. *George is a fine salesman for a spy.* Since Luke hadn't controlled a water sprayer with his joystick before, he wondered if he could demonstrate it without doing something stupid. He tapped George's shoulder. "You think you should show how the robotic arm works?"

"It is easy. Push robot arm button on joystick. Then use joystick. You can do with no training."

Tom pointed to four garden chairs standing next to a folding banquet table on which the tractor joystick sat.

When Luke neared the joystick, he saw it had an extra button with a flexed-arm icon on it. A blue water drop symbol was pasted on a second button. "I see the arm and water buttons, George." Luke sat in the chair by the joystick.

George grinned. "Tom. Let's see how Luke does with robot arm. He never use before. But it so easy a teenager can run it right away."

Tom laughed. "I'm always asking my youngest son about how to use my computer and phone."

Luke sighed. *I'm gonna be embarrassed.* "Should I go ahead?"

After Regina pulled out her phone, she started to film and leaned forward while staring at the video picture on her device's display.

George rubbed his hands together. "Yes, try."

Luke remotely turned on the tractor's headlights.

Tom tapped Luke's shoulder. "See the wooden barrels to the left?"

"Yep."

"Show me how you can run the machine toward them and spray water at them."

Luke nodded. He commanded the farm machine to ease up to the barrels and halt. After tapping the robot arm button, he pushed the water button. Next, using the joystick, he turned the robot arm to aim at the barrels.

George kneeled next to Luke. "Push joystick's red side button."

Luke pushed the side button, and a stream of water hit the middle barrel. "It's easy."

George said, "Push joystick forward."

Luke put forward pressure on the joystick, and the water volume increased. "Yeah, even a middle-aged guy like me can run this."

George turned to Tom. "We also have big water cart tractor can pull. It holds many liters. If I knew wildfire to our west would happen, I would have sent cart to you. But tomorrow I send Belarus Tractor HQ a message. I request we send one for each tractor on loan. If you like water cart, you can buy. No obligation."

"Thanks, George." Tom sat in the chair next to Luke. "Can I try it, Luke?"

"Yep."

Tom wiggled the joystick and backed up the tractor. After touching buttons and wiggling the controller, he commanded the machine to roll closer to the barrels and squirted them with a heavy stream of water. "The joystick works great. I'm sold. I look forward to trying out the water carts." He stood. "George, you got a super product. During our next national park Zoom meeting, I'm going to talk about this tractor."

George beamed. "Thank you, Tom."

Tom stood slowly. He glanced at George. "How about we call it a night? I'm tuckered out." He glanced at a pair of young park employees. "My fellas will put the tractor away. I'll drop you at your hotel."

Luke observed George when Regina latched onto his arm. *He seems starry-eyed even if he suspects she's working for the cartel.*

* * *

10:25 P.M., THURSDAY, MAY 29, 2031, THE SOUTH RIM, GRAND CANYON

As Javier and José approached the Bright Angel Lodge front desk, Javier grimaced and felt his ears turn red. The same young woman with dark brown hair in braids who'd checked them in earlier in the day was behind the counter. He displayed a nervous smile. "You're working a long day."

"A coworker got sick, so I had to work her shift, too, at the last moment."

Javier swallowed. "I'm sorry your plans had to change. But you recognize me, and it's lucky for us because we locked our keys in the cabin. Could you let us in?"

The young woman hesitated for a microsecond, and then Javier opened his wallet and gave her a twenty-dollar bill. "Thanks."

Javier cocked his head. "My name's Hector Castro, in case you forgot."

"I remember you. Follow me."

After Javier and José entered the cabin and the lovely young woman left, José sat on the edge of the bed nearest the door and pinched the skin on his throat. "Don't you think staying here's risky?"

"No. We didn't see any cops or rangers snooping around here lately. But the police could be checking Route 64 right now." Javier glanced at the door. "I'm going to the truck to get my small suitcase. Want me to bring your knapsack?"

José bit his lip. "Won't we have to get up early?"

"Let's sleep in. We know they're heading for Monument Valley tomorrow, and the tracker's on the bus."

"Sure, bring in my backpack. I'm going to shave off my beard and cut my hair."

Javier drew his eyebrows together. "If you look like you did in London, Luke might recognize you from the knife attack."

"Yeah, but people saw me at the cliffside with long hair and a beard when I knocked Luke over the edge."

Javier sighed. "Maybe you're right."

José frowned. "Next time, why don't you take a shot at him? He won't recognize you."

Javier rubbed the back of his head. "Okay, it's my turn." He peered at the dark window. "I need to tell Mateo what happened. I'll tell him a rifle shot may be our best option."

José shook his head. "Mateo won't be pleased."

Javier stared down at the carpet. "Yeah. Luke's a lucky one. It's as if Eutychia, the goddess, is watching over him."

José swallowed twice. "What?"

"You forgot. I studied philosophy and mythology in college. Eutychia is the goddess of good luck. Luke seems like he has more than nine lives."

José nodded. "His number better come up soon, or Mateo will come after us."

TWENTY-FOUR

STANDING outside the three-story El Tovar Hotel in the cool darkness, Regina held George's warm hand and stared up at the star-sprinkled night sky. A gusting, fresh breeze tossed her hair. She couldn't recall a time when she'd seen more distant dots of light in such a black sky. Gazing at the building's main entrance, she saw just one dim exterior hotel light lighting a disk-shaped sign. Though a faint glow leaked from hotel room windows, the escaping light was weak. She turned to view George's face as he surveyed the stars. "George, it's so dark because the park has little outdoor lighting."

"Light pollution harmful when watching stars."

Regina leaned against George and felt his welcoming body.

George squeezed her hand. "Let's go in. I tired."

Regina turned to face him and leaned against his chest. "Before we go inside, let's enjoy one more romantic moment." She felt her lips touch his, and then his strong arms enveloped her as he prolonged their kiss. She sighed. *His mouth is tender for a strong, rough man.*

George peered down into her eyes in the murky darkness. "I like you lot, Regina."

"I'm quite fond of you." She squeezed his sturdy body with her arms. "Let's have a drink together before bed."

"Sure. Nightcap helps the body rest."

Regina felt her body begin to cook inside. "Shall we drink in my room or yours?"

"I have bottle of whiskey in my suitcase." George's voice was husky.

They entered the hotel. Though anxious to get into George's room, Regina stopped for a moment to view the inside lobby walls, which were made of bark-free, varnished logs. *This building must be a large log building.*

She craned her neck and scanned the top of the walls. The tall ceiling was constructed of logs, too. Antlered animal trophies stared down from the log walls. *Are the preserved animals deer or antelopes?*

The pair climbed carpeted steps to George's room. As he used his key card to unlock his door, Regina noticed his strong right hand had a slight quiver. *He wants me. How do I encourage him yet not appear to be eager?* An experienced sex worker, she knew being brash and forward was now a habit of hers.

When George opened the door, Regina bumped him as if by accident. "Sorry, George." *How many times have I done that?*

"That okay. I get bottle from suitcase." Regina knew Wild America Tours had delivered their luggage to their rooms. *My nightgown's in my room. But I don't need it.* She blushed, thinking how nice it would be to cuddle nude in George's arms under clean sheets.

Regina unzipped and then took off her light jacket. "Seems hot in here." She undid the top two buttons of her blouse and sat on the foot of one of two queen-size beds.

George broke the seal on a bottle of Kentucky bourbon with a snap and unscrewed its cap. "I pour you one or two shots? Mix with water?"

Regina shrugged. "Two shots with water." *I don't have to drink it all. But he'll drink all of his.*

He handed her a tumbler of bourbon and water and clinked his glass with hers. "*Za lyubov.*"

"What's that mean?"

"To love." He blushed.

"To love and kisses." She tapped his glass again. *That's an encouraging toast.* Still holding her glass, she leaned into him and kissed his mouth.

* * *

10:35 P.M., THURSDAY, MAY 29, 2031, SOUTH RIM, GRAND CANYON

While Javier sat in an easy chair in his room, he held his satellite phone in his palm. *Should or shouldn't I text Mateo?* Javier took a gigantic breath and eased it out. *If I do it now, he'll have time to digest the information and cool down. If I call him tomorrow and break the news Luke still lives, Mateo may well have a conniption fit.*

Javier bit his lip, and with a jerky motion, he held up his phone so he could focus on its display. Beginning to type with both his thumbs, he watched his Spanish words appear on the phone screen. "I regret to inform you Luke Ryder survived his fall from the cliff edge. He fell a mere eight meters and got caught in a crevice. Park employees rescued him with ropes. He was not injured much. We continue to tail him and will finish the job ASAP. I will text you when the job is done."

* * *

10:35 P.M., THURSDAY, MAY 29, 2031, SOUTH RIM, GRAND CANYON

George felt the smooth, cool glass surface as he grasped Regina's empty whiskey goblet. He placed it and his drink beside the TV set behind him.

Regina fell backward onto the blue blanket on the queen bed, and the warm glow of a bedside lamp made her appear inviting.

George gulped, making steady eye contact with her while he felt his back arch as he lowered his body on top of hers. As if a warm sun toasted him, his body got hotter and hotter when he touched his lips with hers.

Wrapping her arms around his back, Regina sealed her torso against his. He deepened his kiss, and his tongue stroked hers. At the same time, he slid his finger under her belt and touched her soft skin. She sighed and took her lips from his. "Take me, George."

He panted, touching her face with his rough fingers, and began to think in Russian. *She's so fine. I want her no matter what. Even if she's a honey trap. So what?* He unbuttoned her blouse. She peered deep into his eyes, and he could feel her passion penetrate his being as he continued to undress her.

George felt her trembling fingers as she fumbled with his shirt buttons. *She's not faking passion. She likes me, too.*

In a sudden flurry, they removed the rest of each other's clothes. George felt proud he'd taken control of her as they intertwined their arms and legs. He closed his eyes as he took his time to explore her body. After fifteen minutes, she began to moan. "Do it, George."

A flush of passion permeated him. *There's no turning back now.* She'd surrendered to him, and she'd given him permission to do what he wished to do.

After twenty minutes of energetic sex, they remained next to each other, hugging and holding hands. George felt her delicate skin. "You so fine. Why not we keep in touch after trip?"

Regina snuggled against his bare, muscular body. "I would like that." She wavered. "Don't you have a girlfriend?"

A mental picture of Baroness Anne Thorpe flashed into his mind. Then he remembered seeing Anne's body in a pool of blood. "No, she died." He felt a tear begin to work its way from an eye.

The tear must not drip down my cheek. He willed the bead of water to stop, to defy the law of gravity, not to flow from his right eye, the one closest to Regina. Despite his supreme effort, the warm drop escaped, rolling down his cheek. He wiped his hand across his face.

George saw Regina's expression soften in an instant. Shifting even closer to him, she hugged him with tender passion and, with a gentle touch of her lips, kissed him. *She's so comforting.* "I love you, Regina."

Regina held him against her bare chest for a minute, rubbing his back. His muscles relaxed and his vision of Anne's smiling face faded and slipped away like a forgotten dream.

Regina's voice broke into his thoughts. "I haven't felt like this for years, George. We must stay together, but how?"

George felt his mind begin to consider and calculate like a high-speed computer. *I could hire her.* "I need helper cuz I must travel and sell tractors. How 'bout I hire you to be aide?"

Regina buried her face in his chest and kissed him there. Pulling away, she said, "Yes, I'll work for you. I don't care what the pay is. We just need to be together."

George displayed a wide grin, and his eyes sparkled. "I double your pay. I guarantee."

A warm smile formed on her mouth.

George tried not to crush her as he hugged her and envisioned her in a white bridal gown. Would she marry him? Would they have children?

* * *

11:11 P.M., THURSDAY, MAY 29, 2031, SOUTH RIM, GRAND CANYON

Luke's satellite phone rang, and he muted his television. Setting down the TV remote control, he grabbed his phone, which was charging on the table next to his bed, and glanced at the device's display. Rita was calling. "Hello, Rita."

"Sorry I called so late, but I want you to know that two FBI agents from the Phoenix Field Office will follow your Wild America tour bus and keep watch over you and George. They've been driving your way for a while."

Luke sat up straight in his bed against a pillow propped against the headboard. "Has the FBI made any progress investigating my fall?"

"The special agent in charge of the Phoenix office, Brad Boccio, will call you in fifteen minutes and interview you. Tomorrow, he'll send two more agents to look into the South Rim incident."

Luke scratched his head. "There isn't anything else I can tell Brad I haven't told you."

"You might think of something more."

"Okay. Anything else?"

It was after 2:00 a.m. in Kentucky, and Luke could hear Rita yawn and take a deep breath. "If you spot the two agents tailing you, pretend they're not there. Let George know about them, too. We don't want to alert either the KGB or the Mexican cartel guys."

"You sound tired."

Rita yawned again. "Layla and your kids are okay. Your fellow deputies are driving by your farm and keeping their eyes peeled."

Luke felt his eyes droop. "You better git some shut-eye, Rita."

"Yes. I should."

"Thanks fur your help."

"We need to take care of our own, and you're a favorite of mine." Rita disconnected.

* * *

11:40 P.M., THURSDAY, MAY 29, 2031, SOUTH RIM, GRAND CANYON

Regina fell asleep against George's warm body, and her contentment gave her a sense of home and happiness. But then troubling dreams began to drag her into a warped view of the world displayed in a series of strange images. The vision of a man running into Luke at the canyon's rim moved forward frame by frame like a slow-motion sports replay.

Through murky darkness, Regina watched each still picture frame click to the next grainy image, and then the next, and the next. In a flash, she saw the indistinct form of a thin, short man's face. Studying him, straining her inner eyes, she saw he had straggly, long hair and a beard. He was Mexican. Her gut told her so.

I've seen him before, but when and where? Or is this man someone who's similar to someone I know?

Without warning, another snippet of memory began to play back in her brain. She was walking toward the ladies' room in the Cameron Trading Post dining room at lunch. Javier sat near a thin Mexican man with long, shabby hair and a thick beard. The short, skinny man turned away from her in an instant.

Was this the same man who'd bumped Luke, almost sending him to his death, or am I mixing up reality with a dream?

A tapping sound disturbed Regina's nighttime visions. Opening her eyes, she saw George's form rise from the bed, lit by the dim glow of a digital clock. She heard him padding toward the hotel room door. Louder knocking sounded as Regina heard George unlock the deadbolt, and hall light streamed in as George opened the door.

* * *

George was momentarily blinded by the bright hall light. He rubbed his eyes and then ushered KGB courier Mikhail Popov into the room. Closing the door with alacrity, despite his sleepy state, George wondered what had brought Mikhail to his hotel room so late or even at all.

George whispered in Russian. "Is there something wrong?"

"Maybe." Mikhail hesitated. "Who's the woman in your bed? Does she speak Russian?"

* * *

Regina listened as a man whispered to George in a foreign language. *Is it Russian?*

* * *

George rubbed his unkempt hair and stared at Mikhail. "No, she doesn't speak Russian. She's a beautiful Mexican woman on the tour." *What's Mikhail up to? Has he figured out I'm working for the West?*

Mikhail exhaled a soft breath. "I assume she's a fling, not a honey trap." He stopped talking while he considered what to say next. "I saw the incident during which Luke Ryder was knocked over the cliff. It was not an accident. What do you know about it?"

George's brain went into high gear. *What should I tell Mikhail? Rita wants me to keep quiet, but he's not stupid. He needs to trust me.* "As you know, Luke is a Kentucky deputy sheriff. He told me Mexican cartel assassins are after him because he played a key role in taking down the cartel's operation in Lexington, Kentucky."

Mikhail wound his arms around his torso and angled his body away from George. "Why haven't I seen a lot of police investigating the incident?"

George rubbed the back of his neck. *What can I say?* "Luke told me not to tell anyone it was an attempted hit. He said the park rangers turned the case over to the FBI and they've interviewed him. FBI agents don't want people to know they're investigating because it could alert the hit man."

"Seems the FBI's taking a risk. Amateurish." In the room's darkness, George could hear Mikhail scratch his whiskers before he continued. "Did Luke tell you which cartel is after him?"

"It's a Tijuana cartel—*Nuestro Club*—headed by Mateo Guerra." George wondered if he'd gone too far in sharing information. It would lead to certain trouble if the KGB determined Luke worked with the FBI.

Mikhail was silent for a moment. "If we do bring Luke under our KGB wing, we can't have Mexican drug dealers gunning for him. Because Luke's an alcoholic and has a low salary, we should be able to recruit him. By all accounts, he's a first-rate investigator."

George wondered what Mikhail was thinking, took two gentle breaths, and felt his nerves calm. "What do you want me to do?"

"Observe Luke. Does he know about the Army info you gathered or the money you gave Major Green?"

"No." George took three shallow breaths.

"I'll ask our Tijuana police contact to find out about Mateo Guerra and his cartel. Maybe we can do something about them."

"What?"

Mikhail answered at once. "We could offer the Mexican government help in destroying the cartel. We want the Mexicans to become our friends, maybe even allies."

George took a step backward. "It's shocking how fast the world's been changing in recent years."

Mikhail stepped forward and spoke in an even quieter voice. "Yes. First, there was mutually assured destruction by nuclear bombs. Then, so-called peaceful coexistence came about. Now, alliances are in flux. Across the world, politicians make weird economic and raw materials deals."

George felt his eyes tighten as if he were squinting, and bile inched upward inside his throat. "We're pawns on a global chessboard."

Mikhail put his hand on George's back. "Yes, my friend. We're mere puppets controlled by strings operated by oligarchs who simply want more and more power. Ideology no longer matters."

George sighed. "While we play deadly games, regular people merely want decent, simple lives and not bc lorded over."

As Mikhail removed his hand from George's back, George grasped his fellow spy's hand and shook it. "Take care, Mikhail."

"You, too, comrade." Mikhail walked to the door, peered through its peephole, and left the room.

George heard bedsheets rustle, and then Regina spoke. "Who was that?"

"A company courier gave me a price sheet for a new model tractor." George unsnapped his suitcase and then snapped it closed again. *She'll think I put a price sheet in my case.*

"Why didn't he send it to your phone?"

"Too risky. There are corporate spies around who can hack the internet and messages."

"Better get back to bed, dear." Regina's voice sounded rich and sexy but muddied with a bit of stress. "We need to eat breakfast before leaving for Monument Valley."

"You are right, Regina." George got in bed, and tension drained from his body.

TWENTY-FIVE

LUKE HAD BEEN IN BED, but not asleep, for what seemed to him to be hours. In a repeating memory loop, he kept feeling and seeing the instants before, during, and after he'd slid over the canyon's cliff edge, thanks to having been tripped by a skinny Mexican assassin.

I gotta unwind. Cool air should help.

Throwing his bed sheet and blankets aside, he stood, put on his shirt and trousers, and grabbed his subcompact SCCY pistol in its holster. He'd named the weapon Molly. After putting the holster on his belt, he draped his shirttail over the firearm.

Yesterday's attack was a wake-up call. I'm jumpy, so I might as well try to feel safer. He touched his petite pistol attached to his belt and felt confident. The tiny firearm had saved his life in Kentucky months ago when another pair of Mexican cartel *sicarios* had tried to murder him.

Months ago, Luke had killed one assailant with a crossbow in Kentucky, and the little SCCY pistol had done its job stopping the second assassin, a young man who'd been armed with an AK-47. That would-be killer was now in prison. Was the Kentucky incident what yesterday's attack was about? Payback?

Luke's brain was still busy analyzing the tripping attack on the rim of the canyon as he exited his room. To burn off energy, he walked fast to the front door of the hotel and out into the night. He felt a cool, gentle wind and inhaled clean air into his lungs. *The wildfire smoke musta drifted east.* Tilting his head back, he was surprised by how bright the Milky Way was. He breathed in and out four times, and his heartbeat slowed. *This fresh air's working. I'll do a quick walk fur a while, and then I'll be calm enough to git some shut-eye.*

After three minutes, he began to follow a paved pathway into the deep, black night. Because there were no streetlights, he couldn't see far ahead, though his eyes had become accustomed to the near pitch-darkness. He kept up his quick pace while breathing the refreshing air through his nose. All of a sudden, he felt like he was pacing across the sky. *This ain't no dream.* He squatted in midair and held his arms forward, bracing for impact. In a fraction of a second, his two feet hit hard, flat on a gravel surface that felt like it was made of small, rough rocks. He'd landed on his feet and almost stayed erect, except his momentum had carried his body forward. He flew ahead onto his knees while his outstretched palms hit the small pebbles covering the ground. His knees felt jarred, not from falling on them but because they'd been compressed when he'd first landed.

He stood and touched his holstered small pistol. *At least Molly's okay.* He gulped. *Let's not git in the habit of falling, Molly.* He peered down into the darkness at his subcompact weapon on his belt.

Molly, I might need you one of these days again. Reaching into his hip pocket, he found his penlight and turned it on. Turning to stare behind him, he noticed the blacktop pathway above him made an abrupt turn, and he'd walked off its side into thin air to jump six feet down to the ground. *Fortunate I was walkin' fast, or I might've broke a leg.*

He brushed dirt and flecks of gravel from his trousers knees. Leaving his penlight on, he walked back to the hotel. *I gotta git to sleep before the trip to Monument Valley.*

TWENTY-SIX

GEORGE'S EYES moved about under his lids in what is known as rapid eye movement, or REM. In his mind's eye, he saw sunshine in a warm meadow, a plethora of colorful wildflowers, and Regina in the nude as she walked toward him, smiling. Now close to him, he felt her soft tongue probe his mouth. After a minute of enjoyment, he pulled away from her mouth, and she embraced him with tenderness.

He spoke in Russian. "Marry me, Regina." She appeared confounded. *Oh, yes, she speaks only English and Spanish.* He felt his brain switch to English like a stick-shift automobile switching into a higher gear. "Please be my wife, Regina. I love you."

She tilted her head and her silky, dark hair fell across her left shoulder. "*Sí.* I will."

Abruptly, he awoke and felt her presence next to him in the hotel bed, sleeping.

TWENTY-SEVEN

AS JAVIER ENJOYED HIS SLEEP, he was relaxed, half awake, and aware he was snoring. His satellite phone rang, jarring him. Opening his eyes, he peered at the bedside digital clock face. It read five-thirty. *I set the alarm for eight.* Grabbing his mobile phone after the fourth ring, he stared at the device's face. *Mateo's calling.* Now wide awake, Javier sat up. "Hello, Mateo."

"Javier, where the hell are you?"

Javier felt his body shake. He gulped. "In a lodge at the South Rim of the Grand Canyon." He vacillated. "You got my text about Luke?"

"Yes." Javier could hear Mateo breathing hard. "I thought you were a professional. Don't you know the FBI investigates major crimes on US federal property? Do you truly think Luke believes the incident was not deliberate? Get your asses away from there now."

"*Sí, Jefe.*" Javier felt sick to his stomach.

Mateo's tone changed as he continued to speak. "I'm sorry, Javier. I'm worried about you and José. Please go before someone notices you."

"Should we drop this job?"

"No. Sticking a bug on the bus was an excellent idea. Wait a few days before you try again."

"*Sí, señor.*"

Mateo disconnected, and for a moment Javier stared at his phone. Then he rose to his feet and shook José, who was sound asleep in the bed closer to the cabin door. "Get up. We need to go now."

* * *

4:35 A.M., FRIDAY, MAY 30, 2031, TIJUANA

Mateo entered his bedroom and set his encrypted satellite phone on his bedside table. He stared at a blond woman asleep in his bed. Still furious after speaking to Javier, Mateo slipped into bed, pulled the covers over him, and, with a soft touch, laid an arm across the lovely young female next to him. She stirred but did not awake.

Mateo's brain was busy. *Maybe enjoying the feel of soft, beautiful female flesh will calm me.*

But the cartel chief could not stop thinking of Luke Ryder and how the deputy sheriff had dodged death by luck, or perhaps because of the stupidity of his hired killers. Unable to fall asleep again, Mateo began to think of the many ways he could kill Luke.

Mateo then sat up and leaned against the bed's headboard. Out of the blue, an idea came to him. *We'll kidnap Luke's wife and two children, take them to Tijuana, and demand Luke comes to join them—or they'll die. This could work, if Javier and José continue to fail.*

Mateo decided to send men experienced in human trafficking to Kentucky to execute his backup plan. *I'll dispatch Oliver and Tomás as soon as possible.*

* * *

5:40 A.M., FRIDAY, MAY 30, 2031, SOUTH RIM, GRAND CANYON

A disturbing ring sounded from Luke's satellite phone, which sat charging on the polished wooden end table next to his hotel bed. Opening his eyes, Luke groped in the darkness for the device. It displayed Layla's name on its face. "Hello, Layla." Luke rubbed his eyes and turned on the bedside lamp, and its glare blinded him for a half second.

"Sorry to wake you, but I wanted to catch you before breakfast."

Luke cleared his throat. "What's up, hon?" Had Rita told Layla about the attempt on his life?

Layla was quiet as if she were thinking. "Rita told me you were attacked at the canyon rim." Luke heard her sniffle. "You okay?"

"I'm scratched a little. A Mexican tripped me, tried to git me to fall over the side, but I got caught in a crevice twenty-five feet down."

Luke heard Layla take two deep breaths. "I glad you're not hurt bad. Did they catch the guy?"

"No, but two undercover FBI agents are keeping an eye on me and George for the rest of the trip."

"That'll help." Layla gulped. "I have news, too."

"What?"

After a brief lull, Layla spoke. "I convinced Rita and her FBI assistant agent to go because there's no danger here anymore. I told her the Mexicans are out West, not here, and there's no need for her to guard us. We've got the FBI perimeter alarm system, Jim Pike has the deputies on alert in case the intruder alarm goes off, and I can always call 911."

"Did Rita leave?" Luke figured Layla was also upset with Rita because Rita had been sweet on him before he'd married Layla. He'd detected subtle friction between the two women over at least the last year.

Layla took a quick breath. "Yes, Rita left at eight this morning after breakfast."

"It must feel calmer there now." Luke rubbed the nape of

his neck. *The two women musta got on each other's nerves. At least Layla can relax now, and she won't be a mental wreck when I git home.*

Layla sighed. "I feel a hundred percent better." Layla made a kissing sound. "Can't wait until you're back, hon."

"Me, too." Luke smiled and now felt wide awake.

"Have a nice, big country breakfast." Layla's voice sounded sweet, rich, and happy.

"I will."

"Bye, now." Layla disconnected the phone.

* * *

7:45 A.M., FRIDAY, MAY 30, 2031, SOUTH RIM, GRAND CANYON

Dressed in casual, vacation-type clothes, two men entered the Bright Angel Lodge. The first man, FBI agent Erik Lundgren, a tall, wiry man with light blond hair, pointed to the front desk. At the same time, a young, attractive woman stepped behind the counter. "There's check-in." His pale cheeks had colored with a tinge of red.

Felix Hall, the second FBI agent, stocky and of medium height with sandy hair, trained his eyes on the woman behind the lodge's reception desk. He squinted. She was curvy in the right spots and alluring despite the dark circles under her droopy eyes. As she took her time to slide onto a barstool behind her counter, Felix concluded she was fatigued and perhaps had partied most of the night.

As the two men approached the desk, Felix glanced at Erik. "The perp could've booked a room here."

Erik nodded.

When the two agents stopped at the desk, the young lady focused on them and smiled. "May I help you, gentlemen?"

Felix took out his small FBI gold badge and ID card from a leather holder. He showed them to her. "I'm Felix Hall, and this is my partner, Erik Lundgren. We're here to learn about an incident that occurred on the Rim Trail behind the lodge."

The woman perked up, though Felix noted her eyes were a bit reddish, but not bloodshot. She spoke. "I heard about that. Someone ran into a guy, and he fell into a crevice. Lucky for him."

Felix figured she was eager to cooperate. "So, miss, you didn't see the incident firsthand?"

"I was inside. I'd started a second shift because a colleague became ill."

Felix took a half step closer to the counter and concluded the young lady had been awake all night. He smiled. "I wonder if anything unusual happened during your extra shift."

She stared at the log ceiling for a second, and then she eyeballed Felix. "Two Latino men locked themselves out of their room."

Felix raised his eyebrows. "Latino men?"

"Yep. Strange to leave both keys behind, unless you're checking out." She laughed and shot an expression of disbelief at Felix.

Felix leaned forward on the counter. "Could you describe the men?"

"One was quite handsome. The kind of sharp-looking Mexican man you might imagine to appear in a movie. The second guy was short, skinny, and ugly. He had a beard and thick, messy hair." She paused. "Wait a minute. The second time I saw him, he'd shaved, and his hair was short." She paused. "They left about six this morning."

Felix couldn't contain his grin. "Do you have security footage of the front desk?"

The young lady shrugged. "A lightning strike fried all the lodge cameras and the recorder a couple of weeks ago. The system's still not fixed."

Felix focused on the woman's eyes for a moment. "If we send a sketch artist here, could you work with him to create pictures of the two men?"

"Sure." She was quiet for a second. "Was this an accident, like I've been told?" She crossed her arms.

Felix shrugged. "The man who fell sustained injuries and has filed an insurance claim. The government is self-insured, so we'd like to contact the man who seems to have tripped while jogging and caused the accident."

The young lady nodded. "Makes sense."

Felix scratched his hair. *A little white lie sometimes is required.* "Thank you, miss. An FBI artist will be in touch. Please, what's your name?"

"Martha Greer. If you have a card, I can write down my cell number."

Felix reached into his breast pocket and took out two business cards. "Keep one, and call me if you think of anything else."

As Martha scribbled her name and phone number on the card, she said, "I've never dealt with the FBI before. It's exciting." She beamed.

Felix stuck the card with her info into his pocket. "Thanks."

As the two men left, Felix spoke in a low tone to Erik, and the tall man leaned down to listen. "I bet the short Latino dude is the perp."

Erik glanced out the window. "Let's get moving. The Wild America tour bus leaves soon."

Felix increased his pace. "I'm glad you checked out this old, plain sedan from the motor pool. I'd hate to have those two *sicarios* figure out we're tailing the bus."

Erik opened the front door of the lodge and peered at the faded-blue automobile they'd driven to the South Rim. "The Latinos would be stupid as hell to tail the bus after blowing their assignment."

"Yeah." Felix got into the passenger side of the worn automobile. "But lots of crooks are as stupid as snails." Felix furrowed his brow. "I'll call Brad Boccio at the Phoenix office and update him."

* * *

8:00 A.M., FRIDAY, MAY 30, 2031, SOUTH RIM, GRAND CANYON

George and Regina rushed toward the Wild America tour bus parked in the crescent-shaped drive in front of El Tovar Hotel. As George viewed the sky, he saw it was deep blue, and no clouds floated above, though a line of low gloom had formed on the western horizon. Glancing at the bus driver, who was loading the last three suitcases into the underside of the motorcoach body, George felt relief. He turned to Regina. "We almost miss bus."

Regina smiled. "They would've waited a couple of minutes or called us before leaving."

George recalled how he'd hurried to place his suitcase outside his hotel door so it would be ready for the bellhop to take to the bus. George had watched Regina as she scampered down the corridor to unlock her door and shove her huge case into the hallway. Afterward, she'd joked with George, saying they'd get a partial refund if they'd room together for the rest of the trip.

Now, George focused on Regina's graceful body as she climbed up into the coach ahead of him. Sighing, he stepped into the vehicle's narrow aisle.

A cheer from his fellow passengers shocked him. "Hey, George, we had a pool goin' as to who would be the last one on the bus," a big, stocky Texas tourist yelled.

George felt blood rush to his face. "Sorry." His thoughts were in Russian. *In spy school, they taught us never to draw attention to ourselves unless absolutely necessary.* He figured his KGB instructor, Dmitri Zaitsev, would be appalled.

As George neared the amiable Texan who was seated by the aisle, the heavy man gestured at Regina with his chin as she walked past his seat. Then he winked at George and patted the spy's back. "That's okay, George. We like you."

Luke waved his arm from near the tail of the bus, signaling Regina and George. Heidi had rotated all her passengers to new seat assignments.

George stopped, turned, and smiled at the Texan, and the

muscular man gave him a thumbs-up. George resumed walking to the rear seats. *Americans can be friendlier than Brits.* He sat next to Regina.

Grasping her microphone, Heidi stood. "Now that we're all here, we can begin our drive to Monument Valley in Utah." The bus began to move as she spoke. "We're heading for Tuba City, and we'll get there in an hour, where there'll be a rest stop."

She glanced out the window. "It's nice today. After Tuba City, we'll get on US 160 and US 163 and go northeast toward the Navajo Reservation. It'll take us two hours and we'll arrive in Monument Valley. We'll park at the Goulding's Lodge on Main Street, have lunch, and then ride open-air vehicles to see the buttes and mesas."

The big Texan raised his hand.

Heidi took notice of the stocky man. "Yes, Alfred?"

"Kin you tell us more about the buttes?"

Heidi grinned, focusing on the Texan. She used a remote control to turn on the TV monitors above the passenger seats. A still picture of an orange-red desert scene with six buttes, towering like skyscrapers, flashed onto the TV screens. Above the arid land, clouds that could've been gigantic, floating cotton balls dotted a deep blue, big sky.

Heidi glanced across the faces of the passengers in the coach. "This is a panoramic view of Monument Valley. Notice the two tall buttes in the center of the picture. They're called the Mittens because when you look at them from this angle, those two soaring, skinny rock formations resemble the thumbs of two gloves."

George studied the picture on the TV monitor above his seat. To the right of the two Mittens buttes, he saw another large butte with a flat top. At the bottom of the image, a dusty road wove its way into the distance.

Heidi tapped the screen of the TV monitor over her seat. "Monument Valley is in the Navajo Nation and has been the location for many famous Hollywood movies." She inhaled. "Notice the dirt road. You'll be riding open-air vehicles to see the buttes and mesas. It will be a bumpy ride. Be sure to wear dust masks."

George focused on the TV picture of the desert. *It'll be like being in a Hollywood Western movie.*

* * *

8:20 A.M., FRIDAY, MAY 30, 2031, EN ROUTE TO MONUMENT VALLEY, UTAH

The old, faded-blue sedan, an FBI plainclothes vehicle, lagged behind the Wild America tour bus as it sped toward Monument Valley. Agent Felix Hall held his mobile phone in his hand while his partner, Erik Lundgren, drove.

Glancing at Erik, Felix said, "Keep our eyes peeled for a vehicle that could be following the bus."

Erik scanned the cars near him as he guided the worn sedan. "Lots of these people are going to Monument Valley. Many of their cars will appear to follow the bus."

Felix took a cleansing breath and rubbed his hair. "True, but we have descriptions of the two Latinos the Bright Angel Lodge receptionist gave us." He glimpsed at the unfolding landscape outside his passenger-side window. "And the sketch artist should text us drawings of the suspects soon."

As he drove with one wiry hand on the steering wheel, Erik tapped his loose shirt under which he'd concealed his holstered Glock. "I can't wait to nail those two Mexican *sicarios*."

Felix peered down at his phone. With his two thumbs, he began to type a text to Luke. "I'm FBI Agent Felix Hall. My partner, Erik Lundgren, and I are following your bus in our faded-blue older sedan. We are assigned to protect you and George. Please refrain from drawing attention to us." Felix sent the message and included pictures of Eric and himself.

Thirty seconds later, he saw a return text from Luke. "Copy that."

Felix tapped a second text. "Are you armed?"

"Yes. Packing an SCCY pistol. Glock is in suitcase."

Felix again tapped with his thumbs. "Though we're FBI, we'll be using DEA IDs. Don't want to alert anyone about your operation."

Five seconds later, Luke replied. "10-4."

Felix nodded and typed. "Take care. Bye." He turned to Erik. "Luke's carrying an SCCY, a weapon of last resort. He's got a Glock, but it's in his luggage."

Erik shrugged. "But we're armed to the teeth."

Felix rubbed his short, sandy hair. *Uzi submachine guns, shotguns, M16s, except they didn't issue us an M60 machine gun. If the shit hits the fan, we're ready.*

* * *

8:40 A.M., FRIDAY, MAY 30, 2031, TUBA CITY, ARIZONA

After returning their gray rental truck and then leasing a modest, light blue sedan using new identities, Javier and José sat in a coffee shop in Tuba City, Arizona.

As Javier stirred his sweetened coffee, his spoon clanked the inside of his cup. *One excellent cartel benefit is we have extra IDs. The cops are going to have a hard time connecting the dots and finding us.*

Javier and José had also stopped at a drugstore and bought dust masks. On Wild America's web page, Javier had read the company's tours included rides in open-air vehicles to view buttes and mesas. Because the vehicles and the wind kicked up dust, the company suggested wearing dust masks.

José peered at a digital map on the face of his mobile phone to monitor the progress of the Wild America bus during its trip to Monument Valley.

Javier was glad he'd planted a tracker on the bus. He glanced at José. "Where is the bus now?"

José lifted his head and stared at Javier. "They should be here in twenty minutes."

Javier rubbed his temples. "We need to leave soon to stay

ahead of the coach. From here, the trip to Monument Valley takes two hours. I checked us in early at Goulding's Lodge so we can check out the area in advance and consider our options for dealing with Luke."

José gulped down the rest of his coffee. "I'm going to the restroom."

Javier's face tightened as he pressed his lips together. *I wish I could lower Luke into a vat of acid and see him disintegrate.* Thinking about Luke and how the man had been beating the odds against him and avoiding death, Javier felt his tension rise. He recalled reading how Italian and US syndicates had thrown bodies into barrels of chemicals to dispose of corpses. *If I could do it, I'd handcuff the bastard and drop him alive into a vat of lye.*

After José returned to their booth, Javier stood and then drained the rest of the coffee from his cup and placed it on the table. As the two men left the coffee shop, Javier whispered to José, "Let's prepare the sniper rifle in case we get a break and can shoot the SOB."

José shook his head no. "Mateo said to wait. The FBI could be on our tail."

After they got in their light blue rental car, Javier glared at José. "Set the GPS for Goulding's Lodge on Main Street. I booked us a room there."

José shook his head. "You want to keep our reservation?" He turned on the vehicle. "The tour must've booked rooms there if it's the best hotel around."

Javier settled in his passenger seat. "The tour will be in rooms there, according to the Wild America web page. We'll keep a low profile and order from room service."

* * *

11:30 A.M., FRIDAY, MAY 30, 2031, MONUMENT VALLEY, UTAH

A tribal police officer entered the gift shop near Goulding's Lodge. He walked to the counter and smiled at a young

Navajo woman. "Hello, Doba." He held a pair of FBI wanted posters. "May I put these on your bulletin board?"

The young woman stroked her dark hair. "Of course. What are they wanted for?"

The officer handed both of the posters to Doba, and she stared at the drawings of two Latino men. "These guys are wanted for questioning. Someone almost sent a man over the rim of the Grand Canyon to a sure death."

Doba squinted and studied the drawings. "Okay, I'll watch for them." She returned the posters to the officer.

He winked. "Thank you. But remember to call the police if you see one of them. Don't act like you recognize these guys if you do."

She nodded. "I'll be careful."

* * *

10:31 A.M., FRIDAY, MAY 30, 2031, TIJUANA

Mateo typed *https://www.fbi.gov/wanted* into his browser to reach the FBI website page that displays wanted posters. Clicking on the *seeking info* link, he spotted artist's renditions of two Latino men.

His nostrils flaring, Mateo tapped the *View Poster* link next to the image of a drawing that could have been a picture of José. After the enlarged poster filled his computer screen, Mateo judged the sketch was indeed an excellent likeness of José.

The caption under the image read: *DETAILS: The Federal Bureau of Investigation is seeking information regarding the individual sketched here in connection with an incident at the Grand Canyon during which a man was bumped and fell a short distance over the cliff edge. The individual is wanted for questioning. He is described as a Latino male, with long, black hair, a beard, and brown eyes, who speaks both English and Spanish. If you have any information concerning this person, please contact your local FBI office.* Mateo saw there was a link to download the poster.

He figured people might print it and tack it up in public places.

Mateo lifted his chin high, took five deep breaths, and grabbed his encrypted satellite phone. He felt his temples pound as he began to type a text to Javier with two thumbs. "You both are wanted for questioning by the FBI. Wanted posters are on FBI website. Stay out of sight. Wait until end of bus trip to deal with Luke."

Mateo snatched a whiskey glass and a bottle of bourbon from the shelf above his computer. After pouring two shots of the amber liquid into the glass, he tasted the liquor and then gulped down an ounce of it. *Those two bastards better not get caught.*

* * *

11:40 A.M., FRIDAY, MAY 30, 2031, MONUMENT VALLEY, UTAH

As the Wild America motorcoach slowed and entered the Goulding's Lodge parking lot, Luke peered out his passenger-side window. *'Cept for the scrubby vegetation and buildings, the landscape resembles a view from a Mars lander.*

Scanning the area, he noticed one skinny, flowering tree near a long, two-story building where the lodge rooms were. Along the second-story rooms, there was a balcony, and below it, cars sat in parking spaces.

After the tour bus driver guided the bulky coach into a special, large-vehicle parking area, Luke felt the coach come to a stop.

Heidi's amplified voice interrupted Luke's thoughts. "Folks, we've arrived in time for lunch. The restaurant is in the building up the steps."

As Luke followed George and Regina off the bus to walk to the restaurant, Luke got a distant, fleeting glimpse of two men standing on the lodge balcony. Within four seconds, they retreated back into their room. Luke didn't notice one of the men, Javier, had been viewing him with compact binoculars.

* * *

11:45 A.M., FRIDAY, MAY 30, 2031, MONUMENT VALLEY, UTAH

Javier set his compact binoculars on the table next to his room's easy chair and put his feet up on the queen size bed near him. "I might be able to get a decent shot at Luke after he leaves the restaurant tonight when it's dark."

José sat on the other bed and crossed and then uncrossed his legs. "Sounds risky."

Javier's phone chimed. Pulling it from his jeans pocket, he read two texts from Mateo. The first told him to lay low because the FBI wanted to question him and José. The second text said, "Have you two got ahead of the bus yet? If not, get moving."

Javier handed his phone to José. "I admit you're right, José. I won't take a shot at Luke tonight."

José smirked. "Let's drive away, wait somewhere, and make a better plan."

Javier peered down at the floor. "Okay. But since we bought the tickets, let's take the open-air buggy ride and check out the buttes and mesas."

José shook his head. "That's crazy. Someone might recognize us."

Javier stood. "We'll wear the dust masks during the ride. Besides, there's a new COVID outbreak spreading across the West, so we can keep the masks on."

José laughed. "Maybe COVID will kill Luke if we can't."

Javier frowned. "What makes you think we won't take him out?"

José sighed. "Counting our attempt in London, we've failed to kill Luke four times so far. Did I count right?"

Javier slipped on his dust mask. "Come on. Let's find something to eat."

TWENTY-EIGHT

EIGHT OPEN-AIR TOUR vehicles lined up in the parking lot near Goulding's Lodge, and Heidi shepherded her flock of travelers into the first five of the large buggies. They were flatbed trucks with seats in their cargo areas. Light-tan canvas tops on top of the vehicles protected the riders from the blazing sunlight. All of Heidi's riders wore dust masks, including George, Regina, and Luke.

Surveying the brilliant blue, cloudless sky, Luke saw distant, massive, orange-red sandstone buttes and tall, thin spires of rock clustered across the expansive, bone-dry desert landscape. He noticed green plants were few and far between, while a warm breeze carried mini clouds of dust across the unpaved road the tourists would soon travel.

As he relaxed in the rear of the fifth buggy, Luke turned to examine the three non-Wild America open-air vehicles behind him, which unfamiliar tourists boarded. Focusing on two men wearing wide-brimmed hats in the last vehicle in line, Luke watched as they turned away, pulling their collars up to their masks.

Those guys must hope to keep dust from getting underneath their shirts. It's gonna be super dusty. Luke pulled his mask tighter against his face and watched another puff of dust blow across a far-off section of desert.

Turning to face forward, Luke held his satellite phone and readied its camera. As he gazed miles ahead at the horizon, he felt the open-air buggy jerk into gear and move toward a short stretch of paved road. Luke realized the ride over smooth blacktop would soon end because the dirt road into the desert was dead ahead. *It's gotta be a real bumpy ride over the backroads.*

As the open-air trucks ahead of Luke's buggy crossed onto the dirt trail one by one, they bounced. Puffs of dust kicked up by the caravan blew backward into Luke's face. The buggy's Navajo driver picked up a microphone as he drove. "One of the most photographed places on Earth, Monument Valley covers 92,000 acres. Many years ago, it was a seafloor."

The driver clicked his microphone off as he steered around a deep pothole. Even so, Luke felt his vehicle make two big, bone-jarring bounces.

Luke heard the sound of the driver's microphone clicking on again. "Sediments and sandstone filled this seabed area, and after many years, tectonic forces pushed this seafloor up above the surface of the water. After eons, erosion wore away much of the sediments, leaving behind the towering buttes, mesas, and tall sandstone pillars you see today."

Luke took four pictures, but the truck jostled him so hard on the rough road that he wasn't sure how sharp his pictures would be.

The speakers on the buggy crackled with static. "You can ride a horse for miles and see the buttes poking up all around. Also, you might recognize this valley from many Hollywood Western movies. It still is a popular location for filmmakers."

The driver stopped at a viewing area. "It'll be a lot easier to take photos when you're standing on solid ground." He laughed.

As Luke stepped down from the rear of the flatbed truck, he spotted the same two men he'd seen pulling up their collars before the ride had begun. Luke noticed they both glanced at him.

* * *

2:05 P.M., FRIDAY, MAY 30, 2031, MONUMENT VALLEY, UTAH

Javier hopped down from the open-air truck after it stopped at the first photo opportunity location, and from behind his mask, he glared at Luke.

The tall Kentucky lawman loitered under the shade of a tarp draped on top of a twelve-foot-high structure made of galvanized pipes. Three folding banquet tables also stood under the canvas covering. Javier figured vendors used the tables to display souvenirs they sold to tourists.

Keeping their distance, Javier and José watched their human target, Luke, as he stared at a massive mesa perhaps a half mile in length. Backlit by sunlight, hazy dust was blowing past the sandstone megalith.

Turning to José, Javier spoke in Spanish, his quiet voice blending in with the wind. "Too bad this place is filled with people. It would be a wonderful place to shoot the son of a bitch."

José huffed. "As you have told me many times, a hunter must be patient and wait for the right moment."

Leaning closer to José, Javier pulled his wide-brimmed hat down tighter on his head. "Tonight, we can monitor Luke with the night-vision binoculars if he decides to watch the sunset. If the opportunity arises, we can take a shot with the silenced sniper rifle when nobody can see us after sunset."

José shook his head and shrugged. "Remember, the FBI's after us. Mateo said to lay low."

Javier stared at José. "It'll be dark, and if we are lucky, no one but Luke will be nearby. After it's done, Mateo will congratulate us."

* * *

3:20 P.M., FRIDAY, MAY 30, 2031, MONUMENT VALLEY, UTAH

The open-air vehicles returned to the Goulding's Lodge parking area after the mobile tour of the buttes had ended. Stepping from the open-air buggy, Luke caught sight of George and Regina, who'd ridden in a separate flatbed truck, and they soon walked to Luke.

George removed his dust mask and stuffed it into his breast pocket. "This place is like another planet. I noticed scenes I saw before in movies." He grinned. "Too bad Navajos do not need tractors, and we cannot demo for tribal leaders."

Luke took his mask off, too. "Yep, but I guess they don't farm much here, but I'm not sure." He reckoned the main industry was tourism, and he wondered how the Navajos had survived here centuries ago. *They must be a resourceful and intelligent people.* He gazed into the distance of the desert, trying to visualize times in the far past. Surely the desert hadn't changed much in recent centuries.

The sounds of suitcases being removed from the Wild America motorcoach made Luke turn. The tour's bus driver was lining up baggage near the motorcoach.

George put his arm around Regina, who blushed. "We go now, get cases, and take to rooms. Check-in is soon." He glanced at Regina, who peered at the blacktop beneath her feet.

Luke figured the pair would spend the night in one of their two rooms. He smelled the dry air and felt at ease, having seen the wonders of the desert. Also, he noticed George was cheerful.

I never seen him so happy. A woman in his life's gonna help him. Luke nodded at George and Regina. "We better grab our cases and see what our rooms are like."

As the three walked to the side of the bus where their luggage stood, Luke started to think about George Black, a.k.a. Yegor Bulat, a KGB Belarusian spy, a double agent working for the FBI and British Intelligence.

Most people are normal, even if they're spies, police, farmers, Navajos, Brits, whatever. They wanna love and live, have a safe place fur sleeping, and enough food. As a rule, folks are close to the same underneath, no matter where they're from. Crazy politicians and power grabbers just set different people against each other. With any luck, George can quit the spy game and stay in the US like he wants. Is he gonna marry Regina? Luke beamed when he thought of the prospect of the pair exchanging vows.

* * *

After unlocking his room door on the second floor, Luke pulled his wheeled suitcase behind him, left it next to one of the beds, and neared the sliding door of the balcony. The room was cold.

I best reset the air conditioner.

Unsnapping the latch on the patio door, Luke pulled it open and stepped onto the platform outside. The warm sun soothed his skin.

Studying the desert view from a high vantage point, Luke again gawked at the iconic rock formations on the horizon—two small buttes and four rock pinnacles stood between two massive buttes. They were looming large and colored an even deeper orange than they'd been during the open-air buggy tour.

The sun must be hittin' the sandstone at a different angle to make the colors so intense.

As Luke dragged a black iron patio chair away from a small square table on the balcony, he felt the chair vibrate and heard it screech. He sat and peered downward over the patio railing and noticed the rock-strewn desert was darker closer to him.

Too bad we're leaving Monument Valley tomorrow. Sure would be nice to spend time with the Navajos and learn their ways.

Once a game warden, Luke realized Mother Nature hadn't loosened her grip on him. The pull of the untamed places on Earth attracted him like a strong magnet.

What if I went back to bein' a game warden? Have I done the right thing becomin' a deputy sheriff? Would Layla like me to quit? She's sure been stressed for the last week and before that, too.

He blinked and rubbed his chin. Reaching into his shirt pocket, he grasped a brochure to read about the tour's next major destination the following day, Canyonlands National Park in Utah.

He reckoned there'd be a lot of walking at the Sky Visitor Center, the Shafer Canyon Overlook, and then the Grand View Overlook, where a person could survey the canyon for miles into the distance. According to the itinerary, the Canyonlands leg of the trip would take three and a half to four hours.

Luke got up and stuffed the pamphlet back in his pocket.

Might as well check out the gift shop and git Navajo souvenirs for Layla and Angela. Within three minutes, he was going down the lodge steps, heading for the shop.

* * *

3:26 P.M., FRIDAY, MAY 30, 2031, MONUMENT VALLEY, UTAH

After their open-air ride to view the mesas and buttes had ended, Javier and José exited their open-air tour buggy near Goulding's Lodge. Javier rubbed his nose under his dust mask. As he did so, he also peered at the gift shop sign on a small building on the edge of the parking lot. He focused on José. "Let's go in and browse."

"Why?" José pressed his lips together and wavered. "It's better to keep out of sight."

"I want a Navajo souvenir."

José shook his head and adjusted his mask.

Within a minute, the two assassins entered the shop, and at once, Javier spotted Regina. She'd taken off her mask and was examining a bow and arrow set across the store. Signaling with his eyes, Javier suggested José walk to the back wall of the shop behind high shelves of merchandise.

Javier scratched his scalp. *Regina won't recognize me with my mask on, or will she?* He took his time to survey the tourist items near him, and then he felt José tap his shoulder and point at a bulletin board on the far wall.

Turning, Javier caught sight of two FBI wanted posters, and a shiver coursed through his body. A sketch artist had drawn excellent likenesses of him and José. Surveying the area near him, Javier saw no customers close by. He approached the bulletin board and, with a swift movement, he ripped both posters from it and stuffed them into his pocket. He caught José's attention. "Let's get out of here and drive."

TWENTY-NINE

AFTER LEAVING THE GIFT SHOP, Javier and José rushed to their room, retrieved their luggage, and headed for the light blue sedan they'd rented. "Hurry up, José, let's get in the car and roll." Javier walked ahead of José at a quick pace.

José caught up to Javier. "Slow down. People may notice us."

Javier decreased his pace. "I suppose you're right. I'll drive."

"Suit yourself." José took a cleansing breath.

After they'd loaded their vehicle's trunk, Javier double-clicked the automobile's fob key, and José opened the front passenger door and slipped into his seat. Once in the car, Javier slammed the driver-side door, put the vehicle in gear, backed from his parking space, and then pressed the accelerator pedal too hard. The auto's tires squealed on the blacktop, parking lot surface. "Let's get ahead of the bus and stay there."

José rubbed the back of his neck. "Take it easy, or the cops will stop us."

Javier frowned and then sighed. "Again, you're correct."

He took three deep breaths. "I'm irritated. Let's drive to Yellowstone, wait a few days, and hit Luke there."

José nodded. "Waiting three days is smart."

Javier was quiet for a moment. "I'll be happy when this job's done." He let his mind rest for a moment. "After the next stop, you can drive. I'll text Mateo the plan."

THIRTY

WHILE GEORGE NAPPED on their lodge room bed, Regina sat on the toilet lid in the bathroom, her cell phone in her hand. *It was weird how fast Javier and his friend walked away from the gift shop without acknowledging me.*

She began to tap out a text message to Javier. "I saw you two guys in the gift shop. Are you staying in Monument Valley at the lodge? Anything you need me to be on the alert for?" She rubbed the nape of her neck.

A minute later, Javier sent a reply. "We're on the road. Continue to monitor tractor sales presentations."

Regina had a funny feeling in her stomach. *Javier didn't answer my question about the gift shop. He's acting weird. Should I confess to George what I'm doing?* She sighed. *Better not. No way do I want to lose him.*

THIRTY-ONE

LUKE SPOTTED the Wild America motorcoach decorated with its tiger-fur paint job standing in the lodge parking lot. *It's hard to miss the bus cuz it's mostly bright yellow.* He followed George, Regina, and the rest of the Wild America tour group as they boarded the massive bus.

After everyone was seated, Heidi, like a schoolmarm, counted her passengers. "We're all here," she announced. Turning to the driver, she nodded, and he guided the bus toward the parking lot exit.

Luke glanced backward over his seat at George and Regina. "Are we gonna demonstrate another tractor at Canyonlands National Park?"

George grasped the seatback in front of him. "Yes. Chief park groundkeeper will meet us at Shafer Park Overlook. I told Heidi 'bout it."

"They have one of yur tractors?"

"Yes. After we do demo, groundkeeper will drive us to Green River Outlook, and we rejoin tour."

"These national park fellas seem to like your tractors."

George leaned on the seatback next to Luke. "They like cuz my machines cost less."

Luke nodded. "Makes sense. They're quality tractors. But do users really need to run them with remote control joysticks?"

"No. National Park guys think joystick is gimmick. But I tell them AI soon can run tractor with no human needed."

"Unless the AI goes crazy and drives it into a place it shouldn't go."

George shrugged. "There is work to do to make AI better."

At the front of the bus, Heidi stood with her microphone in hand. "Now that we're underway, I'll give you a rundown of what's happening today." She clicked her remote control, and a digital road map appeared on the TV monitors hanging above the passenger seats. "Here's our path to Canyonlands National Park. It'll take three and a half hours to get there, just in time for lunch. We have a nice restaurant picked out where we'll have a group meal." She pointed at the map on the TV monitor above and behind her.

As Heidi talked about the lunch menu, Luke began to wonder about artificial intelligence. Would it ever be able to run a tractor without a person ready to take control in case something went wrong? *What if kids or animals ran in front of an AI-controlled tractor? Is there a chance it could roll on top of a whole row of crops or cut them down if the tractor were weeding?*

Heidi's soprano voice cut into Luke's thoughts. "After lunch, we'll go to the Shafer Canyon Overlook. We'll also visit other vistas, too—at Grand View Point and Green River Overlook. You'll be able to see for miles."

Luke sighed and stared at the passing scenery. *I hope those assassins don't try again.* He felt his tiny SCCY holstered pistol on his belt under his loose-fitting sweatshirt. Touching the weapon made him feel confident.

Heidi clicked her remote control, and an image popped onto the TV screens showing a boat full of tourists floating on a river. "After checking in to our hotel, we'll go to dinner and have a night cruise on the Colorado River. A speaker will describe the canyon while spotlights shine on its walls. Then the lights will go out, and we'll see thousands of stars in the dark sky unpolluted by city lights."

Luke pulled his itinerary from his breast pocket. *What's comin' up for the rest of the trip?*

After Canyonlands National Park, the tour would visit Arches National Park to view several of its 2,000 natural arches. Luke was impressed by the pictures of tall, red rock arches in his itinerary brochure.

During the following days, the bus would stop in Salt Lake City, Utah, for a tour of the Mormon Tabernacle to see and hear its famous organ with its more than 1,100 pipes. Then the motorcoach would travel north through Idaho, following the Snake River to Jackson Hole, Wyoming. After that stop, the group was slated to view the Grand Tetons and, finally, Yellowstone National Park and its geysers, including Old Faithful.

Luke glanced out his passenger-side window and caught sight of a thin, blond man driving a faded-blue sedan, an unremarkable car. Luke sat up straight. *That's the FBI agent, Erik, driving his plainclothes car, and Felix's sitting in the front passenger's seat. I hope the Mexicans don't spot them.*

THIRTY-TWO

FOUR DAYS after driving away from Monument Valley, Javier and José stood on a wooden walkway near the banks of the boiling, acidic water of Lucifer's Rapids. Javier's stomach demanded food, so Javier took off his pack, set it on the cedar planks of the path, and unzipped his backpack. Reaching in, he pulled out a paper bag of fast food and glanced at José. "Want a hamburger? I have two."

José displayed an upturned face. "*Sí, gracias.*"

Javier handed José a burger, and the man wolfed it down. *He must be hungrier than I am.*

Taking his time, Javier unwrapped his cheeseburger, began to eat, and savored it as he leaned back against the wooden railing along the boardwalk. Behind and below him, the roiling, acidic, hot water rapids kicked up a noxious mist.

Bored, Javier pinched a small chunk of ground beef and cheese from under his hamburger bun. Tossing the bit of burger into the boiling water, he watched as the thumb-size chunk of food sizzled and bubbled, swirling in a small eddy near the bank of the creek.

The morsel was breaking down and smoking as it dissolved. Javier smiled.

After he finished his burger, Javier got José's attention. "Where's the bus?"

José took his phone from his hip pocket and touched its on-screen icon controls. Staring at the device's face, he said, "It's running late, but should be here before sunset."

"We'll hit him here when the tour makes its first stop."

* * *

6:45 P.M., TUESDAY, JUNE 3, 2031, EN ROUTE TO YELLOWSTONE NATIONAL PARK

Luke relaxed in his bus seat while he viewed photos he'd taken at several national parks and tourist stops.

George reached over Luke's seatback and tapped him. "You took nice pics. What is that one?"

"A hoodoo rock at Bryce Point."

"Weird how hoodoo rocks eroded to make strange shapes. Looks like picture from another planet."

Luke displayed another image. "This is the Snake River." He paused to switch pictures. "That's a beaver." He tapped his phone again. "And here's the snowcapped Grand Tetons."

George shook his head. "Too bad tour soon will end."

Luke glanced back at George. "Yeah, but we're still gonna see Yellowstone and its bubbling mud, geysers, and hot springs."

His eyes gleaming, George smiled. "Tour was fun, but also sales trip successful. I think we sell two or three machines tomorrow."

Luke checked his wristwatch. "Too bad an accident jammed up traffic cuz we're hours behind schedule. If we're lucky, we'll git to Yellowstone before sunset."

THIRTY-THREE

THE TWO MEXICAN assassins sat in their rental car in a lot near the Old Faithful geyser and some of Yellowstone's other 10,000 hydrothermal features, including Lucifer's Rapids.

Javier felt his satellite phone vibrate in his hip pocket. Grabbing his mobile, he saw Mateo's name on the device's display. "*Hola*, Mateo."

Javier could hear splash noises in the background of the call. *Mateo must be near his pool with a bunch of babes in bikinis.* Then Javier heard Mateo make a sound like he'd exhaled cigarette smoke. "Javier, please report your progress with the Luke Ryder matter."

"We're at Yellowstone National Park. I have the Wild America tour itinerary, and I know the tourists will visit superhot Lucifer's Rapids when they first arrive."

Javier could hear Mateo suck on his cigarette. "How can you be certain the tour will not deviate from their timeline?"

"I can't guarantee they'll follow their plans, but so far, they have done everything on their itinerary." Javier held his chin high. "I put a tracker on the bus, and José's been watching its progress. It should arrive before sunset."

There were a dozen seconds of silence. Was Mateo livid? Javier gulped just as Mateo spoke. "Make it a clean kill. Then get the hell away from Yellowstone."

Javier took two deep breaths. "*Jefe*, I will finish the job, if not today, then by sunset tomorrow."

Mateo's breath whistled as he inhaled and exhaled, and then he spoke in a calmer voice. "Sorry about that, Javier. I am irritated because Luke killed my nephew, and I want the Kentucky bastard dead."

"*Sí, mi Jefe*. It will be done, I promise you."

Mateo disconnected.

Javier stared at his phone. *I better kill Luke today or at least in the next twenty-four hours, or I could be next.* All of a sudden, nausea made Javier feel like throwing up. Acid flowed up his throat, he gagged, and then he plastered his palm against his face.

THIRTY-FOUR

LUKE NOTICED movement at the front of the bus and saw Heidi stand and grasp her microphone. She scratched the mike with her finger, making an amplified rubbing sound to alert the tourists she was about to make an announcement.

"As some of you may have noticed, we've entered Yellowstone's South Entrance. Almost two hours from now, we should arrive before sunset in time to see the Old Faithful geyser as well as Lucifer's Rapids, the new acidic, boiling creek formed by the 2029 earthquake."

Her fingers bumped her microphone as she glimpsed at the TV monitor above her head. After she clicked her remote control, an aerial image of Yellowstone popped onto the screen.

"This is before the quake." She pushed a button on her remote, and a second photo appeared. "Here's the same view after the temblor. Notice the big changes."

Luke recalled seismologists had feared the June 19, 2029, temblor could have been a warning sign that an even larger, more devastating earthquake might follow. Thankfully, a colossal quake did not happen then. Still, scientists feared such a massive temblor could have set off a super volcano, which might well have wreaked destruction across neighboring states and even worldwide.

As Luke stared at the aerial photo of Yellowstone after the June 2029 quake, Heidi switched to a picture of a rushing stream and a wooden boardwalk following its bank.

Heidi coughed. "This slide shows one of the biggest changes—a new, fast-moving stream of boiling, acidic water, which averages ten feet deep. It's called Lucifer's Rapids. Shortly after this hellish waterway formed, rangers observed a whitetail deer slip into it and die. Hours later they tried to recover what they could of the deer, but all that was left were bones. The current carried the rest of the remains away."

Heidi scanned the faces of her audience of tourists. Luke noticed most of his fellow passengers appeared shocked by the story of the poor deer that had lost its life. Heidi took a deep breath. "Of course, you'll get to stroll beside Lucifer's Rapids on the boardwalk. I warn you not to dip your toe in to test the water." Her captive audience chuckled.

Luke thought their chortles sounded nervous.

Heidi continued. "Don't stand too near the edge unless you want holes burned in your trousers or socks." There were more shaky snickers.

Heidi clicked her controller to show a new picture of a geyser pumping steam into the azure sky. "This is a young geyser called Ann's Geyser, named for a ranger who had retired the day before the big quake." Heidi showed a picture of an elderly woman dressed in a ranger uniform. "Ann's Geyser is one of four new ones that sprang to life when the temblors hit. We're fortunate Old Faithful and other famous geysers are behaving as they have for years."

Glancing out the bus window, Luke noticed five bison and three mule deer. The sun was low on the horizon.

THIRTY-FIVE

JAVIER SAT in his rental car in a parking lot near Lucifer's Rapids, loading four extra magazines with bullets. *Better to have too many rounds than not enough.*

José watched as Javier shoved bullets into his mags. "Where are you going to carry all those magazines?"

"In my sweatshirt pockets. It'll be dark by the time I take a shot, and nobody will see them."

"You have enough ammo to take on a half dozen police." José showed a sarcastic grin.

Javier sighed. "You never know what could happen. Let's hope we finish the job tonight and get the hell out of here." Javier glared at José. "Check out the drone and get it ready."

José shrugged and reached into the back seat to grab the cardboard box where he'd stored the new drone.

* * *

8:38 P.M., TUESDAY, JUNE 3, 2031, YELLOWSTONE NATIONAL PARK

As the Wild America tour bus pulled to a stop in a parking lot near the Old Faithful geyser and Lucifer's Rapids, Heidi spoke into her microphone. "Be sure to carry a flashlight with you because it gets dark fast."

Luke stood, grabbed his backpack from the overhead compartment, and pulled out his penlight. He sat down and touched his SCCY holstered pistol, which he'd concealed below his loose-fitting sweatshirt.

You're nice to touch, you little equalizer. The weapon made him feel unafraid and ready for anything.

Heidi tapped her microphone. "Folks, let's get out there and see Lucifer's Rapids before sunset."

* * *

8:40 P.M., TUESDAY, JUNE 3, 2031, YELLOWSTONE NATIONAL PARK

Felix and Erik, the two FBI agents who'd been following the Wild America tour bus, sat in their car in the far corner of the parking lot where the tour's yellow, tiger-striped motorcoach had stopped.

Felix, the shorter agent, walked away from the faded, plainclothes FBI car and stared away from the crowd of Wild America tourists exiting their bus. He caught sight of a sign pointing toward the famous geyser, Old Faithful, and then turned to his fellow agent, Erik, whose blond hair was lit by the setting sun. "Old Faithful could erupt soon."

Erik glimpsed at a brochure he held. "Its eruptions are more or less regular, but they vary from every forty-four minutes to two hours apart." Erik stared at a large number of people walking toward the geyser. He studied the crowd and noticed many people were speaking Spanish. *There must be a tour group from Latin America. It'll be harder to pick out the two suspects who went after Luke if they're here.*

The Wild America tour group began to follow Heidi toward Lucifer's Rapids. Eric nodded toward Luke and the rest of his fellow tourists. Then Erik and Felix began to tail them at a quick pace toward the acidic, boiling waterway.

* * *

8:41 P.M., TUESDAY, JUNE 3, 2031, YELLOWSTONE NATIONAL PARK

Javier inserted a wireless earbud into his ear canal. "Ready, José?"

"*Sí.*" José appeared jumpy to Javier.

Staring at José, Javier said, "Let's do a quick sound and picture check with your phone." The drone camera sent audio and video to both José's and Javier's encrypted satellite phones.

José activated the speaker phone on his device and spoke. "Testing one, two, three. Testing."

"I read you loud and clear." Javier studied José's face. The short, skinny man blinked as if he had something stuck in his eyes. *He's as rattled as a man ready to make his first parachute jump. Then again, he's had plenty of practice flying the drone since we left Monument Valley.*

Javier sighed as he screwed a silencer onto the muzzle of his big blue pistol.

José cleared his throat. "It's not too late for me to rig the drone with C-4 explosives. You could fly it into Luke and blow him to bits."

Javier stowed his firearm in the holster under his extra-large sweatshirt. "A C-4 blast would be super loud and could kill bystanders. The cops would swarm this place." Javier eyeballed José. "The combined sounds of my silenced pistol shot and the noise of rushing water will make it hard for people to realize Luke's been shot."

José sighed.

Javier grinned. "Tell me which way to go and how far from Luke I am."

"Got it." José saluted. "Best of luck."

THIRTY-SIX

THE SUN WAS DIPPING below the horizon at Yellowstone National Park. Like a grammar school teacher, Heidi led her Wild America tour group along the wooden walkway near the banks of the hellish stream, Lucifer's Rapids.

At the tail end of Heidi's group, Luke stopped in the semidarkness. He stood on the planks of the new wooden pathway that ran parallel to the acidic water cascading below him. Nearby, chatting tourists were hard to hear because of the din of the boiling rapids.

Luke stared into the caustic creek through the gloom. Though the bright, thin line of sunlight on the western horizon shot a weak glow his way, it was faint as starlight when it reached the boardwalk where he stood.

The sound and the nasty odor of the speeding water sharpened his hearing and sense of smell. Stirred up as it rushed around boulders and smaller rocks near the stream banks, the water emitted a noxious mist. As Luke held the wooden railing near the roiling rapids, the stench of the rising, acidic air made him almost sick to his stomach.

His eyes adjusting to the growing darkness, Luke spotted George and Regina walking ahead of him. The scant remaining light leaking from the horizon silhouetted the pair. When Luke spied Regina embrace and kiss George, Luke smiled, despite the unhealthy atmosphere.

Standing tall, Luke focused on the lovers. *Will they start a long-term relationship?*

* * *

8:46 P.M., TUESDAY, JUNE 3, 2031, YELLOWSTONE NATIONAL PARK

Javier studied José, who seemed jittery. Holding a mini-drone aircraft, José exited their rental car just minutes before the sun would set, though rays of light were still creeping over the horizon.

As José set the battery-powered aircraft on the sedan roof, Javier remained inside the automobile, peering through the passenger-side window with his night-vision binoculars. *This night-vision option works well.*

After José got back into their car and picked up the drone's remote controller, which included a small video screen, he glanced at Javier. "See the Wild America group yet?"

Javier pulled the binoculars away from his eyes. "Yes. Launch the drone. I'm leaving."

Javier exited the car, slammed its door, and began to walk at a brisk pace toward Lucifer's Rapids. He heard the soft buzzing of the drone as José commanded it to zoom upward and then head toward the Wild America tourists—including Luke—who stood on the wooden walkway close to the creek's steaming, hot bank.

Javier touched the silenced pistol under his loose sweatshirt and felt invigorated. His lips formed a maniacal grin in the growing darkness. *Tonight, you die, Luke Ryder.*

* * *

8:47 P.M., TUESDAY, JUNE 3, 2031, YELLOWSTONE NATIONAL PARK

The sound of the fast-moving, steamy waters of Lucifer's Rapids grew louder as FBI Agents Felix Hall and Erik Lundgren neared the wooden walk by the toxic waterway. Posing as undercover DEA agents, they had shadowed the Wild America tour group, including Luke and George. The agents carried their service firearms under their loose-fitting shirts.

The nasty smell of the stream almost made Felix gag, and he turned his gaze away from the rushing waters to peer behind him. Though the sound of splashing water was loud, a hard-to-discern, high-pitched buzz made him stare upward into the dark sky. "You hear that, Erik?"

"What?"

"I heard a hum, maybe a drone." Felix drew his firearm. "A drone zoomed down at a ranger after Luke was tripped by the canyon rim."

"Yeah." Erik also removed his weapon from his holster.

THIRTY-SEVEN

IN THEIR RENTED, burgundy cargo van, two human traffickers, Oliver Marenco and Tomás Villaruz, traveled toward Luke Ryder's Kentucky farm under the cloak of darkness as there were no streetlights in this rural area.

The warm night air felt sticky to Oliver, a tall, lanky man. He had big hands, a large head covered with thick, black hair, and a Fu Manchu mustache dangling from his upper lip. Fearing failure, he was willing to do anything to complete an assignment. An ambitious workaholic, he was in charge of tonight's mission to kidnap Layla Ryder and her two children. He rubbed the back of his head and glanced at Tomás, who suddenly stopped the van in the middle of the deserted roadway.

Pointing through his passenger-side window, Oliver commanded, "Park behind that bush."

Tomás nodded and began to guide the vehicle off the road into the grass. He mumbled, "I'll be glad to get back to a civilized city after this job's over." Five-foot-three-inches tall with a full head of curly hair, he stopped the van, turned off its lights and motor, and unbuckled his seat belt.

Oliver rolled down his passenger-side window and

glanced at Tomás. "I wish you'd shower more often. You smell like a pig." Oliver sighed. *Tomás also has breath as foul as a stray dog's halitosis.* In the dim light, Oliver focused on Tomás's rotten teeth. *No wonder his mouth is so odoriferous.*

Tomás rolled down his driver-side window, narrowed his eyes, and squinted sideways at Oliver.

Oliver sighed, opened a hip flask, and took a sip of Kentucky bourbon.

Mateo had given the traffickers orders to capture Layla Ryder and her two children—a baby boy and a young girl.

Flashlight in his left hand, Oliver took a printout from his breast pocket and unfolded the sheet. It was a copy of a hand-drawn map of Luke's farm with notes written on the margins of the diagram. Mateo had reported Javier had sketched the drawing when he'd lain low in a cheap motel after his first attempt to kill Luke had failed.

Earlier, during daylight, the two traffickers had driven past Luke's farm and hadn't seen police vehicles parked there. Next, the men had parked under a dense stand of trees near the farm's fence. Every once in a while the men had taken turns peering through binoculars at the farmhouse and barn. Again, they had seen no police or anyone else except Layla, her older daughter, and her baby boy when they'd eaten dinner outside at a picnic table.

Oliver took a deep breath, held it, leaned close to Tomás, and then exhaled. "Let's go in the rear door. I'll kick it in, and we'll grab them." He thought for a moment. "Have tie wraps?"

Tomás felt in his side pocket. "*Sí.*"

Oliver straightened up in his car seat. "After we secure the woman and the kids, you get the van and park as close to the back door as you can get."

Tomás nodded.

Oliver reached for his car door handle. "Let's go."

* * *

Layla sat at her kitchen table with a steaming cup of coffee. The aroma was soothing, and she was glad FBI Agent Rita Reynolds had departed with her fellow agent. After a Latino man had tried to shove Luke over a cliff at the Grand Canyon, Layla had argued the would-be killer or killers had followed Luke to its South Rim. She recalled her exact words. *"There's no immediate danger, and your FBI perimeter detection system and cameras will sound off if there's an intruder. I can call 911 if I need help."* Rita had then agreed to leave.

Layla sighed. *It was comforting to have Rita watch us for a while, but she has a crush on Luke. I'm glad she left. She was getting on my nerves.*

Layla glanced into the living room. Since Angela had been unable to sleep, Layla had let her stay up late. Layla saw that Angela was playing a video game.

The baby was asleep in a wooden cradle next to Layla. She reached down, rocked it, and smiled, and then her thoughts turned to Luke. He'd tried his best to downplay the attempt on his life at the Grand Canyon, but she knew better.

It must've been a close call. I've got to convince him to stay clear of the FBI. Seems like he's in more danger when he works with them. The bureau better catch those Mexican cartel guys soon.

A beeping alarm sounded. Layla's lips trembled as she glanced at the surveillance camera image displayed on a TV monitor on the counter by the refrigerator.

Holding pistols, two men were walking from the road down the driveway. Layla's mouth turned dry. "Angela, go down into the basement and hide."

Her eyes wide, the little girl dropped her electronic game and ran to the cellar steps.

Layla grabbed the baby, scampered after Angela down into the basement, and set the sleeping boy on a couch cushion on the floor. She turned to Angela. "Lock the door and don't open it unless I tell you to do it."

"Yes, Mama." Angela's eyes brimmed with tears as Layla

scrambled back up the stairs and shut the basement door. She grabbed her cell phone, engaged the deadbolt on the back door, and dialed 911.

"What's your emergency?"

"Two men with guns are walking up my driveway. I'm Layla, Deputy Ryder's wife."

"Help is on the way. Don't hang up."

Layla knew it could take five minutes or more for a squad car to arrive. She set her phone on the kitchen table and glanced at the TV monitor. The two men were at least seventy feet from the back door. Seeming to take their time, they glanced around as if to make sure no one else was nearby.

After pulling her keyring from her pocket, Layla unlocked a kitchen drawer and grabbed her Beretta pistol. Next, she ran to the gun cabinet in the living room, opened it, and grasped Luke's semiautomatic 12-gauge shotgun. Luke had taught her how to fire it. *It has a hell of a kick*, she recalled.

After shoving her pistol into her jeans pocket, she cradled the shotgun, stooped, and walked into the kitchen.

The TV monitor showed the two men near the back door. *Are they going to kick in the door?* She gulped, and fear raced through her body. Shaking, she kneeled by the kitchen table as her elbow bumped an open plastic bottle of ketchup, knocking it to the floor. The slippery red sauce spread underneath her. She glimpsed at the TV security monitor and saw the taller of the two men raise his leg as if about to kick the back door down.

When he threw his booted foot at the weak door, Layla raised the shotgun and aimed at the entryway. Her left foot slid on the slimy ketchup. As she slipped, the shotgun fired, its pellets hitting the ceiling above the door.

The gun's strong kick pushed her backward, and she fell flat on her back on the slick mess on the floor. Three deafening pistol shots rang out, and the shots splintered the flimsy back door. The slugs hit the refrigerator behind Layla.

She raised the shotgun. The big man fired two more rounds through the thin door. He kicked it down. Layla fired. The tall, lanky man, hit by a swarm of shotgun pellets, died as he fell.

Layla watched the security monitor as the second man fled along the driveway, running toward the road.

Russell, her baby boy, screamed, his cries muted by the basement door. Layla also heard little Angela whimpering between Russell's piercing cries.

Breathing in and out six times, Layla tried to calm herself as she focused on the dead intruder's eyes. They were wide open and motionless.

Layla waited, almost frozen in place, and then she began shaking, not able to stop. Despite her fussing baby and Angela's weeping, Layla decided to wait for the police to arrive before getting up and comforting her children. For one thing, she didn't want Angela to see the dead man whose blood had started to creep toward the spilled ketchup. And would the second man return?

After what seemed like an eternity, Layla heard sirens.

* * *

Holding his Glock ready to fire, Kentucky Sheriff Jim Pike peeked around the door frame, over the body of a tall Latino, and spotted Layla, stunned and sitting in a slimy, red mess. *Is she wounded?* "Layla, are you hit?" He heard a baby crying—*Luke's boy, Russell?*

Jim saw Layla take deep breaths, and then she whispered, "I think I'm okay. I knocked ketchup down when the guy kicked my door." She shook like an aspen tree in a strong breeze. Jim and Luke had been boyhood friends, and now—still best friends—they both worked in law enforcement. *I'm blessed I don't have to call Luke to give him the worst news ever.*

"Any more bad guys around?"

Layla shifted, pulling her feet closer to her torso. "I don't think so. On the TV monitor, I saw another Latino run away down the driveway toward the road after I shot this guy." She hesitated. "I have to check on Angela and the baby in the basement." She released the shotgun, let it slip into the spilled ketchup, grabbed hold of the tabletop, and stood.

Using caution, Jim stepped around the dead man. *He's full of buckshot.* "Layla, keep the kids in the cellar while we process the scene. Best Angela doesn't see this."

Layla nodded and took a step toward the basement door. Just then, Deputies Jesse Reagan and Michele Johansen surveyed the situation from outside the back door, focusing on the carnage in the farmhouse kitchen. Jesse asked, "Everything under control, Jim?" He focused on Jim's back.

Jim turned. "Yep. Another perp fled. Take a couple of guys, set up a perimeter, and search the farm for a perp who appeared to be Latino. Michele, go with Layla down into the basement to check on her two kids."

"Yes, Sheriff." An inch over five feet tall, Michele was careful not to disturb the crime scene as she stepped into the kitchen. Her straight, shoulder-length, dishwasher-blond hair bobbed as she moved toward the basement door and Layla.

Layla spoke. "Jim, the FBI video machine must've recorded everything. The recorder's in the bottom right kitchen cabinet."

Jim glanced at the cupboard and then caught Michele's attention. "Ask Layla what happened and take notes, too."

Michele nodded.

From outside the back door behind him, Jim heard a noise, and then a high feminine voice asked, "Jim, can I process the scene yet?"

Turning, Jim saw crime scene investigator Alice Strom, her braided blond pigtails hanging over her shoulders.

He pointed at the cupboard. "First, open the cabinet and review the FBI digital video recorder footage. It will show the incident. Get a freeze frame of the perp who fled. We need it for an APB ASAP."

"Yes, Sheriff." She paused. "I set boxes of crime scene footies and gloves outside the door. Everyone should wear them if they enter the scene." She thought for a second. "Unlock the front door. Everyone should enter there from now on."

"I agree."

Alice spoke with a quiet yet perky voice, though the situation was serious.

Jim furrowed his brow. *The two bastards must've been hired by the Tijuana drug czar, Mateo.*

Jim glanced at the bullet holes in the refrigerator. *Layla's lucky she's not dead. Slipping on the ketchup saved her life when she fell.* Even though Jim was an even-keeled man, calm under pressure, he inhaled two deep breaths and took his time to let the air out of his lungs. He scanned the crime scene. *We have a lot of work to do here.*

Alice slipped on a pair of blue nitrile crime scene gloves, put covers over her shoes, and stepped toward the cabinet where the video recorder was stored.

* * *

8:50 P.M., TUESDAY, JUNE 3, 2031, YELLOWSTONE NATIONAL PARK

While manipulating his joystick, José stared at the drone controller's video screen. *Why does Javier insist on hitting Luke when a crowd of witnesses are around?* Squinting, José recognized a half dozen of the tourists from the Wild America tour. Then he spoke into his encrypted satellite phone that he'd set to the hands-free mode. "I saw Luke. He's next to the barrier by the acid creek, thirty meters ahead of you. George is farther back."

* * *

"Thanks, José." Catching sight of Luke, Javier threw his shoulders back and grinned, his facial expression obscured by the waning light of the setting sun. *This time, Luke will die.*

Javier lifted his black sweatshirt and pulled his large, silenced pistol from its holster. "Back me up, José. Watch for rangers." Javier pressed his earbud so it was snug in his ear. "Call me if you spot a problem."

José whispered, "Okay."

Cloaked by the fast-darkening night, Javier walked toward Luke's position.

* * *

José gulped and shook his head as he flew the drone over Luke, Javier, and Lucifer's Rapids.

I'll drive away from here if this fails. He shifted on his seat in the rented car that sat in the parking lot. *At least this time, Javier is taking chances instead of me.*

* * *

10:53 P.M., JUNE 3, 2031, LUKE'S FARM

While Layla stood in the cellar, she held her baby and patted his back. He appeared to be falling asleep, worn out from screaming during the attack by the tall Mexican.

Turning to Deputy Sheriff Michele Johansen, who stood nearby with little Angela, Layla said, "It's important I phone Luke."

Michele smiled. "You better call him before Jim starts asking you more questions." Angela was gripping Michele's hand and eyeballing Layla.

Layla set the now sleeping baby on a couch cushion on the basement floor, withdrew her cell phone from her ketchup-soaked jeans, and touched Luke's name on her contact list. She heard ringtones.

* * *

8:53 P.M., TUESDAY, JUNE 3, 2031, YELLOWSTONE NATIONAL PARK

A humming sound caught Luke's attention. *Is that a drone?* The hum blended in with the hisses of the boiling stream.

Lucifer's Rapids sounded and smelled worse to Luke the longer he stood on the wooden walkway above the scalding and acid-infused stream. When his satellite phone began to ring, Luke turned toward the western horizon, still lit even after the sun had set, and pulled his mobile device from his pocket. Layla was calling. Strong fumes rose from the roiling channel and affected his nose. He coughed. "Layla."

Loud, creaking sounds came from the wooden walkway behind him, and Luke began to turn.

As Luke completed his turn toward the creaking sound, he focused behind him into the gloom to his right.

In the semidarkness, he saw a tall, thin Latino raising a big, blue-black pistol equipped with a silencer. A shock of alarm traveled through Luke's chest like an electric jolt.

As he thrust his right hand toward his belt to grab his tiny SCCY pistol, Luke's phone tumbled away.

* * *

10:55 P.M., TUESDAY, JUNE 3, 2031, LUKE'S FARM

All of a sudden, Layla heard Luke's phone fall and bounce, and the call disconnected. Focusing on Michele, she said, "Luke dropped the phone. I'll call again."

Michele pressed her lips together, still holding little Angela's hand.

Layla tapped Luke's name again, and his phone rang, but after twenty-one rings, she hung up. "I'll try again later."

* * *

8:56 P.M., TUESDAY, JUNE 3, 2031, YELLOWSTONE NATIONAL PARK

As his phone fell, Luke dove toward the boardwalk, his miniature pistol now in his hand. The phone came to rest, stuck between two planks. An instant later, a spark-filled muzzle flash lit the darkness as the Latino's firearm discharged. Cracking like a whip, a bullet zipped past Luke within an inch of his ear. Now on his knees, Luke heard the pop of a second shot, and a thud sounded behind him on the pathway's cedar planks as he staggered sideways, off-balance. *Where's George?*

Crashing toward the wooden walk, Luke fired twice, a fraction of a second before landing on his side.

THIRTY-EIGHT

THE ODOR of spent gunpowder mixed with the fumes of the fast-moving, acidic creek. Javier's blue-black pistol smoking in his hand, Javier felt a fleeting moment of superiority after he'd fired two quick rounds at Luke. A split second later, there was a pop, and a punch-like force hit Javier's shin. *What was that?* Fright struck him like a bolt of lightning. *I'm hit.*

Feeling his numbing leg collapse like a dynamited, imploding skyscraper, Javier knew he couldn't guide his sideways fall. His body careened toward the raging mix of boiling water and acid. As he crashed against the wooden barrier on the edge of the cedar-plank walkway, a flash of hope traveled through him. Then the fencing broke. Doom invaded his brain.

Like a motion picture projector showing just one frame per second, time crept forward like molasses oozing from a cold bottle. The last moments of Javier's life played out in extreme slow motion. The smell of fumes rising from the searing, acidic water lingered in his nostrils, triggering nausea, and bile rose into his throat, burning its insides. His body fell and twisted in the steamy mist above the ten-foot-deep acidic rapids. Javier gawked in disbelief at the angry, sizzling stream below him as he plummeted in slow motion toward it. *Is this punishment for my sins?*

Now an inch above the maelstrom of water swirling around boulders, he dreaded what was next. As he struck the scalding water, severe pain stabbed his body. His skin fell away bit by bit, peeling off like layers of melted plastic. Then there was darkness.

* * *

10:59 P.M., TUESDAY, JUNE 3, 2031, LUKE'S FARM

Standing in Luke's basement, Sheriff Jim Pike glanced at his deputy, Michele, who had a comforting arm wrapped around Luke's young stepdaughter, Angela. The little girl also leaned against the female deputy. *I wonder how traumatized Angela is. She's gonna need therapy, and Layla will need help even more.*

He kneeled next to Luke's young daughter. "Angela, you know I'm a friend of your daddy and mama."

"Yes."

"Close your eyes and lean into Officer Johansen's chest after she picks you up. In a few minutes, your mama will meet you upstairs after I talk with her. Okay?"

The little girl gulped. "Yes, Sheriff Pike."

She's one scared little girl. Jim stood. "Michele, please carry Angela upstairs, but be sure to shield her eyes from the scene. Here are booties and nitrile gloves you need to wear."

Michele nodded and put on the shoe covers and gloves. In less than a minute, she was carrying Angela upstairs.

Layla eyeballed Jim. "Thanks for making sure Angela doesn't see bad stuff."

"It's the least I could do." He observed Layla for a moment. "It was my fault not to provide a deputy to be on the lookout after the FBI left."

Layla grimaced. "No, it was my fault. Rita and the other agent were willing to stay here, but I convinced Rita there was no danger because the cartel hit men were out West."

Jim fingered an unlit cigar. Once in a while, he'd light one and puff on it, but he didn't inhale. "I'll ask Michelle and Deputy Jesse Reagan to stay here the rest of the night. Another deputy will relieve them tomorrow morning."

Layla gulped. "Thank you."

Jim noticed Layla had stuffed her small pistol in her jeans. "Did you fire your Beretta?"

"No, I didn't need to." Layla began to tell Jim about what had happened that night. As she neared the end of her story, she stopped speaking. She choked up. Her eyes welled up with tears, and she began to weep.

Jim put his arm around her shoulders. "Let it all out."

Layla sobbed for more than a minute, and then she regained her composure. After wiping her eyes and nose with her sleeve, she coughed. "When the man kicked down the door, I fired the shotgun." More tears flowed down her face.

Jim patted her back. "If there's anything else, you can tell me later."

* * *

9:02 P.M., TUESDAY, JUNE 3, 2031, YELLOWSTONE NATIONAL PARK

The two FBI agents tailing Luke had rushed toward the sounds of four shots—two muted reports and then a pair of weaker pops. An instant later, they heard a loud splash and a scream. The blond agent, Erik, yelled, "Someone fell in the boiling creek."

Felix started to run. "Hope it's not Luke."

* * *

In horror, José had watched the night-vision video feed displayed on his drone controller. After Javier had crashed through the fence along the creek and into the lethal water, José felt nauseous.

Seconds later, José spotted two men with drawn firearms sprinting toward the scene, where Luke Ryder was standing up, holding a small pistol. Luke appeared unharmed.

José guided his drone into a dive, and the small whirly-bird smashed into the caustic waters of the blistering creek. He reckoned the little aircraft's plastic parts would sag and melt in the steamy waterway. Odds were the rapid current would carry the destroyed parts away.

I must go now. Starting the rental car's motor, José drove from the parking lot. Still wearing a pair of rubber gloves, he tossed the drone controller out of his window into the vegetation on the side of the road. *Should I head for Tijuana or use one of my false IDs to enter Canada?* Taking a deep breath, he said out loud in Spanish, "Canada, here I come."

* * *

Javier's piercing scream had echoed as he'd collapsed and splashed into the steaming waters of Lucifer's Rapids. Luke's ears ringing, he stood and rushed to the broken railing at the same instant Javier's cries stopped. The man flopped like a hooked fish in the stream of turbid, acid-infused water. Then the flailing assassin became stuck, wrapped around a jagged boulder in the raging water. Grabbing a wooden board from the broken barrier, Luke thrust it toward Javier, who failed to grab it and stopped moving. Then Luke tried without success to guide the body toward him with the piece of shattered cedar.

Is he unconscious or dead? The Mexican assassin's body now appeared as lifeless as a freshly killed lobster that had been steamed in a pot of boiling beer. Suddenly, a wave of splashing water dislodged the limp, blistered corpse, and a strong current dragged it downstream faster and yet faster.

A high, shrill cry sounded behind Luke. "Help!" Luke turned and caught sight of Regina in the dingy darkness holding George, who'd collapsed onto the planks of the walkway. "He's shot."

A gurgling noise, a gasp, and a hacking cough sounded behind Luke through the blackening night. Luke dreaded what he'd see as he approached the wounded spy.

Dropping the shattered board from the barrier, Luke rushed toward George and Regina, tripping and almost falling. "Where's he hit?"

George coughed. "In my arm."

* * *

Conscious, George was on his back on the blood-soaked wooden walk, and Regina was with him, pressing her small leather purse against a wound where Javier's bullet had struck George's upper left arm.

Luke saw tears leaking from Regina's eyes, and George was blinking and groaning. Luke felt like lightning had hit him, and at the same time, he was angry. "George, hang in there, buddy. Hit any place besides your arm?"

"No."

After running back to grab his satellite phone from a gap between two boards, Luke dialed 911.

Luke felt his heart skip a beat.

"What's your emergency?"

"A man's shot in the arm. He's bleedin' a lot."

"We have your exact location in Yellowstone Park. Ambulance is on the way. Stay on the line."

"I'm puttin' you on speaker." Luke set his phone on the wooden walkway and turned to Regina. "I'm gonna cut off George's shirtsleeve and then put on a tourniquet. Keep pushin' on the wound."

Regina nodded.

Using his penknife, Luke sliced George's shirtsleeve off at the armpit level and glanced at Regina. "Lift the purse, and I'll pull off the sleeve. Then put the purse back over the wound." In a quick motion, he slipped George's shirtsleeve downward and tossed it aside. To Luke, the bullet appeared to have cut through all the layers of George's skin but missed the arm's bones. Pulling a clean cotton handkerchief from his back pocket, Luke twirled it to form a rope and then tied it four inches above the wound. "Regina, hold his arm up. That'll help stop the bleeding."

She did as instructed.

George whispered, "It not bad."

Loud footsteps echoed behind Luke. "DEA. We heard shots." The agent, who'd spoken in a deep voice, held a pistol at his side. A taller blond man, also grasping a firearm as well as a flashlight, stood next to the first agent, scanning the area, searching for potential threats.

The first FBI agent glanced around, his pistol ready to fire. "Where's the shooter?"

Luke pointed toward the broken barrier. "I shot him. He fell into the boiling, acid water. Ain't no way he lived."

"Any more bad guys around?"

Luke shrugged. "I don't know, but I didn't see anyone else."

"You Luke Ryder?"

"Yes."

The first agent scanned Luke. "You hurt?"

"No."

"Rita Reynolds sent us." Sirens sounded in the distance.

The tall blond man's flashlight beam focused on George. "How bad is he?"

Luke glanced at George. "A bullet hit his arm. It's a flesh wound." Luke wiped his sleeve against his eyes and turned around. Both agents still held their service weapons at the ready.

The sound of sirens was loud. Luke saw an ambulance skid to a stop in the gravel parking lot not far from the boardwalk. Two emergency medical technicians rushed from their vehicle and raced toward Luke and the two agents.

Luke yelled, "Where you gonna take the wounded man?"

An EMT slowed down and said, "Jackson Hole Hospital."

After the two EMTs knelt by George and Regina, the shorter agent caught Luke's attention. "Let's talk over there and let the ambulance crew do their work."

* * *

Regina watched as the two EMTs checked out George and bandaged his wound. She kissed him before they loaded him onto a stretcher and then loaded him into the back of the ambulance. Tapping one of the EMTs, she asked, "Can I ride with him? I'm his girlfriend."

"Of course."

"Thanks." Regina gulped and walked closer to the back doors of the ambulance. After Regina climbed into the rear of the emergency vehicle, the two techs got into the front of the ambulance, leaving her alone with George. Putting her hand on his head, she stroked his hair and peered deep into his eyes. "I love you, George."

George turned his head, making eye contact with her. "I love you, too." He smiled, though he was pale.

She peered down at the white, steel floor of the emergency transport for a moment and then stared at him. "I'm going to confess something to you, though."

George lifted his head a bit. "What?"

"I was working for the man who shot you and tried to kill Luke. But he lied to me because he said he wanted to find out who your customers are so he could make sales for his company."

With small motions, George nodded. "I thought so. What government you work for?"

"Government?"

"US? Russian? Belarus?" George cocked his head.

"Javier told me he works for a company from Tijuana, a

competitor of your company. I was supposed to text him what you were doing and who your customers were. But he seemed more interested in Luke than you."

"So, you are honey trap?"

"No. I had no idea Javier was going to shoot at someone." She leaned close to George and kissed his lips. "George. I'm not lying. I love you. Please believe me." Her chin shook, and tears streamed down her face. "I wouldn't have told you about this if I didn't love you... I'd be running."

George patted her back with his right hand. His eyes appeared watery to Regina. "I love you, too, even if you are not who you said you are." He pulled her closer to him, and they kissed again.

She sighed and pulled away from his kiss. "Are the police going to arrest me after they find out Javier hired me to spy on you?"

George shook his head no. "Don't tell them. I will not."

"Okay."

George rubbed her back with his right hand. "If you need job, I hire you to be my assistant, like I said before. I need to sell tractors in US and maybe Mexico, too."

Regina wiped the tears from her face, smearing her makeup. "Yes, George, I'll work for you, even if you don't pay me." She kissed him again. "Later, I'll tell you more about me."

George grinned. "I need personal nurse, too. You will live with me?"

"Yes." She kissed him again.

George smiled and cocked his head. "Later, I tell you more about Belarus, my home country, and my old job."

Careful not to squeeze his injured arm, she gave him a half hug. *How will I ever tell him I was a call girl?* Another tear dribbled down her cheek. *He's saved me from the life.*

* * *

FBI Agents Felix Hall and Erik Lundgren stood with Luke in a brightly lit area a hundred feet away from the Wild America tourists. They'd returned to gather around Heidi after park rangers had secured the area. Now that the crime scene was lit by floodlights shining from park service pickup trucks, Luke got a chance to closely observe the two FBI agents who'd been assigned to follow and guard him and George. The two men wore vacation garb, including loose shirts so they could conceal their sidearms. Luke scratched his fast-growing beard. *They don't stand out like some FBI agents.*

Felix extended his hand to Luke. As they shook, the agent said in a low voice, "I'm Felix Hall. I'm pleased to meet you in person." He glanced toward his partner. "This is Erik Lundgren." Luke nodded at Erik, and the man winked.

Felix let go of Luke's hand. "We've been briefed in detail about your mission with Yegor Bulot, a.k.a. George Black."

Luke glanced back and forth at the two agents. "I'm glad yur up to speed." Luke kept his voice volume down, though the sound of the rushing, caustic water in Lucifer's Rapids muffled his words.

Felix took a step closer to Luke and leaned toward him. "We know about George's handoff to KGB operative Mikhail Popov, and we've been told he's trying to recruit you."

"Yep."

"Our team has Mikhail under surveillance. He's been following you and George." Felix paused. "If he contacts you about this incident, tell him the DEA thinks the guy who shot at you and hit George was involved in an unrelated drug deal gone bad."

Luke nodded. "Okay. I'll call Rita to find out what she wants to do about Mikhail."

Felix wrinkled his nose. "I talked to her an hour ago. She said she wants you to tell Mikhail the Mexican cartel is after you because of the Lexington undercover operation you worked."

Luke felt his satellite phone vibrating in his pocket,

pulled the device out, and saw Rita was calling. "I gotta take this. It's Rita."

Luke stepped away from the two FBI agents and answered his satellite phone. "Hello, Rita. I guess you heard what went down here."

"No, but I have bad news." Rita's voice sounded higher to Luke, as if she were stressed and worried.

"What?" Luke's mind galloped a hundred miles per hour. *Is Layla okay? Did those Tijuana cartel bastards hurt her?*

"Two Mexicans, we think Mateo's guys, came after Layla. She killed one with your 12-gauge shotgun. She and the kids are okay. The perimeter alarm worked, and Layla spotted them coming."

Luke gulped and wiped a tear from his eye. "Did Angela see anything gruesome?" Luke pictured his stepdaughter, Angela, perhaps unable to speak, emotionally scarred for life.

"No, Layla quickly moved Angela and the baby into the basement, called 911, and got the shotgun. One man kicked in the back door, and she shot him."

Luke shook his head. "Thank God Russell and Angela are okay. But Layla's gonna need help. I gotta git home ASAP."

"I'll book you and George a flight from the Jackson Hole Airport. You're at Yellowstone, right? What happened there?"

"Minutes ago, a Latino fired at me. I shot him in the leg, and he fell into boiling creek water and died. George got hit in the arm, and an ambulance took him to the hospital. It didn't look like a bad wound to me."

"I'll check with the hospital. Which one?"

"Jackson Hole Hospital."

"If they release him soon, you two can fly to Lexington together. I can debrief him here."

Luke coughed. "He's got a new girlfriend, Regina, who's on the tour. They're serious, stayin' in the same hotel rooms. She got in the ambulance with him."

"I'll call George. I could get her a reservation, too, if she wants one."

Luke reckoned Rita would tell George to say his company set up the airplane reservations. "What are you going to ask George to tell Regina?"

"We'll think of a cover story. I'll text you about it."

Luke glimpsed at the two FBI agents loitering nearby. "Your two guys, Felix Hall and Erik Lundgren, are interviewin' me now."

Luke could hear Rita exhale. "I'm going to insist the Tijuana police raid *Nuestro Club*'s villa." She took a moment to consider the situation. "Let me talk to the two agents."

"Sure." Luke handed his phone to Felix. "Rita wants to talk with you."

* * *

While Felix was speaking to Rita, Luke noticed something white blowing and tumbling across the wooden walkway, lit by the floodlights mounted on the rangers' pickup trucks. Running across the boardwalk, he leaned down and snatched a business-size envelope a moment before it would've fallen into the boiling creek.

Luke reached into the envelope and pulled out a short letter. Staring at it in the semidarkness, he saw his name and his farm's Kentucky address written on a hand-drawn map of his property. There was one sentence. *"Mata mi enemigo."* The paper was signed MG. *That's gotta be Mateo Guerra's initials, the cartel boss. The Latino who just shot at me is one of the two guys who shot at me back on the farm. The guys who attacked Layla were other men.*

* * *

After Felix returned Luke's phone to him, Luke walked away from the flashing emergency lights and floodlights into the darkness.

Glancing behind him, Luke saw the two agents approach the Wild America tourists. He figured Felix and Erik would continue to pose as DEA men when they spoke to the people on the tour. If asked, the agents would describe the incident as a drug deal gone wrong.

Because I was behind the rest of the Wild America folks, no one in the group saw me shoot.

Luke continued to walk farther from the scene of the shooting. *I wonder how George's doing.*

Luke decided to ask the agents to drive him to the Jackson Hole Hospital to check on George after they'd finished interviewing the Wild America tourists.

As Luke wandered into much blacker shadows, ever more distant from the crime scene, he heard faint, almost imperceptible noises, like the rustling of bushes.

In moments, he became accustomed to the near-total darkness of the night, and he shifted his attention toward the source of the sounds. All of a sudden, he spied two sets of eyes glowing in the coal-dark shadows. The eyes moved back and forth as if investigating the strange activity on the boardwalk next to the boiling rapids.

What kind of animals are they? Just as Luke was wondering about the mysterious eyes, one of the rangers' pickup trucks began to turn around, and its floodlights illuminated two wolves for an instant. As if lit by the flash of a strobe light, the image of the two wolves scampering away into the deep, ebony night was like a picture taken by a still camera.

Beautiful animals. I wouldn't mind workin' as a ranger. Luke's love of wildlife and the outdoors made him forget the attempt on his life for the moment.

Although he was already shrouded in blackness, Luke closed his eyes to visualize the wolves he'd just seen. One was more than three feet tall and at least a hundred pounds, perhaps even a hundred and thirty pounds. The second animal was smaller, though its stomach appeared bigger. Was the petite one a female soon to give birth? Luke recalled wolves mate for life and live in packs of four to seven animals.

The pair of wolves had stood by logs near lush green bushes and grass. Behind the wolves, Luke had spied three trees with white trunks and dark patches where bark had fallen away. *Are these birch? Maybe they're aspens?*

Glancing back at the flashing lights near the crime scene, Luke began to feel jumpy again. *I gotta call Layla. She needs me now.*

* * *

11:08 P.M., TUESDAY, JUNE 3, 2031, LUKE'S FARM

Deputy Sheriff Michele Johansen rested on a hassock near Layla, who sat in a comfortable easy chair in the master bedroom, holding her daughter, Angela. "Don't worry, honey. Daddy's friends are going after the bad men who knocked down the back door." Layla kissed the top of her daughter's head and glanced at baby Russell in a deep sleep in a bureau drawer, now serving as a temporary cradle. Though her stomach was unsettled and her nerves fired so much her hands shook, she felt better when she gazed at Russell, who seemed like a fragile angel.

Angela buried her face in Layla's breast and clung to her. Now tilting her head backward, Angela kept her eyes focused on Layla's face. "Mama, what were the loud noises, the booms, and popping?"

Layla felt her throat constrict. *I'm about to lie to my daughter.* "The bad men used explosions to knock in the door." She was silent for a moment, considering what to say next. "The noises scared me, too, but the bad men are gone. They're afraid of Daddy's friends, Sheriff Pike and his deputies. The bad men won't come back." Layla felt a tear flow down her cheek, and with a swift swipe of her hand, she wiped it away. *I hope I don't have to lie to her again.*

Angela frowned. "Will you sleep with me tonight?"

"Yes, dear."

Musical tones from Layla's phone sounded. Layla gulped and withdrew the device from her jeans pocket. Luke was calling. "Luke, I'm glad you called. Just a sec." She caught Michele's attention. "Could you sit with Angela?"

Michele smiled. "Yes." She stood and then sat on the carpet near the easy chair, and Layla handed Angela down to the deputy sheriff, who embraced Angela. "Let's talk about how nice it is to be a deputy sheriff."

Angela nodded.

Layla spoke into her phone as she left the master bedroom. "You hear that, Luke?"

"Yep."

His voice sounded calm to Layla. *But he's hard to read.* She took a massive breath. "I'm going into the living room, and we can talk. I miss you so much."

* * *

Through his phone, Luke heard Layla walking toward the living room. He was thinking fast. *How can I tell Layla the Mexicans tried to kill me again? Or should I tell her I know the Mexicans came after her tonight, too? What should I say first?*

Luke heard Layla bump her phone. "We can talk now." Layla sounded stressed. "The Mexicans just tried to kill me."

"Rita called and told me. She's booking me a flight home soon. You okay?"

"Yes." All of a sudden, Luke heard Layla begin to breathe fast. *Is she hyperventilating?* After three seconds, she spoke. "I killed one with the shotgun. The other man ran away." Strong sobbing pounded Luke's ear through his satellite phone. Then Layla blew her nose and took a deep breath.

"Layla, are you hurt at all?"

"No. The kids are okay, too. Jim and a team of deputies are here." Layla took two loud breaths and, with force, drove air from her lungs. Then she inhaled more oxygen. "Thank

God the perimeter alarm went off, and I saw them coming on the security camera monitor."

"There were just two?"

"Yeah, the deputies are after the second guy. The first Mexican kicked down the back door, and I fired." Layla began to sob again, and after fifteen seconds, she calmed down. "Sorry, hon."

"Pretty soon, I'll git on a plane, and I'll be there." He peered at the bright lights shining across the boardwalk crime scene. "The nearest larger airport is at Jackson Hole."

"Jim told me Rita's on her way here." Layla sniffled. "I'll be okay. A lady deputy sheriff's with me, too. The crime scene people are investigating and will stay here all night."

Luke figured now was the time to tell Layla about the attempt on his life. His throat tickled, and he hacked. "Layla, I gotta tell you something. Tonight, another Mexican tried to kill me, too. I shot him in the leg. He fell in a creek and died. I'm okay."

Layla began to hyperventilate again. After five seconds, she recovered. "This is too much."

"I found a note dropped by the man. It had a map of our farm and house. I think the guy who attacked me tonight is the one who shot at me by the barn."

Luke heard Layla breathing easier again, and then she said, "Between us, we took out two bad guys." She sounded stronger, like killing a man wasn't a big deal. But Luke knew that wasn't the real Layla.

She's street smart, and now she's comin' across as tough—it's her defense mechanism kickin' in, even though she's a soft, sweet, emotional, caring woman. Because she'd been a high-class prostitute, Luke reckoned Layla had learned to appear tough to have a better chance of survival.

Luke heard himself begin to talk. "I'm havin' second thoughts about bein' in law enforcement. It'd be nice to be a game warden again or a park ranger."

Layla was silent for a moment, and then she spoke.

"Didn't they fire you from your game warden job because of your drinking?"

"Yeah." Luke peered at his shoes in the dim light.

"I suppose you could be a full-time farmer instead."

"It's an option." Luke wavered. "If nothin' else, I'll tell Rita I'm done with FBI gigs for now."

Layla sounded like she was breathing in a normal manner again. "We should talk everything over when you get here. I know Jim's your best friend, and he bent over backward to get you the deputy sheriff job."

"I could switch and work as a crime scene investigator."

"If those Mexicans keep coming after us, you might want to keep your deputy sheriff job until they stop harassing us."

"Yep." Luke nodded to himself. "Hang in there, my honey. Two FBI guys are walking this way to talk to me some more. I'll hang up now. But I'll call back soon as I can."

"Love you, darling. Bye." Layla disconnected her device.

If Nuestro Club cartel keeps this up, I may have to go after Mateo myself. Luke felt his face flush in the cool darkness. A gust of wind rustled his hair, and at first, it calmed him, but then he began to worry about Layla again. He watched as Felix and Erik approached, taking their time, chatting, surveying the crime scene.

As he waited for the two agents, Luke wondered how killing a man would affect Layla. She might already be suffering from post-traumatic stress disorder, PTSD. *I could git Carol Cuddy to help Layla. The sooner, the better.*

Carol Cuddy, Luke's ex-girlfriend, was a psychologist who'd helped him analyze criminals and even himself. *I'll call Carol tomorrow and see what she can do.* Carol was now dating Jim Pike, though she was still Luke's platonic friend.

Luke recalled Carol explaining PTSD to him. Its symptoms included bad dreams and troubling thoughts. Carol had told him PTSD often lasted a month but could persist for years. Luke knew extreme PTSD might lead to suicide.

I hope Carol knows how to treat PTSD.

Luke sighed and began to wonder about his stepdaughter, Angela.

What did she see? Carol had said young kids were less prone to be distressed by trauma, but following an upsetting incident, they might show its effects during play.

Could Carol counsel both Layla and Angela?

Felix came closer. "Rita says we should take you to the hospital after we're done here."

Luke nodded. "Thanks."

THIRTY-NINE

JOSÉ STOPPED his rented vehicle by the side of the road in the darkness, opened the glove compartment, grabbed a flashlight, and stepped into the night. Shining the portable light's LED beam around, he found bushes where he could relieve himself. After his bladder was empty, he stared at the stars and relaxed. *I better call Mateo and tell him what happened.*

José grabbed his encrypted satellite phone from his jeans pocket and touched Mateo's name on the device's display. The phone rang seven times, and José's finger hovered above it, about to disconnect his call. *I should text Mateo instead of calling.* All of a sudden, Mateo answered. "What in the hell are you calling so late for, José?"

"Javier is dead. Luke shot him, and Javier fell in a creek of boiling, acid water at Yellowstone."

Mateo coughed. "Are you still near the scene?" Mateo's voice sounded like he was still half-asleep.

"No. Two men armed with pistols ran forward to Luke. Park rangers rushed in, too. I left."

Mateo exhaled. "What is your next move?"

"I don't know. Luke is like a tiger with nine lives." José

took a mini-second to think. *I shouldn't tell him I'm going to Canada.* "I'll lay low for a couple of weeks."

Mateo sounded like he'd yawned. "I'm going to Northern California to check out our new operation. Head there. I'll text you an address."

"It's critical to stay out of sight." José bit his lip. "It could be a while with an all-points bulletin out for me."

"It's your call."

"The FBI issued wanted posters with drawings of us. Javier ripped two of them off a wall in a shop at Monument Valley."

"Okay. Lay low. I know about the posters. Call me in three weeks."

"*Sí, Jefe.*"

Mateo disconnected.

FORTY

THIRTY-TWO MILES FROM YELLOWSTONE, George sat dressed in street clothes, perched on a chair next to his hospital bed.

Regina sat on her large suitcase next to George's luggage. When agents Felix and Erik had driven Luke to the hospital, they also had transported Luke's, George's, and Regina's luggage in a newer, large SUV the FBI had provided them to replace their smaller, faded-blue sedan.

Tired, Luke held a cardboard cup of steaming coffee. No one in the room had spoken during the last three minutes. Luke sipped his coffee. *Everyone's tired after stayin' up all night. Good thing Rita's got us on the same flight.*

They were scheduled to take off from Jackson Hole Airport. After a stop at Chicago's O'Hare, they'd fly to Lexington.

Luke smiled. *I'll be happy to be home back on the farm.* He glanced at Regina. *I hope George sticks to his cover story that he's just a tractor salesman from Belarus. But I shouldn't worry. He's a seasoned spy.*

Rita had hired a limo to take the three of them from the hospital to the airport after George was released.

Regina stood. "Excuse me. I'm going to go to the ladies' room." She smiled and left.

Luke caught George's attention. "I think I'm done with FBI fur a while."

George shifted his arm in his sling and wrinkled his brow. "You still will be spokesman for Belarus Tractor Company on your farm, though?"

"Yep, I made a deal. But I'm quitting the cloak-and-dagger stuff as of now. I won't take sales trips with you."

George wrinkled his brow. "You think FBI will trust me to be on my own in US?"

"They'll have to." Luke took a sip of his coffee. "Don't worry, we'll still be friends. But I gotta be close to home to protect Layla and the kids from the Mexicans."

"I understand." George tapped a foot on the tile floor. "I wonder if UK-US-Belarus Agricultural Pact is working like politicians said it would."

"Yur sellin' lots of tractors. Farmers and other people like your machines. The countries are trading crops, too." Luke bit his lip. *Of course, the intelligence agencies of all of the parties to the pact are using it to spy on each other, too.*

George fingered his sling and then glimpsed at Luke. "My friend Mikhail wants to partner with me and buy farm in US. Maybe in Kentucky." George leaned forward and spoke in a quieter voice. "We both try to quit spy business."

"I'm glad you may retire from spying." Feeling his pulse throb in his temples, Luke let his mind rest for a moment. "Like I said before, most people, no matter where they're from, just want a cozy house, food, friends, and freedom."

George made steady eye contact with Luke. "Tractor-type machines can be war fighters, but are better for farm work."

Luke tossed his empty cardboard coffee cup into a wastebasket. "Yep, just like a sturdy boot's needed fur war, but it's better fur walking across your own farm."

George grinned. "Peaceful coexistence is good. I hope makes comeback."

Luke heard Regina's shoes clicking on the hallway before

she re-entered the room. "The nurse says she's bringing a wheelchair for George because the airport limo's outside. Another nurse said she'd help with the suitcases."

Luke stood. *I can't wait to git back and hug Layla. She needs me, and I need her.*

* * *

11:00 A.M., WEDNESDAY, JUNE 4, 2031, JACKSON HOLE AIRPORT

KGB courier Mikhail Popov approached Luke from behind while the Kentucky lawman bought sandwiches for himself, George, and Regina.

Luke felt someone tap his shoulder. As he turned, Luke saw the Belarusian spy, who was dressed in casual clothes, including an *I love New York* baseball cap.

"Remember me, Luke?"

"Yep. Yur George's friend from the Belarus Tractor Company."

Mikhail drew his eyebrows together and whispered, "I heard he was shot in the arm."

Luke sighed as he glanced across the terminal corridor. He spoke in a low voice. "Yeah." He stared at Mikhail. "I'm to blame in a way."

Mikhail avoided eye contact and put his hands in his pockets. "I don't see how that could be." He touched Luke's shoulder and guided him a step farther away from people near the fast-food eatery.

Luke's ears turned red. "George told you I'm a deputy sheriff in Kentucky. I helped break up a Mexican drug cartel's operation near Lexington. The cartel's gunnin' fur me, and George got hit by one of their bullets."

The KGB spy blinked and spoke in a soft voice. "That this cartel wounded one of our valued employees has upset our management in Minsk. Please tell me more details about the incident at Yellowstone. My company may wish to complain to Mexican authorities via our embassy."

A sandwich shop employee in a white uniform called after Luke, "Sir, here's your order."

"Thanks." Luke nodded and walked to the woman in white, who handed him the bag of food he'd ordered and three drinks on a cardboard tray.

Luke looked at Mikhail. *What's the KGB up to? This espionage stuff is gettin' too risky. I don't need a bunch of spies attacking my family, too.* His hands full, Luke gestured with his head for Mikhail to step aside so the two men could talk farther away from the crowd of fast-food customers.

Leaning against a concrete pillar, Luke spoke in a whisper. "Mikhail, your company doesn't have much of a chance of takin' down a Mexican cartel."

Mikhail stood tall. "I have contacts in the Mexican government, and George is my best friend. No matter what Minsk decides, I'm going to complain about this cartel. I wish to get the most information I can when I bitch to the Mexicans."

Luke wet his lips. "Mateo Guerra is the head of *Nuestro Club* cartel. Its headquarters is in the Tijuana region in a large villa. I don't know anything else about 'em."

Mikhail clasped Luke's arm. "Thank you. We don't want you hurt, either." He stared at Luke for a moment. "My company would still like you to be in our employ, helping George to demonstrate our farm machinery when your schedule permits."

Luke glimpsed far down the terminal corridor and caught sight of George, his arm in a sling. He sat next to Regina. Luke turned to face Mikhail. "I appreciate yur offer, Mikhail, but I figure it'd be better if I don't help George with his tractor sales on the road. There'd be less chance of him gettin' hurt again."

Luke thought Mikhail was forcing his smile. "Don't be hasty. The Belarus Tractor Company and George like you. Maybe merely one or two sales trips would suit you."

Luke smiled. "I'll think about it."

"That pleases me." Mikhail glanced at his wristwatch.

"My flight boards in five minutes. Tell George to heal well. I'll call him soon."

"Okay."

Mikhail began to run toward a gate at the end of the terminal, his knapsack bouncing on his back.

Luke started to walk at a slow pace toward George and Regina. *I wish I could be a game warden again.* He envisioned walking through the wilds of Kentucky and began to relax.

But I can't turn my back on Jim and the Sheriff's Department. There's no way I could disappoint my best friend, Jim, the guy who gave me the chance to be his deputy and helped me deal with my drinkin' problem. Then again, Layla would like me to quit bein' a deputy sheriff and get a safer job.

Luke saw George wave. *I'm feelin' relieved to get the hell out of here.*

FORTY-ONE

LUKE OPENED THE NEW, reinforced, steel back door leading out of his kitchen and stepped onto the pristine redwood platform under the patio roof.

Luke held his chin high, turned, and then examined the exterior of the attractive entryway, painted a light brown.

Layla didn't waste time using the FBI bonus money to get a super strong door installed and a new patio built. He was happy the bureau had helped her find excellent workmen who'd completed the job of repairing the inside as well as the outside of the house a week after the attack by the Mexican human traffickers.

Pulling a new cedar picnic table closer to his two older ones, he smelled the air, perfumed by flowers and trees. The light breeze was warm, not too humid, and the weather was fair with puffy, white, cumulus clouds drifting across the blue sky from the west.

Soon the gang will be here, maybe in a half hour. He moved Russell's cradle near the end of the new table, close to where Layla would sit.

Rita had called minutes ago and said she had surprising news—Mateo Guerra's villa outside Tijuana had been destroyed. She'd tell him all about it, but not until after she'd arrived at the farm.

Luke sat down next to Layla's place at the table and stared across his fields. *Who took out Mateo's house and compound? Must be a hell of a tale. Is Mateo dead? Has Nuestro Club drug cartel been wiped out?*

The sound of a car crushing gravel in Luke's driveway alerted him one or more of his guests were arriving. He stood and walked around the corner of the house at the instant Rita pulled her tall, black sports utility vehicle to a stop near his bright red barn.

Walking toward her SUV, he smiled and opened the driver-side door. "Thanks for coming, Rita." He held her hand as she stepped down from the tall vehicle. She blushed. *I shouldn't have helped her down. No use encouraging her. And Layla would get irritated if she saw me touch Rita's hand.*

With her free hand, Rita held a clear plastic carton that held a cheesecake. She gave it to Luke. "I wouldn't miss your party." She started walking with Luke toward the picnic tables. "I came before the rest of your guests so I could speak with you alone about the attack on Mateo's compound."

Luke pointed to the new picnic table. "Have a seat. Can't wait to hear about it."

Rita opened her purse, pulled out a white business envelope, and handed it to Luke. He tilted his head to the side and shifted on his cedar picnic table seat.

What's this? Turning its flap up, he saw the envelope contained small snapshots. They showed the aftermath of a wildfire or perhaps burned-out ruins after a bombing. A brick chimney, scorched metal appliances, and a swimming pool filled with floating debris remained among the ashes.

Rita leaned toward Luke and spoke in a quiet voice. "That's what's left of Mateo Guerra's house and estate."

Luke put his hand on his chest. "Is Mateo dead?"

Rita's brow wrinkled. "We're not sure."

"Why not?"

"We sent a crime scene team to help the Tijuana police investigate. They found human bones, including skulls, but we don't have Mateo's dental records. The fire was so intense it burned up DNA."

"What else did the CSI folks find?"

"The initial blasts were caused by C-4 plastic explosives. Investigators found bits and pieces from at least a dozen drones. Neighbors heard loud humming—like the sound of a swarm of bees flying toward Mateo's place at two in the morning."

Luke rubbed his chin and felt his whiskers with his fingertips.

Who'd send a swarm of suicide drones to destroy a drug lord's headquarters and kill who knows how many people? Would a rival drug cartel do it? The Tijuana police? The FBI? After all, wasn't it in the early 1990s that the FBI launched a teargas attack on the Branch Davidian cult's compound in Waco, Texas? A fire started, and seventy-six cult members died.

Luke focused on Rita. "Who attacked Mateo's villa?"

"The Tijuana police deny it. I'm told FBI people were helping them to plan a raid, but the attack took place before the Tijuana police could conduct their operation." Rita gazed across Luke's fields. "One possibility is another Tijuana cartel, *Los Animales Locos*, did it, but they and *Nuestro Club* signed a peace treaty two years ago."

Luke crossed his arms. "Somebody did it."

Rita whispered, "Some of us think the KGB destroyed Mateo's place. The Tijuana police say someone from the Belarusian embassy contacted them and offered to help fight drug cartels in Tijuana."

"Interesting."

Rita bit her upper lip. "You told me how George's friend, Mikhail Popov, the KGB courier, tried to recruit you to help George sell more tractors. Didn't he tell you the KGB takes care of its own?"

"Yep."

Rita smiled. "I bet you a bottle of ginger ale that the Belarusian KGB did it."

Luke scratched his knee. "Is *Nuestro Club* wiped out?"

"No. We have intelligence that a bunch of them moved to Northern California. But we don't know much yet."

Luke looked up and saw more guests were arriving, and then he heard another vehicle driving from the road toward his barn. He glimpsed at Rita. "That could be George and Regina."

Rita stood. "I better take this cheesecake inside and help Layla with the food." She looked at Luke. "Please hold off on speculating with George about the origin of the fire at Mateo's compound."

"Okay."

* * *

Layla brought a platter of steaks outside and set them at the end of a serving table she'd set up at the edge of the patio. She grinned. "Dig in, folks. We have fried chicken, steaks, veggies, potato salad, desserts, and enough other food to feed an army."

Luke thought Layla appeared much less stressed after his friend, psychologist Carol Cuddy, had conducted therapy sessions with both Layla and his stepdaughter, Angela. As he'd suspected, both Layla and Angela suffered from PTSD after Layla had shot the Mexican man who'd kicked in the back door.

As guests began to line up at the serving table, Luke took Carol aside. "How's Layla doing?" Luke knew Layla was an expert at hiding her emotions, and she could smile even when she was sad.

Carol whispered. "Layla's a strong woman and is responding well to therapy. I believe she's surmounted most of the effects of PTSD. I predict in a couple of weeks she'll be in good shape. As for Angela, she's a little trooper. Layla shielded her, and Angela didn't see the dead man. That was super helpful. She heard scary sounds, but she's done well, too."

"Thanks, Carol."

"I'm glad to help. Don't worry, I won't bill you."

Luke cocked his head. "I'd like to pay you something."

"Not necessary." She winked, smiled, and got in line with Sheriff Jim Pike, her date.

Luke stood in line behind George. The KGB double agent, who no longer wore his arm sling, followed Regina in the serving line and began to scoop potato salad onto a paper plate.

Grabbing a paper plate, Luke piled a steak, potato salad, and mixed vegetables on it. The food smelled delicious, mainly the odor of the steak, which caused his mouth to water. Luke smiled at Layla. "You sure set out a fine selection of food. I'm proud of you."

Layla grinned. "You helped, too, hon." She turned and focused on George. "I heard you bought a farm at the other side of the holler."

George set his plate on a picnic table. "Yes, I did." Then he grasped Regina's hand and glanced at her. She nodded and whispered, "Go ahead."

George blushed and stood, holding a spoon in his hand. He tapped it against his water glass and surveyed the guests around him, who included Rita and other FBI agents, Sheriff Jim Pike and Carol, and several deputies with their wives and girlfriends. "I announce I and Regina will marry."

The picnic tables vibrated as the diners clapped and cheered. "Also, I buy farm in holler with help of Belarus Tractor Company. I will farm it between tractor sales trips."

Luke beamed. "Congrats, George." Luke scratched his ear. *That caught me by surprise, 'specially Belarus forkin' out money for a farm.*

"Thank you, everyone." George pulled Regina to him and hugged her.

Rita sat across the table from Luke, and he cocked his head and asked, "Did you know about this?"

She grinned. "Yes, and I kept it secret. All's copacetic. Talk to you about it later."

Luke glanced at Layla, and she shrugged when Rita turned her focus on George. Luke bit his lip. *I'll check with Rita right after we finish dessert.*

* * *

As the picnic party guests were tossing their paper plates into a wastebasket, Luke gestured at Rita to step aside with him. He spoke in a low voice. "Now that I'm bowing out of yur FBI dealings with George's tractor sales trips, what's gonna happen?"

"We trust him." She stopped speaking and glanced at Regina, whose shapely figure was catching the attention of three of the male deputies who were speaking with George. "As for Regina, we checked her background. I won't tell George we learned she was a high-class call girl in Vegas."

Luke was quiet for a moment as he thought. *Layla was an escort, too, and she's a fine, loving woman. Regina seems to be okay.* Luke cleared his throat. "Just cuz Regina has a past she's prone to hide, don't mean she isn't a good woman."

Rita stared at Regina and then focused on Luke. "We have no evidence Regina broke the law. In 2026, Nevada changed state law to permit prostitution in all the state's counties, not just in certain locations. Then Las Vegas passed a city ordinance to regulate and allow it within city limits."

Luke shrugged. "Okay."

Rita eyeballed Luke. "Any chance you'll be able to help the FBI once in a while other than with the KGB stuff?"

"Not in the near future." Luke peered at the rest of his guests. "I need time. And I gotta protect my family."

Rita cocked her head. "Makes sense. If I learn more about Mateo and *Nuestro Club*, I'll let you know."

"Thanks."

Rita glanced at Layla. "I'll say goodbye to Layla." She patted Luke's forearm.

* * *

10:00 P.M., WEDNESDAY, JUNE 18, 2031, LUKE'S FARM

In the dim but warm glow of a bedside lamp, Luke watched his alluring wife take her time to shed her clothes. Layla smiled at him with a playful grin. Nude, she slipped into bed and cuddled with him. Her soft, ample breasts were warm against his bare chest as she stroked his arms. At first, he felt delicious relaxation, but without warning, her closeness and gentle movements began to hasten his desire to have her. Now, he felt wide awake. *She feels so feminine.*

Pulling her face to his lips, he kissed her, and then he began to fondle her body with his fingertips, examining all of its contours. Taking his time, he kissed her torso. After ten minutes of embracing and stroking her shapely figure, he sensed her desire to make love had grown to a desperate level. He felt her heart beating quicker as he held her close, and she began to breathe faster. She peered deep into his eyes. "Do it."

She wrapped her body around his. They made sensuous, unembarrassed love only as two people who were so comfortable with each other could. Though their lovemaking had begun with small movements, it grew more and more intense until they were in a frenzy that ended in mutual bliss.

Then they cuddled, and she rubbed his back and whispered in his ear. "I hope the Mexican drug cartel has forgotten about us."

Luke rolled over and focused on Layla's eyes. "Before the picnic, Rita showed me snapshots of buildings burned to the ground. They were the ruins of Mateo's Tijuana villa. Drones attacked it with C-4 plastic explosives."

"Is *Nuestro Club* cartel destroyed, and is Mateo dead?"

"It's unknown if Mateo is dead or alive. The Tijuana police found the bones of many people but couldn't ID him."

Luke waited and added, "The FBI learned some of his cartel members have fled to Northern California."

"Who blew up the cartel's villa?"

"I'm not sure." Luke took a breath. "Mikhail, George's KGB friend, spoke with me when I was out West. I told him I thought Mateo had ordered a hit on me at Yellowstone. Mikhail said he'd ask friends in the Tijuana police to investigate *Nuestro Club*, but I suspect the KGB decided to teach *Nuestro Club* cartel a lesson cuz the cartel's assassin wounded George."

Layla put her head on Luke's chest and kissed him.

Luke peered deep into Layla's eyes. "Could be the cartel guys are done goin' after me. For sure, one Mexican assassin is out of commission. Boiling, acid water in Lucifer's Rapids ate him up except for his bones." Luke scratched his scalp. *If the cartel tries again, I'm going after them myself, even if I have to go to Mexico.*

He felt Layla slip her arms around his chest and press herself against him. She spoke with a soft voice into his ear. "It's nice to be skin to skin." After a moment, she pulled the blankets around them.

Luke felt warmer as their body heat became trapped under the thick covers. *While she's in bed, I wonder if she feels more protected from the outside world and its criminals, crazy politicians, wars, and spy agencies.* Luke touched Layla's face. "There's somethin' else you'll be glad to hear."

Layla raised her eyebrows. "What?"

"I told Rita I won't keep workin' with the FBI. George will be okay on his own because he loves America and won't turn on us. He loves Regina, and I bet he'll stay in the US forever."

Layla showed a smile that grew larger. "I'm glad. What about the other KGB guy you told me about?"

Luke sat up with his bare back against the bed's headboard. "I told him I don't have time to go on sales trips." Luke's mind zipped back to his memories of the surprising treaty the US, UK, and Belarus had signed in 2029. It enabled the three countries to trade farm products and machinery as well as a limited amount of inexpensive military equipment. He rubbed his chin. *It's strange how politicians flip-flop. We traded with Vietnam after the Vietnam War and with Germany and Japan after World War II.*

Layla's eyes sparkled. "I'm glad you decided to quit the spy biz."

"Yeah. I don't need to be a pawn in a worldwide chess game." Luke nodded to himself. *Why do a power-hungry few end up in control, cause wars, and spy? Bein' a local deputy sheriff's okay cuz I'm helping regular people.*

Layla placed her head against Luke's chest. "Thinking about something?"

"Yeah, George helped teach me most people are good underneath. Just a few are bad."

Layla glanced into Luke's eyes. "You should run for office."

"I'm not the type." Luke's inner voice started speaking to him again. *Fur now, I'm gonna stay in law enforcement cuz I believe I gotta protect the innocent. I'm strong enough to fight evil and win.*

Layla kissed his lips. "You're more thoughtful than I've seen you in months."

Luke smiled and felt confident. "I think I learned a lot during these last three weeks."

"What?"

"Stand up for what's right, and fight evil if you must."

ACKNOWLEDGMENTS

I thank my wife, Sheryl, a retired English teacher, for her thoughts, critical edits, and encouragement. She has helped me with this and my other books as well. I'm also indebted to my editor at Rough Edges Press, Rachel Del Grosso, for her patience, expert suggestions, and friendliness.

IF YOU LIKE THIS, YOU MAY ALSO ENJOY: THE FINGER TRAP

A TONY FLANER MYSTERY BOOK ONE
BY JOHNNY WORTHEN

When half measures don't get you the whole truth...

Tony Flaner is a part-time comedian and full time commitment-phobe who has never been able to stick with anything in his life. After his fourteen-year marriage ends in divorce, Tony's life takes a dramatic turn when a drunken party ends in murder.

With his life on the line, he must uncover the identity of the mysterious girl who was murdered and how they ended up together in the first place. This undertaking is not just about clearing his name—Tony needs to prove to himself and everyone else that he can finish something for *once in his life*.

But when Tony discovers that his fate is intertwined with that of the mysterious girl he hardly knew—and that their lives are connected like a Chinese finger trap—he unknowingly embarks on a journey full of twists and turns around every corner.

Can Tony Flaner finish this one task and clear his name before he gets sent to prison for a murder he didn't commit?

AVAILABLE NOW

ABOUT THE AUTHOR

John G. Bluck was an Army journalist at Ft. Lewis, Washington, during the Vietnam War. Following his military service, he worked as a cameraman covering crime, sports, and politics—including Watergate for WMAL-TV (now WJLA-TV) in Washington, D.C. Later, he was a radio broadcast engineer at WMAL-AM/FM.

After that, John worked at NASA Lewis (now Glenn) Research Center in Cleveland, Ohio, where he produced numerous television documentaries. He transferred to NASA Ames Research Center at Moffett Field, California, where he became the Chief of Imaging Technology. He then became a NASA Ames public affairs officer.

John retired from NASA in 2008. Now residing in Livermore, California, he is a novelist and short story author.